Her lips grazed over ███ **the warm smoothness** ███ ███ **She inhaled a deep draft of** ıııs **spicy, smoky scent. Her well-honed sense of discretion warned her that she should not linger so close to Hadrian, but her body was slow to respond. The unexpected thrill of those sensations held her captive there, hovering over him.**

Before caution had a chance to intervene, his kisses swept along the sensitive flesh just below her jaw, moving over her chin and finally upward to meet her approaching lips.

This kiss had a deliciously familiar feel, but it held a subtle thrill of novelty, too. She sensed a tender restraint on his part, which appealed not only to her physical desires but also to her wary heart.

Her heart had good reason to be wary, painful memories reminded her—all the more because she had allowed herself to feel something for her husband. But that could be more than enough to scorch her if she risked playing with fire.

Abruptly she drew back, ignoring the protest of her pleasure-deprived senses.

Hadrian caught her hand. 'Don't go.'

Author Note

Welcome to the second book of my new series, **Gentlemen of Fortune,** about the self-made men of Vindicara Trading Company! While I love reading and writing about dashing aristocrats, I've always had a fascination with the man who makes his own fortune and charts his own destiny. Such men make great romance heroes because they have large, definite objectives and intense motivation to succeed. They will fight for what they want and refuse to let anything or anyone get in the way of achieving their goals—even when it comes to love.

Ford Barrett, Hadrian Northmore and Simon Grimshaw all left Britain for various reasons, going half way around the world to make their fortunes. Now, though they have money, power and success, they discover those things mean nothing without a special person to share them. As destiny throws three unique women into their paths, these driven men discover that achieving material success was easy compared to the challenge of forging a close, passionate relationship that will last a lifetime.

Bought: The Penniless Lady is the story of Hadrian Northmore, who overcame terrible tragedy to make his mark in the world. Returning to England to launch his brother's political career, he discovers that Julian was killed in a duel, leaving behind a young son. Desperate to claim this last remnant of his family and fulfil the mission that has driven him to succeed, Hadrian will do anything to gain custody of his nephew. Even if that means wedding Lady Artemis Dearing, whose family he holds responsible for his brother's death. The reserved spinster reluctantly agrees to a marriage of convenience to provide for the child she loves so dearly. But Artemis soon discovers she and her nephew need more from Hadrian than his fortune. In return, they can give him something far more precious than worldly success—if only he will let them!

I hope you will enjoy *Bought: The Penniless Lady* and those of the other **Gentlemen of Fortune**!

BOUGHT: THE PENNILESS LADY

Deborah Hale

MILLS &
BOON®

First published in Great Britain 2010
Harlequin Mills & Boon Limited,
Eton House, 18-24 Paradise Road, Richmond, Surrey TW9 1SR

© Deborah M. Hale 2010

ISBN: 978 0 263 22276 0

Harlequin Mills & Boon policy is to use papers that are natural, renewable and recyclable products and made from wood grown in sustainable forests. The logging and manufacturing process conform to the legal environmental regulations of the country of origin.

Printed and bound in Great Britain
by CPI Antony Rowe, Chippenham, Wiltshire

In the process of tracing her Canadian family to their origins in 18th century Britain, **Deborah Hale** learned a great deal about the period and uncovered plenty of true-life inspiration for her historical romance novels! Deborah lives with her very own hero and their four fast-growing children in Nova Scotia—a province steeped in history and romance!

Deborah invites you to become better acquainted with her by visiting her personal website www.deborahhale.com or chatting with her in the Harlequin/Mills & Boon online communities.

Novels by Deborah Hale:

A GENTLEMAN OF SUBSTANCE
THE WEDDING WAGER
MY LORD PROTECTOR
CARPETBAGGER'S WIFE
THE ELUSIVE BRIDE
BORDER BRIDE
LADY LYTE'S LITTLE SECRET
THE BRIDE SHIP
A WINTER NIGHT'S TALE
   (part of *A Regency Christmas*)
MARRIED: THE VIRGIN WIDOW*

**Gentlemen of Fortune*

Look for the final story in
Deborah Hale's
Gentlemen of Fortune
WANTED: MAIL-ORDER MISTRESS

This book is dedicated with love
to my nephews Ian, Andrew, Bradley, Ben,
Dane and Sean and my nieces Melissa,
Amanda and Kate. I wish you all the
success and happiness in the world!

Chapter One

Sussex, England—April 1824

The summons Lady Artemis Dearing dreaded had come at last.

Scooping up her small nephew, she pressed her lips to his silky hair, which was the same honey-golden shade as his late mother's. If only she could absorb some of his innocent optimism and head-strong courage! She needed both, desperately.

Oblivious to his aunt's distress, the child wriggled in her arms, chortling with the simple joy of being alive and loved. For an instant, his sunny spirits made Artemis forget her lingering grief and worries for the future.

With the tip of her little finger, she traced the shape of his mouth and his dimpled chin, which reminded her so keenly of her brother. It comforted her to know that part of her sister and brother lived on in this dear child. She must not fail him as she had failed them.

"Please, my lady," said the housemaid who'd been sent to fetch Artemis, "the master wants you to come straightaway. He'll only be in a worse humor if you keep him waiting."

"Of course, Bessie." The fragile bubble of happiness inside Artemis collapsed at the mention of Uncle Henry. Having waited fifty years with little hope of inheriting the Bramber title and estate, the new marquis seemed impatient to make up for lost time. "Can you watch Master Lee for me? I daren't take him with me and if I leave him in his cot, he'll only cry."

Cry indeed. He would scream at the top of his sturdy little lungs. He was still too young to understand that such outbursts were unseemly. The last thing Artemis needed during her interview with her uncle was Lee's piercing shrieks echoing through the decorous stillness of Bramberley.

"But, my lady…" Bessie backed away with a regretful grimace "…I'm that far behind with my work already. The master wants the State Apartments aired and dusted, floors scrubbed and windows washed. How am I to get that done on top of all my other duties when I'm being sent to run messages and pressed into service as a nursemaid?"

Artemis stifled a flicker of vexation. A few months ago, none of the servants would have dared refuse an order from the mistress of the house. Since her brother's death, so much had changed at Bramberley…none of it for the better.

"Please, Bessie?" Artemis hated to stoop to bargaining, but she had no choice. "I will not be long, I promise. And once Lee is asleep tonight, I will come and help you scrub."

"That wouldn't be fitting, my lady!" The offer seemed to shock Bessie into agreement. "Very well, I'll take him, but I reckon he'll cry anyway, being away from you. You've got him well spoiled."

Perhaps she did indulge the poor child, Artemis admitted privately, but how could she do otherwise for a tiny orphan everyone but she seemed to wish had never been born? How could she keep from clinging to the last person in the world she had left to love?

"If you take him down to the Green Gallery and let him walk from one chair to the next, he'll never notice I'm gone." Artemis gave the child a final kiss, then thrust him into Bessie's arms. "Just keep a tight hold on his leading strings so he doesn't fall."

Brushing past Bessie, she rushed from the nursery. Lee was less likely to fuss if she left him quickly, while Uncle Henry was more apt to fuss if she kept him waiting.

Artemis arrived in the library out of breath with her heart racing. After taking a moment to compose herself, she knocked, then entered at her uncle's bidding. As she crossed the threshold, she inhaled the dry, musty aroma of old parchment and leather. That smell revived heartening memories of her adored father.

Her two uncles sat in a pair of matched brocade armchairs. Artemis willed her knees not to tremble as she made a respectful curtsy. "You wished to see me, Uncle Henry?"

"I did, my dear." The Marquis of Bramber pressed his long, thin fingers together and rested his chin upon them. "I have some very encouraging news to share. After the past year of bereavement and scandal, the Dearing family may soon put all that unpleasantness behind us."

Wrenching as the events of the past year had been, Artemis did not want to put them behind her. That would be like turning her back on the memories of her brother and sister. Since she knew better than to contradict her uncle, she stood in composed silence, waiting for him to continue.

He did not keep her in suspense. "I have made Mrs. Bullworth an offer of marriage, which I hope she will accept."

"Mrs. Bullworth?" Artemis could not keep her tone from betraying surprise and distaste.

She had heard plenty of gossip about Harriet Bullworth over the years. The former actress had been kept by a succession of gentlemen before marrying a wealthy banker three times her age. After his death left her a rich widow, Mrs. Bullworth had made no secret of her intention to buy her way into the highest peerage possible.

The prospect of such a brazen adventuress usurping the place that had belonged to a succession of the most refined ladies in the kingdom horrified Artemis.

"You heard correctly." Uncle Henry's iron-gray brows contracted in a severe frown that brooked no argument. "The lady is a most suitable choice for many reasons, not least of which is her comparative youth. The duty of propagating the Dearing line has fallen to me and I will not shirk it. A man of my years looking for a younger bride is in no position to pick and choose. Particularly when the size of his fortune does not match the luster of his pedigree."

Duly chastened, Artemis lowered her gaze. "I understand, Uncle. Of course I want the Dearing line to continue."

Her show of deference seemed to appease her uncle. "I knew I could count on your support, my dear. You have always been a paragon of loyalty and duty. If only your unfortunate brother and sister had followed your example, we might not have found ourselves at this pass."

Any gratitude her uncle stirred by praising her loyalty, he forfeited by criticizing her brother and sister. "Perhaps if you had not forbidden Daphne to see Julian Northmore—"

Uncle Henry gave a dismissive flick of his fingers. "That is all water under the bridge."

Some long-suppressed spirit of rebellion made Artemis itch to seize a pair of heavy bookends and hurl them at her uncle. Prudence restrained her. Now that Uncle Henry was head of the family, she could not afford to antagonize him—for her nephew's sake as well as her own.

"You have been a model of familial duty," Uncle Henry repeated. "Caring for your sister and her unfortunate child. I am certain the family can depend upon you to act for its greater good."

Artemis sensed a lurking threat in her uncle's praise. "What *greater good* might that be?"

"The one of which we just spoke, of course, and you endorsed." Uncle Henry sounded impatient. "My finding a wife and begetting an heir."

At the risk of annoying him further, Artemis asked, "What do your plans have to do with me?"

"You must appreciate Mrs. Bullworth's position, my dear—the impropriety of her living at Bramberley under the same roof as an illegitimate child."

Uncle Edward gave a fastidious shudder. "Not to mention the

harm you have done your own reputation, keeping the child with you for so long."

"I have always been perfectly scrupulous about my reputation, Uncle. I fail to see how caring for my dead sister's child should damage it. As for Mrs. Bullworth's propriety—" Artemis bit her tongue to keep from saying something that might make Uncle Henry lose his temper. "I sympathize, of course, but you cannot turn Daphne's child out of Bramberley. He is barely a year old. He has nowhere else to go, any more than I do."

"You will always have a home at Bramberley," said Uncle Henry. "But the child must go. I should have insisted upon it sooner, but I feared being parted from her infant might be the death of your sister. Now that she is gone and the boy is weaned, surely some place can be found for him."

The fear that had stalked Artemis since her sister's death now pounced, threatening to rip her wounded heart to pieces. "Please, there must be some other way. Bramberley is such a vast place and so much of it unoccupied. Could I not move with Lee to a room in the north range? No one would ever have to know we were here."

"*I* would know." Uncle Henry looked thoroughly shocked at her suggestion. "I mean to give Mrs. Bullworth my word of honor that the child will not be living under her roof, and I refuse to be foresworn. You know as well as anyone, the word of a Dearing is sacred."

"Surely our responsibility to an innocent child of our own blood is sacred, too? If he cannot stay at Bramberley, find us a little cottage on the estate or give me some money to take him farther away." It would be a wrench to leave this sprawling old mansion crammed with rich history. But giving up the child, who was her only remaining link to her brother and sister, would be a hundred times harder.

"Out of the question." Uncle Henry seemed surprised and vexed by her reluctance to bow to his wishes. "It would reflect badly on the family when we most urgently need to restore our good name."

"I cannot hand him over to strangers," Artemis protested. "He is such a little fellow and so attached to me since his mother died."

"Attached? Nonsense!" The marquis turned up his nose. "A child that age is more vegetable than animal. As long as it is clothed, sheltered and given adequate nourishment, it will be reasonably content. By the time the boy is old enough to reason, he will have long forgotten you."

If that were true, the thought did not comfort Artemis. Even if Lee forgot her, she would never forget him or cease to yearn for him. Perhaps because he was so small and helpless, so entirely dependent upon her, she'd permitted him to creep into her aloof, solitary heart.

Before she could devise an argument that might sway her uncle, he rose from his chair, signaling the end of their interview. "I have made my decision. The child must go. You have two weeks to find him a place you deem suitable. If he is not gone by then, I shall take matters into my own hands."

Though a dozen desperate emotions raged in her heart, reticence and deference were so deep a part of her character Artemis could only murmur, "I understand, sir."

"That's a good girl," said Lord Henry. "Be assured, as long as I am head of this family, *you* will always have a home at Bramberley."

As long as she did not try to keep Daphne's child with her. The marquis was too well-bred to put his threat in such bald terms, but Artemis knew that was what he meant. She had a fortnight to find Lee a good home and reconcile herself to parting from him. Or she would be cast out into a harsh world without friends or resources to scrape a living for herself and her nephew.

As she hurried away from the library, gusts of impotent rage buffeted her, while waves of despair threatened to sink her spirits.

Over and over, she cursed the name of the man who had killed her handsome, dashing brother and ruined her beautiful, vivacious sister. "Damn all Northmores!"

* * *

"Hadrian Northmore, what are you doing on this side of the world?" Ford Barrett, Lord Kingsfold, strode across the drawing room to greet his business partner. "Did *Tuan* Farquhar expel you from Singapore for trespassing on his authority again?"

In spite of Ford's hearty tone, Hadrian sensed something amiss. Had he come too late to prevent the British government from handing Singapore over to the Dutch?

"Farquhar has been replaced as Resident." Hadrian wrung his partner's hand. "Before you ask, I had nothing to do with it. I've come to represent our fellow merchants in treaty negotiations with the Dutch. Whatever else the Foreign Office has to concede, they must not give up Singapore. The volume of trade has more than tripled since you left. Before long it will be more profitable than Penang."

"You don't need to persuade me." Ford looked so relaxed and content, he appeared to have grown younger in the two years since Hadrian had last seen him.

Could that be on account of the fair-haired beauty who stood by the window with a young child in her arms, patiently waiting for an introduction? Hadrian had been surprised to receive word of Ford's marriage—to his cousin's widow, no less. He wished his partner better luck in marriage than he and Simon Grimshaw had found.

Before leaving Singapore, Hadrian had been charged with fetching back an English girl to be Simon's mistress. Simon had suggested he find one for himself as well, but Hadrian shrank from the prospect. A mistress was too much like a wife to suit him.

"You will not need to persuade the government of Singapore's commercial value, either," Ford continued. "They signed the treaty last month. In exchange for Bencoolen and some other concessions, the Dutch have agreed not to oppose British occupation of Singapore. I wish you and Simon could have been here to celebrate the good news. Now that you are, I must call up a bottle of champagne so we can drink a toast."

"Not champagne." Hadrian grinned. "Arrack is the only proper drink for toasting the future of Singapore. But first, I must beg the honor of introductions."

"To my charming ladies, of course." Ford beckoned the woman to join them. "Forgive me, my dear. My partner's unexpected arrival drove all civility from my mind. Allow me to present Mr. Hadrian Northmore, senior partner of Vindicara Company. Hadrian, this is my wife, Laura, and our daughter, Eleanor."

"I am delighted to meet you at last, Mr. Northmore." Sincere pleasure beamed like sunshine from the cloudless blue of Lady Kingsfold's eyes. "I have heard so much about you from my husband. No one could be more welcome at Hawkesbourne."

The little cherub in her arms stared gravely at Hadrian. The moment he met her gaze, she turned bashful, hiding her face in her mother's shoulder.

"The pleasure is mine, ma'am." Hadrian bowed. "I would wish my partner joy, but I see he has already found it."

"Indeed I have." Ford's doting gaze rested on his wife and daughter with such obvious adoration, Hadrian scarcely recognized the grim, guarded man he'd once known. "After we raise our glasses to Singapore, we must drink to my good fortune."

"If you will excuse us, gentlemen," said Lady Kingsfold, "we shall leave you to your toasts. Eleanor must have her nap or she will be too cross for anyone but her papa to tolerate. I shall have Mr. Pryce fetch you a bottle of arrack. You must stay the night with us, Mr. Northmore. I hope my husband can persuade you to visit longer."

"I accept your gracious invitation for tonight, ma'am." Hadrian looked forward to becoming better acquainted with the woman who had worked such a transformation on his partner. "But tomorrow I must press on for London to see my brother. He is my other reason for returning to England. I mean to do whatever it takes to win him a seat in Parliament."

It had been his mission for more than fifteen years—to put his brother in a position of power, from which he could work to reform the worst abuses of the mining industry. Abuses Hadrian had experienced firsthand. Abuses that had nearly wiped out their family.

All the warmth drained from Lady Kingsfold's smile. She and Ford exchanged a furtive glance, which revived Hadrian's earlier instinct that something must be wrong. As she fled the room without another word, her young daughter began to cry.

"What is it?" Hadrian demanded. "Is my timing off for that as well? Has there been an election already?"

Ford shook his head. "Not for another year or two. It's just… Have a seat, won't you? Pryce should be along soon with the arrack."

Hadrian had never seen his partner so shaken. It did not bode well. "Damn the arrack and damn the chair! Whatever you have to tell me, spit it out, man. Julian's landed himself in trouble, hasn't he? Has some little fortune hunter got her claws into him? I told you to warn him about women of that sort."

"I did!" cried Ford. "It isn't that. Damn it, Hadrian, I thought the news would have reached you. Your brother is…dead."

"That can't be!" Hadrian staggered back. "Julian is not yet five-and-twenty and he's scarcely had a day's illness in all that time."

He and his brother came from hardy stock, bred in the harsh beauty of the Durham dales, tested in the dark depths of the northern coal mines. It took a lot to kill a Northmore.

"He didn't die of an illness." Ford inhaled a deep breath that seemed to suck all the air from the large room. "He was killed in a duel over a year ago. If it is any consolation, the end came quickly. His opponent was not so fortunate."

"A duel! Who with? Over what?" Dueling was the folly of gentlemen who cherished their highborn honor. Hadrian had worked and planned to launch his brother into the highest tier of English society. But not for this.

Had the young fool forfeited his life over some stupid gambling debt or an insult spoken in the heat of drunken anger? Hadrian cursed himself for not taking the lad in hand sooner. But how could he? He'd been halfway around the world, making the fortune that would have put Julian in Parliament to be a voice for those who had none.

Now Hadrian's fortune could have been dust for all it mattered. Because Julian was dead, his promising young life snuffed out like the rest of their family.

"His opponent was my neighbor, the Marquis of Bramber," replied Ford. "He was wounded in the duel and died a few weeks later in great suffering. Their dispute was over a young lady."

"I might have known. Was the little minx playing them off against one another?" He'd make her regret it if she had.

"Nothing like that!" Ford shook his head vigorously. "The lady was Lord Bramber's sister. She is dead now, too, poor creature."

"Poor creature?" Deprived of its rightful targets, Hadrian's anger fixed on his partner instead. "You sound sorrier for your fine neighbors than you do for my brother!"

"I pity *everyone* involved," Ford protested. "It was a terrible tragedy that never should have come to that."

"Then why did you not stop it?" cried Hadrian. "If you could not talk sense into this neighbor of yours, you should have been able to warn Julian."

"I tried to intervene when it began." Ford sounded defensive. "But I was told to mind my own business. When it all came to a head, Laura and I were abroad. I'd meant to return to Singapore, but... my plans changed. I had a great deal going on in my own life just then."

"Too much to care what happened to my brother?" Hadrian grabbed Ford by the arm. "Did you forget promising me you'd look out for him? Or would that have interfered too much with your grand new life as lord of the manor?"

"I hope you know me better than that." Ford wrenched his arm free. "I tried to talk to your brother, but he did not want my advice any more than he wanted to stand for Parliament. He only wanted your money to pay off the debts he'd incurred from idle living."

"That is a lie!" Hadrian stabbed his forefinger into his partner's chest, hoping to provoke a fight.

Landing a few good blows might vent the dangerous head of rage building inside him. And if Ford struck him hard enough, it might knock out the nagging fear that he was somehow to blame for his brother's death.

But Ford refused to be goaded, damn him! "It's the truth. Julian was a rash young fellow used to getting his own way. He acted improperly, but he did not deserve to die for it. Looking back, of course I wish I'd done more. But I never thought it would go so far."

"You let me down, after all I did for you." Turning away from his partner, Hadrian headed for the door before he said or did something he would regret even more. "Perhaps folk like you never feel a sense of obligation to folk like me."

As he strode away, the volatile brew of shock, desperation and fury within him threatened to collapse, leaving him as empty and dead inside as his brother. As dead as the Northmore family, of which he was now the last surviving member.

"Before you storm out of here," Ford called after him, "don't you want to know what became of the child?"

"Child?" That word stopped Hadrian in his tracks. It stirred the ashes in his heart like a breath of air, coaxing the dying embers to glow again. "What child?"

Chapter Two

"Dearest child!" Artemis lifted her nephew to her shoulder, inhaling his sweet baby scent as if it were the only air worth breathing. "I will do *anything* rather than give you up!"

They were heading back to Bramberley on a mild spring day, after visiting one of the tenant farms where Uncle Henry wanted her to place her nephew. After meeting the childless couple and judging their manner toward Lee, Artemis was determined not to let them have him.

"I could tell you didn't like them," she crooned. "The woman so coarse and her husband so gruff. It's not a child they want, but a future servant. The impertinence of that woman, saying she'd soon cure you of being so spoilt. I shudder to think what her cure might be. It made me so angry, I wanted to give a most uncivil answer."

She hadn't, of course—probably couldn't if she tried. All her life she'd been taught to avoid strong emotion in favor of well-bred decorum and reserve. Even with those she loved most dearly, she'd never been able to express her true feelings. It grieved her to think her brother and sister might have gone to their graves, never knowing how much she'd loved them.

Somehow it was easier with her nephew. Perhaps because he was so tiny and helpless, she'd been able to break through her deeply in-grained reserve and demonstrate her affection for him. Now her fear of losing him made Artemis clutch the child too tightly. He began to struggle against her embrace, demanding to be let down.

"Very well, you can walk for a while." She blew a rude, wet kiss on each of Lee's plump cheeks to make him laugh, then she set him on his sturdy little feet.

He crowed with delight at getting his own way. His lively gray eyes sparkled with quicksilver curiosity.

As he staggered forward over the high weald heath, Artemis clutched the leading strings of his frock to help keep him upright. "You're happy to be away from Bramberley, aren't you? Out here, you can explore and make as much noise as you like."

A foretaste of homesickness gripped her when she contemplated leaving the crumbling Tudor mansion that had been her beloved home for more than a quarter of a century. Her only comfort was the thought that more modest quarters might be better suited to rearing a busy little boy. If only she could secure such a place and find the means to pay for it.

Preoccupied with her worries and watching that her nephew did not wander into a patch of nettles, Artemis failed to notice they were not alone, until a pair of dark boots and trousers appeared in view. With a spirited shriek, Lee pelted toward them, flinging his stout little arms around one lean leg.

"I beg your pardon, sir!" Artemis dived to extract the gentleman from her nephew's grip. "I did not notice you standing there or I would have held him back."

A vague sense of annoyance bristled within her. Why did this man not have the courtesy to announce himself, rather than silently observing them while she was unaware of his presence? Really, it was tantamount to spying! She would pick up her nephew and make as dignified an escape as possible under the circumstances.

Lee had other ideas. He clung to the stranger's leg with stubborn determination, protesting his aunt's efforts to dislodge him with loud howls. After several unsuccessful attempts, Artemis had no choice but to pry his small fingers from the gentleman's trousers.

If there was a more humiliating position in which a lady might find herself with a strange man, Artemis did not want to imagine it! Her head was directly level with the lap of his trousers, which she discovered to her consternation, when she happened to glance that way. As she struggled to detach Lee's stubborn grip, her fingertips frequently grazed the stranger's firm, muscular thigh. By the time she managed to pull her wailing nephew away, her breath was racing and her face ablaze.

She looked up into the stranger's face at last, expecting an expression of shock, embarrassment or, if she was very fortunate, amusement. Instead a pair of cold, granite-gray eyes fixed upon Lee with dangerous intensity.

"He's a strong-willed lad." The stranger's deep, masterful voice carried easily over the child's howls of frustration.

Artemis could not tell whether his words were meant as praise or censure. But the northern cadence of his speech immediately put her on guard. In spite of his well-tailored clothes and air of authority, this was no gentleman. The scoundrel who'd destroyed her family had spoken like that.

Bouncing Lee in her arms to quiet him, Artemis fixed the stranger with a haughty glare. "He is a good boy. Your sudden appearance must have dismayed him. May I ask what business leads you to trespass on Bramberley land?"

The stranger seemed in no hurry to enlighten her. "Surely if I'd frightened the child, Lady Artemis, he would have run away instead of sticking to my leg like a plaster. If you'd left him where he was, I reckon he'd be better pleased."

Her antagonism toward the man intensified, even as her fingertips tingled from their recent contact with his leg. Sweeping a critical gaze over him, Artemis found little to approve. He was bigger than a gentleman ought to be—tall and broad-shouldered with a thrusting chest and an intimidating presence. His hawk nose and the sharp arch of his dark brows gave him a predatory air.

That must be what made it so difficult to catch her breath. That, and the veiled threat of him calling her by name.

"Do you presume an acquaintance with me, sir?" she demanded. "You must be mistaken. I have never seen you before in my life."

She was perfectly certain of that. She would have remembered his devilish looks more clearly than those of a handsomer man. And yet, there was something vexingly familiar about this stranger.

"It is true we have never met before," he replied. "But I have heard of you as you may have of me. My name is Hadrian Northmore and that boy is my nephew."

The name hit Artemis like a bolt of lightning. Hadrian Northmore—brother of the man who had destroyed her family. No wonder she'd loathed him on sight!

"I have heard of you, Mr. Northmore." She tilted her chin, so she could look down her nose at him. "Your vulgar fortune was much bandied about to excuse your late brother's disreputable conduct."

"You think my fortune vulgar, do you?" His fierce visage darkened like a thunderhead. "I suppose it is tainted by the sweat of my labor, unlike an *elegant* fortune gained without effort from tenant rents, investment or inheritance. Others may have sweat, bled or even died to earn that money in the beginning, but distance cleanses it, so as not to stain the delicate hands of ladies and gentlemen."

The man exuded contempt for Artemis, her family and her entire class. Though she considered it beneath her dignity to respond to such ill-bred insolence, she could not let it pass unanswered.

"You are putting words in my mouth, sir, and I will not stand for that. A fortune like yours is not vulgar on account of how it was earned, but how it is spent. People like you think everything in life can be bought and sold. You do not understand there are things upon which one cannot put a price. Honor is not for sale. Love cannot be hired or auctioned to the highest bidder. True breeding cannot be purchased."

His lip curled in a sneer of salty scorn. "You cannot have seen much of the world if you believe such nonsense. The law courts are full of men who would sell their honor at a bargain price. As for ladies and love, the *marriage market* did not get its name for nothing."

Those words struck Artemis like a backhanded blow. She knew many people viewed marriage as a transaction to secure material comfort or social advancement. Bad enough when both parties entered into such a union with their eyes open to the cold calculation of it all, but when an inexperienced girl was flattered by false attention into an imprudent attachment...

That had almost happened to her. Thank heaven she'd heeded the call of duty in time to save herself from worse hurt. Her impulsive, wayward little sister had not been so fortunate.

The thought of Daphne roused Artemis from her fierce concentration upon Hadrian Northmore. She'd been so preoccupied with him, she had almost forgotten her sister's child. The dear little fellow might have fallen from her arms for all the heed she'd paid him.

But when she forced her attention back to Lee, she realized his cries had subsided. He'd nestled against her shoulder and fallen asleep. She must not let Hadrian Northmore make her neglect her duty to the child a moment longer.

"I bow to your superior knowledge of all things mercenary, sir. Now you must excuse us. My nephew needs his rest." With as much poise as she could muster while carrying a sleeping child who weighed well over a stone, Artemis strode away from Hadrian Northmore. She hoped never to set eyes on the man again.

But his voice pursued her. "*Our* nephew, don't you mean, Lady Artemis?"

That shocking, threatening truth made her knees buckle. She stumbled over a tussock of hardy golden gorse.

As Artemis struggled to catch her balance without dropping her nephew, Mr. Northmore lunged toward her. His powerful arms encircled her and the child, gathering them to his broad chest. In a desperate effort to clear her head, she drew a deep breath, only to fill her nostrils with his scent—an unsettling fusion of smoke, spice and sheer masculine vitality. It did nothing to steady her. Quite the opposite, in fact.

"You should be more careful." His gruff mutter sent a surge of warm breath ruffling her hair. "I do not want any harm coming to this young lad. Fancy, all our bickering and jostling hasn't woken him. He must have the Northmore gift for being able to sleep through anything."

Those words forced Artemis to rally the balance and composure Hadrian Northmore had shaken so badly. Planting her feet firmly beneath her, she shrank from him. "I will thank you to release me at once and refrain from presuming to tell me how to tend *my* nephew."

Mr. Northmore started when she spoke, as if he had not realized how long and how tightly he'd been holding her.

"Would you rather I'd let you fall on your face?" he growled as he let her go and backed away.

All her life, Artemis had found it disagreeable when strangers came too close to her. She'd often wished she could erect a wall to keep a safe, private space around herself. As she grew older, she'd discovered that a cool gaze and an air of aloofness held most strangers at bay. Whenever someone did trespass, restoring her personal boundaries afterward always brought a rush of intense relief.

What made this time so different? Perhaps Hadrian Northmore's overpowering presence was too potent to be easily dispelled. His dangerous yet intriguing scent clung to her. Every part of her where he had touched smoldered with a vexing heat.

Those bewildering sensations sharpened her tone. "I would rather you had never come here in the first place!"

It was the rudest thing Artemis had said to anyone in her whole life. Yet she could not deny the savage thrill of striking a verbal blow against the man whose brother had destroyed her family.

Before he could reply in kind, she added. "Since you neglected to answer my question, I must ask again, what brings you to Bramberley?"

Was it possible he'd come to beg her pardon for what his reckless young rogue of a brother had done? To make some token gesture of restitution in the only medium he understood—hard cash? Though no amount of money could heal her grief or soften her resentment, Artemis was prepared to accept it for Lee's sake.

That tantalizing hope wrought a shift in her perception of Hadrian Northmore. His towering height no longer seemed so threatening. His dark, brooding features looked rather attractive.

But when he answered her question, his reply ripped the breath from her lungs and set every nerve in her body on fire. "I want the child."

Hadrian had not realized how desperately he wanted custody of his nephew until the lad staggered toward him.

The child did not look much like a Northmore with his fair coloring, plump cheeks and dimpled chin. But there was an appealing sturdiness about him. His boldness, energy and determination all proclaimed their kinship.

Perhaps Julian's son had sensed it, too—pelting toward his uncle with the instinct of a fledgling returning to its nest, latching on to his leg with amazing strength for such a small creature. And how he'd resisted when his aunt tried to pull him away—stubbornly clinging to what he wanted, hanging on against overwhelming opposition! Once the battle was lost, he'd protested the injustice at the top of his lungs. But when that did no good, he hadn't wasted energy whimpering or sulking. Instead he'd put the setback behind him and promptly gone to sleep, gathering strength for his next challenge.

Hadrian was determined to put up an equally resolute fight to claim his nephew. And he would *not* lose, for he possessed the strength and means to overcome the chief obstacle keeping them apart—Lady Artemis Dearing.

For all her slender, alluring delicacy, Hadrian did not underestimate his opponent. There was a glint of regal valor in her striking blue-violet eyes and a ring of icy antagonism in her dulcet voice.

Though her haughty disdain stung, he could not stifle a grudging flicker of admiration for anyone with enough spirit to stand up to him.

After an instant of dazed silence, Lady Artemis fixed him with a glacial glare. "You may *want* my nephew all you like, Mr. Northmore. But you will never get your hands on him, of that I can assure you. I suggest you spare us both any further unpleasantness by going back to wherever you came from and leaving me to raise him in peace."

With a contemptuous arch of her dark brows, the lady turned and walked away. This time she took care not to tilt her chin so high and risk tripping over the uneven ground. No doubt she wished to avoid repeating the indignity of being caught in the arms of a man she'd defied and insulted.

Hadrian would not have minded swooping to her rescue again, if necessary. He'd been unprepared for the rush of satisfaction that had surged through him when he'd clutched her and the child tight against his chest, saving them from harm. But if Lady Artemis thought she could dismiss him like one of her servants, she was very much mistaken.

He strode after her. "I can assure *you,* I have no intention of being so easily discouraged. I am accustomed to getting what I want and it will take more than a little unpleasantness to deter me."

The lady stiffened when she realized he was following her, but she did not stop or glance his way. "Perhaps this is the first time you have hankered after something your money cannot buy, sir. My nephew is not a commodity for purchase. I would not consider parting with him for any sum you could pay."

"In my experience, people who claim they cannot be bought are only trying to drive up their price." Hadrian kept a sharp watch for her reaction.

It was all part of the bargaining process—bid, refusal, counter-offer, bluff and call. Success often depended upon the ability to predict an opponent's next move or gauge his weakness. But Lady

Artemis proved difficult to decipher. Her blatant contempt for him was so intense it masked any subtler reactions. It did not help that Hadrian found himself distracted whenever his gaze lingered upon her.

Searching her eyes for a hint of fear, he was lured to plunge into their bewitching depths. When he studied her lips for a tremor of uncertainty, he caught himself wondering if they had ever been properly kissed.

The lady shook him out of such wayward thoughts with a derisive sniff. "Clearly we move in very different circles. Even if I were so shamefully degraded as to consider peddling my own flesh and blood, you would be the last person to whom I would sell him."

"You forget," Hadrian snapped, "the boy is *my* flesh and blood, too. If we were in the Orient, their system of justice might compel you to give him to me as compensation for the murder of my brother."

His words made Lady Artemis walk faster. "I count myself fortunate to live in a civilized society where an innocent child would never be so barbarously consigned."

Was a system of justice based on restitution more barbarous than one that would hang a starving child for stealing food?

Before Hadrian could voice that indignant question, Lady Artemis pressed on, her speech broken by frequent gasps for breath. "Even if such 'eye for an eye' sanctions were applied in England, you would surely be the one to owe *me* compensation. My brother may have caused the death of yours, but he put *both* my brother and sister in their graves, as well as dragging our family through the mud."

"The duel was your brother's idea," Hadrian protested. "I am certain if it had been left up to Julian, no one need have come to harm."

Though he knew antagonizing Lady Artemis would only make it harder to gain custody of his nephew, Hadrian could not help himself. She'd had more than a year to come to terms with this sordid tragedy and carry on with her life. As far as his heart was concerned, his brother's death might have happened only yesterday. With one vital difference...

It was far too late to hold a funeral, don mourning garb or perform any of the usual rituals that helped the bereaved make some sense of death's profound mystery. Only by confronting Lady Artemis Dearing, in place of her brother and sister, could he purge some of the poisonous feelings that possessed him.

"What choice did my brother have?" She shifted her grip on the sleeping child. "He had to defend my sister's honor against the man who had callously seduced her and got her with child out of wedlock."

As they crested a bit of rising ground, the great house appeared like a stately dowager with all its lofty spires and gables. Hadrian knew better than to suppose he could follow Lady Artemis through the imposing gatehouse. What he had left to say, he must say quickly.

"Was that precious *honor* worth the lives of two men in their prime? Where I come from, a girl's father or brother would give the fellow a sound thrashing, then haul the pair of them in front of a parson. By the time the babe was born, nobody would remember or care when it was begot."

Something caused a hitch in the lady's regal stride. Was she growing tired? Or had his barb found its mark?

"No doubt things are a great deal simpler where you come from. If families like mine took such a lax attitude to this sort of disgrace, it would be an open invitation for unscrupulous rogues to seduce their way into our ranks. No unwed lady of quality would be safe from their odious attentions."

This time it was Hadrian's step that faltered. "Are you saying my brother bedded your sister against her will?"

"Not strictly against her will, perhaps, but certainly against her discretion and the wishes of her family." Her outraged tone warned Hadrian she would never permit wanton passion to lure her from the narrow path of propriety.

"You said Julian put your sister in her grave. Did she die in childbed, then?" Hadrian's throat tightened. "If you hold him responsible for that, many a loving husband must bear the blame for his wife's death."

"My sister survived the birth, though it was difficult and certainly weakened her." Lady Artemis kept her eyes fixed upon the house, clearly eager to reach the sanctuary of its imposing walls. "She died eight months later, her spirit broken by the consciousness of how her innocent folly had brought shame upon our family and led to our brother's death."

Hadrian stifled a troublesome spark of sympathy for the dead girl. "So you admit it *was* her fault and not my brother's."

Lady Artemis cast him a sidelong glance of scathing contempt. "If you had any finer feelings, you might understand that people may bear an undeserved sense of responsibility, even when they are not to blame."

The last thing Hadrian expected was for her offensive words to bring him an unaccountable rush of relief. No doubt it was the last thing she intended. "If my brother's child is such a scandalous stain on your family's reputation, I cannot understand why you refuse to give him up."

Lady Artemis practically ran the last few steps to the gatehouse. Once beneath its stone archway, she turned to skewer Hadrian with a challenging glare. "He is all I have left, Mr. Northmore. I cannot expect you to understand how that feels. I will not give him to you to ruin his character with too much money and too little attention."

Her accusation knocked the wind out of Hadrian. She was completely wrong about him not knowing the devastation of such a loss.

Perhaps sensing her advantage, Lady Artemis pressed on. "For his sake, go away and leave us in peace."

Without waiting for an answer, she stalked off into the courtyard.

The child stirred then and opened his eyes. Spotting Hadrian, he reached a small hand over his aunt's shoulder toward his uncle.

"I am not going anywhere!" Hadrian bellowed after Lady Artemis. "I will do whatever it takes to get my nephew!"

Chapter Three

"Hush, dearest!" Half an hour after her confrontation with Mr. Northmore, Artemis had still not succeeded in quieting her nephew.

She'd tried feeding him, changing his linen, bouncing him in her aching arms until she feared they would be wrenched out of their sockets. Nothing had worked. After a year of caring for Lee day and night, Artemis recognized the difference between a hungry cry, a weary cry or an injured cry. This was one she had not heard often—a wail of bloody-minded vexation.

"Hush!" she begged him again, practically driven to tears herself. "This won't endear you to Uncle Henry. He may toss us both out tonight and have done with it."

She would give anything for an hour's peace to review her limited options and decide what to do next. The sudden appearance of Hadrian Northmore had made an already desperate situation far worse. Despite her brave boast about never letting him have Lee, Artemis feared she might soon have no choice.

Even if she'd been willing to entrust Lee to one of Bramberley's tenants, Mr. Northmore could easily bribe such people to give him the child. If she defied Uncle Henry's orders and got them expelled from Bramberley, she had no money to provide for her nephew. Even if she could find work as a governess or companion to some ailing dowager, she would never be permitted to keep a child with her. Which would place her right back where she'd started.

Heaving a dispirited sigh, Artemis sank onto the nearest chair and took her nephew's weight onto her knees. For a moment his cries quieted. Then he inhaled several deep, wet breaths and began to howl again.

"You must get your temper from the Northmores." Artemis struggled to wipe his dribbling nose with her handkerchief. "Your eyes, too. They are the very same shade of gray as his."

That should have not come as a surprise, but somehow it did—this intimate connection between the child she loved and the man she loathed. Was it possible Lee sensed it, too?

"You would go with him in a trice, wouldn't you, ungrateful little creature? What would become of you then?" What *would* become of him? She'd been so preoccupied with venting months of pent-up frustration upon Hadrian Northmore, she had never bothered to enquire about his plans for the boy.

Now that she'd purged some of those dangerously intense feelings, Artemis found herself able to view the situation more objectively. Was it possible her interests and Mr. Northmore's might not run altogether contrary? After all, they had one important thing in common—they both wanted Lee when no one else seemed to.

"I vowed I would do anything to keep you." Artemis cuddled the crying child close and drizzled kisses over his tear-streaked little face. "And Mr. Northmore threatened to do anything to get you. Perhaps we need to find out just how far each of us is willing to go."

Lee seemed to endorse her idea. Or perhaps he was only responding to her kisses and calmer tone of voice. His cries lapsed into a series of sniffling hiccoughs. Artemis rubbed his back while she talked through her plans.

"I cannot let Mr. Northmore know how desperate our situation is. I am certain he is the kind of man who would not scruple to exploit an adversary's weakness. So I must act quickly, before he discovers mine."

Summoned to the inn's back parlor, Hadrian paused on the threshold. "Why, Lady Artemis, this is a surprise."

Not only was he astonished that she'd sought him out after their hostile exchange the day before, she scarcely looked like the same woman he'd happened upon while scouting out Bramberley. If it had not been for her haughty manner and formal way of speaking, he might have mistaken her for a nursemaid taking his nephew for an outing in the fresh spring air.

Today she looked every inch the daughter of a marquis, from the toes of her kid slippers to the crown of her chip hat. A footman in full livery lurked beside the door. This was what Hadrian had pictured when Ford first mentioned Lady Artemis Dearing.

She acknowledged his greeting with a cool half smile. "Perhaps now you will understand how I felt when you appeared out of the blue yesterday, Mr. Northmore. After we parted, I had an opportunity to reflect upon our conversation and repent my incivility. I have come to apologize for any offense I may have given."

Her speech was a model of polished courtesy, expressing all the proper sentiments. Hadrian did not believe a word of it. Given a choice, he would far rather receive pithy insults from the lady's pretty lips than insincere apologies.

What had brought her here, then, if not genuine regret for the way she'd abused him yesterday? Was she hoping to scare him off with a show of grandeur?

"That is most gracious of you." Determined to demonstrate he could play her game, Hadrian reached for her slender, gloved hand and lifted it to his lips. "I hope you will disregard anything I may have said in the haste and heat of temper."

Speaking of heat, he could not forget the unwelcome spark that had crackled through him when her fingers brushed against his leg.

Or when he'd caught her and his nephew in his arms. An echo of it kindled in his lips as he inhaled a faint whiff of lavender from her glove.

"Of course." Her answer sounded a trifle breathless.

Hadrian glanced up to see a flattering hint of color blossom in her cheeks.

Her hand jerked back as if she feared he might bite off one of her fingers. "I was hoping we could discuss the matter you raised yesterday. This time without haste or temper, but calmly as civilized adults."

Did she doubt him capable of calm discussion and civilized conduct? Though he'd made a show of accepting her apology, Hadrian resented the insults Lady Artemis had hurled at him during their first encounter. And he would *never* forgive her family for bringing about his brother's death.

"I would welcome the opportunity." Her sudden willingness to negotiate made him wonder if her position was as strong as he'd feared. "Where shall we talk?"

"Why not here?" Lady Artemis glanced around the rustic room with a massive brick hearth at one end. "I took the liberty of speaking with the innkeeper. He assured me we would not be disturbed."

Anticipating Hadrian's agreement, she seated herself on a sturdy armchair upholstered with horsehair.

"Very well." Hadrian sank onto a matching chair opposite her. "By *the matter,* I presume you mean my intention to seek custody of my nephew."

"Just so." Lady Artemis hesitated, as if trying to decide how to begin. "I am curious to learn more about your plans for Lee and to discover why you want him so badly. Have you no children of your own?"

The unexpected question made Hadrian flinch. He hated being reminded of that tiny grave in the Company cemetery at Madras. "I am not married, nor do I intend to be."

Once had been enough to convince him marriage and a family were not his destiny.

"Then who would care for Lee, Mr. Northmore? I understand you have been very successful in the East Indies trade. Would you retire from it and settle permanently in England, as Lord Kingsfold has done?"

Hadrian shook his head vigorously. "I have fared well in the Indies, especially since moving my business to Singapore, but most of my fortune is invested in my company. I must return after Christmas when the East Indies fleet sails."

Before he could answer her other question, Lady Artemis cried, "You would drag a small child half a world away from everyone and everything he has ever known?"

"Of course not!" Did she think he was mad? "The tropical climate is a scourge on European children. My partner's young daughter seems to thrive on it, but she is an exception. My friend Raffles lost three of his four children to disease in half a year."

He did not speak of his own bereavement. That was none of this proud lady's business. "I would find someone trustworthy to care for the child here in England and see that he is given every advantage money can buy."

Lady Artemis edged forward in her chair. Was she going to remind him what she'd said yesterday about all the things his money could *not* buy?

"I am vastly relieved to hear you do not intend to uproot Lee and take him off to such an unhealthy place." For the first time since they'd met, she seemed to regard Hadrian with approval. "But surely you must understand why I cannot give up my sister's son, a child I have cared for since he was born, to be brought up by strangers?"

"Yes...well..." Put like that, his plans for the lad did sound rather unfeeling.

Hadrian reminded himself there was a world of difference between his idea of caring for a child and that of people like the

Dearings. His nephew would not pine for a woman who stopped by his nursery now and then or took him for an occasional stroll.

But there was a note of urgency in the lady's tone he could not deny. "No caretakers, however well paid, could have the same concern for Lee's welfare as his blood relatives. He is such a little fellow and you will be so far away. How would you know if such people were providing him with proper care?"

"I have eight months to find someone suitable. Surely by then…" Hadrian refused to admit how much her suggestions unsettled him. As did the reminder of his greatest weakness—time. Any legal measures he might take to gain custody of his nephew would not be swiftly resolved. Especially against a family as well connected as the Dearings. To keep the child, Lady Artemis had only to delay until Hadrian was obliged to return to Singapore.

And he had as good as told her so.

If the lady realized it, she did not gloat over the fact. "Perhaps our aims are closer than they might first appear, Mr. Northmore. I want to raise Lee to be a gentleman of honor, as I promised his mother. You have the admirable intention of providing him with every material advantage. Rather than fight over him like those two women in the story of King Solomon, could we not cooperate to give our nephew the best possible upbringing?"

The suggestion sounded reasonable enough. And Lady Artemis looked so appealing with her subtle, twilight beauty. It made Hadrian want to agree, if only to coax a smile from her. Then he recalled some of the insults she'd hurled at him the day before. He also recalled how his brother had been killed for presuming to make love to her sister.

"Cooperate in what way?" He peered into the blue-violet depths of her eyes, striving to fathom her true motives.

"Is it not obvious? If you take custody of Lee, you will need someone to supervise his upbringing when you return to the Orient. I wish to continue caring for him, but I do not find Bramberley well suited to raising a high-spirited young child. Surely the most reasonable course…"

A clutch of hot coals began to smolder in the pit of Hadrian's belly. "You mean you would be willing to take my *vulgar* money to live in high style in your own establishment?"

Her eyes flashed with outrage, but she maintained her facade of courtesy. "That accusation is most unworthy of you, sir. However great your fortune, you could not possibly provide me with accommodations to equal Bramberley. But a grand house is not necessarily the best place to bring up a child. I had something more modest in mind."

She had a valid point, much as it vexed Hadrian to admit. Anyone else he hired to care for his nephew might be tempted to enrich themselves at the child's expense. Artemis Dearing's wealth set her above mercenary considerations. Was it possible his suspicions about her were unfounded?

"I beg your pardon, ma'am. I cannot help but wonder why you would be willing to do this for me. Especially considering your attitude toward my brother. Yesterday you said I was the last person in the world to whom you would give your nephew. What has changed your mind?"

Hadrian Northmore was a dangerous man. Artemis had sensed it from the moment she'd first glimpsed him on the heath near Bramberley. Now, as she scrambled to contrive an excuse he might believe, she was more certain than ever.

Though it sickened her to contemplate taking his money to care for her nephew, she reminded herself it was for Lee's sake. If his uncle agreed to her proposal, they would never have to be parted and Lee could have all the advantages she would never be able to provide for him otherwise. Surely his mother would have approved, even if it cost Artemis her pride?

"What changed my mind? Why, *you* did, sir, by explaining your plans just now, so that I could see your gaining Lee did not have to mean I must lose him. Also, much as it pains me to admit, my sister did care for your brother. I do not believe she would want me to keep their son from you."

"If I agreed to this arrangement, would you permit the lad to bear my family name?" The severe set of Mr. Northmore's wide mouth warned Artemis this mattered a great deal to him.

Her tongue burned with the urge to refuse his presumptuous demand. Who were the Northmores, after all? Nothing but *mushrooms*—so called because they sprang up fast out of the dung. Her family had been in the first rank of British society for centuries. The third Marquis of Bramber had borne the canopy over King Charles I at his coronation. His grandson, Viscount Singlecross, had helped put down Monmouth's Rebellion. Lady Lettice Dearing had been a lady-in-waiting to Queen Anne.

Nothing but the thought of Lee's stout little arms around her neck and the sweet gurgle of his laughter could have compelled Artemis to reply, "If you insist."

"I do." Mr. Northmore's harsh tone made those two words sound like a threat.

Artemis refused to be intimidated. "Though I do not understand why it matters."

His powerful hands tightened around the arms of his chair. "It matters because my nephew is the last of our line. I am determined to rescue my family from the brink of extinction and raise it to a place of prominence, from which it will never be threatened in future."

That proved precisely what she had suspected—the man was nothing but a power-hungry social climber. Artemis strove to keep her lip from curling.

"Prosperity is no guarantee of survival, sir. Many a noble house has died out for lack of heirs." The Dearings might soon be among them, thanks to this man's brother.

"They haven't enough good red blood." Hadrian Northmore did

not bother to hide *his* contempt. "Whatever our other faults, my family does not shrink from breeding."

The man had already made her blush once, when he'd kissed her hand in the manner of a true gentleman. Now he did it again with a most ungentlemanly remark. Artemis had good reason to know the Northmores did not shrink from breeding—even outside the bounds of matrimony.

"Are we agreed, then?" Artemis hurried on. "You will provide for all Lee's material needs, while I attend to his upbringing?"

"Not so fast, if you please." Hadrian Northmore leaned back in his chair, resting his strong, jutting chin against his raised fist. "I foresee some difficulties with this proposed arrangement of yours."

"Such as…?"

His narrowed eyes ranged over her in a way that made Artemis squirm. "An unwed lady living on her own—wouldn't be proper, would it? The lad already has one strike against him, being born on the wrong side of the blanket."

"I always conduct myself with the utmost propriety, sir. I resent your suggestion that I would ever do otherwise, particularly with an impressionable young child in my care."

If it were possible for her to stray from the path of strict decorum, a man like Hadrian Northmore might tempt her. That unwelcome thought shook Artemis to the solitary, sensible core of her being.

"I am not saying you would *do* anything improper." His tone implied that he did not think her capable of it. "I am only saying it might *appear* so. Appearances matter to the kind of people I want the boy associating with once he's older."

It galled Artemis to admit the truth of that. Members of the *ton* could get away with the most despicable wrongdoing, provided they were discreet. Yet a perfectly harmless incident could bring down the full weight of society's censure, simply because it had the appearance of impropriety. If anyone had seen her out on the heath yesterday in Hadrian Northmore's arms, it could have ruined her reputation. If he were a gentleman, honor would have dictated he make her an offer of marriage.

That improbable notion sent her pulse into a skittish dance, which Artemis struggled to ignore. "I am certain I could find a respectable chaperon, if you felt it was necessary. Have you any other objections?"

Mr. Northmore nodded. "Such a handsome lady is bound to attract suitors, especially if she is in control of her young ward's fortune. Where would it leave the lad and me if you decided to marry? I will not have some man I've never met in a position of influence over my nephew."

Did he expect her to be flattered that he'd called her handsome? Hard as Artemis tried to dismiss the compliment, she could not. He'd tossed it off in such a blunt, careless way, as he might have declared the sky was blue or the grass green. For the third time in less than an hour, Artemis felt the blood rise in her cheeks.

"I am nine-and-twenty years old," she replied, as much to remind herself as to inform him. "I have long been on the shelf. Even if some other gentleman were shortsighted enough to fancy me handsome, marriage holds no attraction for me. My nephew...*our* nephew is the only gentleman with whom I wish to share a home. Unless..."

The maddest idea possessed her, born of desperation in the face of Hadrian Northmore's frustrating resistance. "Unless *you* were prepared to marry me...entirely as a matter of convenience, of course."

For once the man looked lost for words. Artemis congratulated herself on that small victory. She hoped the threat of having to wed her would make the alternative, of merely employing her, more attractive.

Before he could recover his voice, she rattled on with counterfeit eagerness, "Such an arrangement would answer all your objections, would it not? I would be a perfectly respectable married woman with a husband working abroad. No one would raise an eyebrow over my living arrangements. And you would not have to worry that I might marry anyone else in your absence. Since neither of us is inclined to wed in future, it would create no encumbrance."

As she spoke, Mr. Northmore's dazed stare tensed into a scowl of profound concentration. Or perhaps it betrayed his deep aversion to the idea of marrying her.

Given their vast differences and mutual bitterness, that was quite natural and all to the good, Artemis told herself, disregarding a foolish pang of humiliation. She did not want to marry him either, not even as a pure formality. The greater his distaste, the more anxious he would be to accept a less drastic alternative.

Hadrian Northmore sprang from his seat and began to pace in front of the hearth, one hand tucked behind his back while he rubbed his chin with the other.

"You know, that may not be as daft a scheme as it sounded at first." His words stumbled out in a disjointed mutter, as if he were trying to persuade himself.

Good heavens! He wasn't actually considering it, was he? For the first time in her life she'd acted on an impulse and look where it had landed her.

"You are too polite, sir." Artemis endeavored to undo the damage. "It is a ridiculous idea. I see that now. Let us think no more of it, I beg you."

He seemed too lost in his own thoughts to heed her. "I could adopt the lad as my heir. If we married, you and he would both bear the Northmore name. By the time he is old enough for school, the scandal of his birth may be forgotten and people might assume he is our son."

"Perhaps so, but—"

"Say no more, Lady Artemis. You have persuaded me." Hadrian Northmore strode toward her. Seizing her by the arms, he raised her to her feet as if she weighed no more than a feather. "For the sake of our nephew, you *must* marry me!"

Chapter Four

If anyone had predicted he'd ever consider marriage again, let alone to the daughter of a marquis, Hadrian would have laughed in his face. Yet, here he was, not simply *considering* marriage to Lady Artemis, but quite determined to go ahead with it. His hands clamped around her slender arms as he awaited her answer.

"You and I marry?" Her eyes darted anxiously. "Surely you cannot mean that. We only met yesterday and we did not get on well."

Her reluctance only strengthened his resolve. "We have our differences, I'll admit. But we have one vital interest in common—the welfare of our nephew. Besides, it is not as if we will have to share a home for the rest of our lives. After a mere eight months, we will have no need for any contact beyond an annual exchange of letters."

Before she could reply, the footman called out from his place by the door, "Begging your pardon, my lady. Do you need any help?"

With a guilty start, Hadrian realized how it must look to the servant—him looming over Lady Artemis, holding her so close. He might appear to be threatening her, or perhaps taking liberties. Both notions unsettled him in different ways.

Abruptly he released the lady and stepped back.

"Thank you, Roger." Her answer sounded calmer than she appeared at close range. "I am in no danger from Mr. Northmore. If I require your assistance, I will not hesitate to call."

Lowering her voice, she directed her next words at Hadrian. "Would it not be easier to provide me with a house and money for Lee's expenses?"

Her reluctance reassured Hadrian. If she'd been eager to accept, it would have put him on his guard. "Think of the gossip and the harm to your reputation if anyone discovered you were living at my expense out of wedlock. I do not wish to bring more scandal upon your noble family. So it must be marriage or we will have a fight on our hands. Which do you choose?"

Expectant silence stretched tighter and tighter as he waited for Lady Artemis to make her decision. Hadrian felt a strange rush of danger and exhilaration, as if he were teetering on the brink of a high cliff above treacherous blue-violet waters. Though the lady's delicate features remained impassive, Hadrian fancied he could hear the low hum of her thoughts as they raced through her mind.

Then her chin tilted a trifle higher and she announced, "I suppose I must choose marriage."

"Excellent!" Only two days ago he had glimpsed his family and all his plans laid waste. Now they seemed to rise from the ashes.

The force of that dizzying turnabout pushed him toward Lady Artemis, his lips seeking hers as if to claim the spoils of victory.

The fine contours of her features, her flawless alabaster skin and her cool, detached manner all gave the impression she was not a real woman at all, but a classical statue that had somehow gained the power of movement and speech. It surprised Hadrian to find her lips so soft and warm beneath his. The unexpected pleasure tempted him to press it further. Then he remembered to whom those sweet lips belonged.

Before Lady Artemis could sputter with indignation, or slap his face, he drew back, speaking as if nothing had passed between them. "Now that you have consented, shall we set the date?"

"Soon." Lady Artemis sounded dazed by his sudden kiss. "As soon as you can procure a special license."

Her insistence on haste seemed odd, given her prior reluctance. Perhaps she wanted the wedding over with quickly, before she could change her mind.

Hadrian did not want to risk that happening. "Soon it shall be. I will go up to London at once to make the necessary arrangements."

"Lee and I will await your return." Lady Artemis made a formal little bow. "Send a carriage to Bramberley to collect us for the wedding."

As she swept from the room with majestic grace, Hadrian's mouth fell open just enough for the tip of his tongue to emerge and swipe over his lips, as if he expected the elusive flavor of her kiss to linger.

As she finished packing during Lee's nap, Artemis caught herself gazing into space, lost in the memory of Hadrian Northmore's swift, bewildering kiss.

For all its abruptness and vigor, it had not been rough or possessive. Indeed, the smooth heat of his lips had been a far more agreeable sensation than she would ever have anticipated. Not that she'd anticipated a kiss from Mr. Northmore in her wildest dreams.

Was this how his brother had ensnared her sister—luring Daphne to defy her family and risk ruin for the sake of a few fleeting moments of pleasure in his arms?

That thought rekindled the outrage that had smoldered in Artemis's heart for more than a year. How could she have agreed to wed into the family of her brother's killer? Not only agreed, but proposed the preposterous idea in the first place! No matter how desperate her circumstances, no matter how businesslike an arrangement it was meant to be, such a union could not be right.

Tiptoeing into the nursery, she gazed down at her nephew, asleep in his cot. A sweet, brooding ache swelled in her bosom.

"I would do anything for you," she whispered. "But this feels like such a betrayal of your mama and uncle."

She could still picture her brother's handsome face, contorted with reckless rage, on the day he'd discovered Daphne was with child. *"Damned if I will let that ill-bred scoundrel marry into this family!"*

It had been the most dreadful row—Leander ranting like a madman, Daphne sobbing violently, Artemis pleading for them both to exercise some restraint. The memory of it still made her bilious. What would her brother say if he knew she would be the means of a Northmore marrying into the Dearing family? Would his ghost rise from St. Botolph's churchyard to haunt her?

Artemis shook off a passing qualm. What was there to fear from her dead brother when she had two living uncles to face? Sooner or later she would have to inform them of her plans. Though she knew better than to expect a violent quarrel, she would almost have preferred it to Uncle Henry's cold, severe rebuke or Uncle Edward questioning her family loyalty. All over a course of action to which they had driven her.

A sudden idea tantalized Artemis with its promise. Perhaps there was still a way she could escape the predicament she had talked her way into. Blowing a kiss to the sleeping child, she tiptoed out of the nursery and went in search of her uncles.

She found them in the library, sipping their brandy.

"Uncle Henry, Uncle Edward." She curtsied. "I have some news."

"Found a suitable place for the child, have you?" asked Uncle Henry. "He must be gone by the end of next week, remember. I have invited Mrs. Bullworth to Bramberley and mean to propose to her in the Great Hall."

"Lee will definitely be gone by then." Artemis squared her shoulders. "As will I. I have accepted an offer of marriage from Mr. Hadrian Northmore. The wedding will take place as soon as he returns from London."

"Northmore?" Uncle Henry glowered. "Any relation to—?"

Artemis nodded. "He is Julian Northmore's elder brother. The one who made such a great fortune in the Indies with Lord Kingsfold. He is eager to take responsibility for his brother's child. He means to make Lee his heir."

"Then give him the child, by all means." Uncle Henry gulped a drink of his brandy. "But you cannot think of wedding such a man. It is out of the question!"

"Why?" Artemis could scarcely believe she was challenging the authority of her uncles. "I am well past the age of consent. Mr. Northmore is willing to provide a home for me *and* for my sister's child. That is more than I can find at Bramberley."

"Remember your rank and lineage," Uncle Henry urged.

"Remember the trouble his miserable brother made for this family," Uncle Edward added.

The second factor weighed far more heavily upon Artemis than the first. "I am only following your maxim, Uncle Henry. Sacrifices must be made for the good of the family. Though you may not choose to acknowledge him, Lee is my family. To keep him, I would marry the devil if I had to. And Hadrian Northmore is hardly that."

The man wanted to raise his family to the kind of prominence hers had once enjoyed. Was that so contemptible? Some distant forebearer must have had the ambition and good fortune to elevate the Dearings.

"Think of the talk." Uncle Henry set aside his glass. "Just when the other scandal was finally dying down."

Was he afraid her actions might cost him the rich bride he sought to snare?

"Break it off, Artemis," he entreated her. "If you have your heart set on keeping the child, perhaps something can be done. It will not be necessary for you to wed that odious man."

There it was—precisely the concession she'd hoped to wring from her uncle with the threat of marrying Hadrian Northmore. If she and Lee left Bramberley straightaway for some remote spot, Mr. Northmore would have little chance of finding them before he was obliged to return to Singapore. She would have what she wanted without being bound to the man who provoked far too many intense, unwelcome feelings in her. The man who would always be a reminder of what she had lost.

But as she prepared to accept her uncle's terms, a pang of conscience made Artemis hesitate. How would *she* feel if Hadrian Northmore took Lee and sailed off to the Indies where she could not follow? She would consider herself wickedly wronged, of course. Then how could she contemplate doing something similar to him? Another factor also weighed on her decision. It was one even Uncle Henry could understand.

"If you had made that offer last week, sir, I would have accepted most gratefully, but now I must decline."

"Why on earth…?" her uncle sputtered.

"Because I have given Mr. Northmore my word." Artemis struggled to subdue her misgivings. "And you have always told me the word of a Dearing is sacred."

"The solemnization of a marriage is always a sacred privilege." The vicar of St. Botolph's beamed at Hadrian as they stood on the steps of the old church awaiting his bride's arrival. "But never more than in this case."

"I am glad you approve." Hadrian was not sure what the vicar meant. "To be honest, I'm relieved you are willing to perform the ceremony, under the circumstances."

"More than willing." The vicar pushed up his spectacles. "Honored. Delighted!"

He was a slight, middle-aged man with thinning white hair and mild blue eyes. His air of naive charity was difficult for a practical man like Hadrian to fathom, though he found it rather disarming.

His face must have betrayed his puzzlement, for the vicar offered an explanation. "Your marriage to Lady Artemis exemplifies a true

Christian spirit of reconciliation after the tragic events of the past. I pray Our Lord will richly bless your union."

Reconciliation with the Dearings? It was all Hadrian could do to keep from venting a blast of bitter laughter in the vicar's face. At the same time, it troubled his conscience to receive undeserved praise for such virtuous motives. His marriage to Lady Artemis was based on hard necessity and cold mistrust, nothing more.

"We both want what is best for the child." Unable to meet the vicar's innocent gaze, Hadrian pulled out his watch and flicked it open. Then he peered up the road. "I hope Lady Artemis has not changed her mind."

It had taken him three days haunting the Doctors' Commons in London to secure the special license. Every hour his impatience had grown as he remembered her plea for haste. What if she had second thoughts and decided to fight him for the child?

The vicar gave an indulgent chuckle. "If I had a shilling for every nervous bridegroom I've heard utter those words, I could easily fill the parish poor box."

Hadrian contorted his mouth into a mirthless grin. He doubted any other groom had such good reasons for fearing his bride might not show up for their wedding. After a final glance at his watch, he clicked it shut and stuffed it back in his pocket.

The rumble of horses' hooves drew his gaze back to the road. He recognized the yellow post chaise he'd dispatched to Bramberley to fetch Lady Artemis and his nephew.

He strode toward the entrance to the churchyard, a wrought-iron gate set in a low stone wall. When the carriage came to a halt, he pulled the door open and prepared to hand Lady Artemis out. Instead, she bundled his nephew into his arms, then climbed from the carriage without his assistance.

The child let out a squeal of laughter and wriggled his sturdy arms and legs. It was like trying to hold a squirming piglet. Conflicting inclinations warred within Hadrian. Part of him wanted to hoist the lad in the air, like a prize he'd won after a hard-fought contest.

Another part warned him to be careful. It would be far too easy to grow attached to this appealing little fellow.

Holding the lad in an awkward grip, Hadrian peered past Lady Artemis into the empty interior of the carriage. "Where's his nursemaid?"

"He does not have one." Her tart tone suggested the question was ridiculous, perhaps even offensive. "I told you I have cared for him from the moment he was born."

So she had, Hadrian admitted to himself. But he could not believe she'd meant the day-to-day routines of tending a child this young: feeding, dressing, washing, changing linen, and soothing him when he was ill.

His nephew's squeals took on a fussy note.

"Hold him up to your shoulder," Lady Artemis advised, "so he has a good view of everything. Then perhaps he won't be so anxious to get down and walk about."

Turning away from him, she greeted the vicar with grave courtesy.

Reverend Curtis bowed. "As I was telling Mr. Northmore, it gives me great pleasure to preside over your nuptials. I consider this a most gratifying symbol of Christian forgiveness between two families who have—"

Lady Artemis stiffened. "Thank you for permitting the ceremony to take place here. Dearings have worshipped at St. Botolph's for centuries. I cannot imagine being married anywhere else."

"Will the Marquis and Lord Edward be joining us?" asked the vicar.

"I am afraid that will not be possible. My uncles are...indisposed at present."

Hadrian could guess the cause of their indisposition. He wondered if Lady Artemis had risked a permanent breach with her uncles in order to do the right thing for her nephew. That possibility kindled a reluctant glimmer of admiration for her.

Perhaps to forestall any more awkward comments from the vicar,

Lady Artemis began walking toward the church. "Have witnesses been arranged?"

The vicar nodded. "My sister and the parish clerk have agreed to witness the ceremony and sign the register."

Hadrian trailed after them with his nephew in his arms. Just as Lady Artemis had predicted, the child gazed around him, taking everything in. Whenever his eyes met Hadrian's, he flashed a wide, wet grin. If his aunt had tended him since his infancy, she'd done very well. The lad appeared healthy, happy and reasonably clever for his age.

They entered the church, which was softly lit by scattered candles and spring sunshine filtering through the stained glass of the altar window. It depicted a cloaked monk holding a traveler's staff. The place reminded Hadrian of another old country church, far to the north.

As they followed the vicar down the aisle, Hadrian's small nephew seemed to decide the church was too quiet.

"Ah-do-ma-ba!" He made a sudden grab for Hadrian's ear, doing his best to yank it off. His other hand found Hadrian's nose and gave it a sharp twist.

"Ow!" The pain shocked Hadrian back into the broad northern dialect of his youth. "Giveower and whisht, ye blasted wee bug—"

Artemis let out a horrified gasp that cut him off before he blurted out something very rude in church.

Taking advantage of his momentary confusion, she wrenched the child out of his arms. "I will thank you not to take such a rough tone with Lee. He is far too young to know what he is doing."

Her icy rebuke stung Hadrian more than his hot outburst seemed to have bothered their nephew. The wee imp chortled as if he knew he'd done something naughty and managed to get away with it.

Hadrian rubbed his smarting nose. "He's none too young to start learning to mind."

He sensed she wanted to fling a pithy retort at him, but by now they had reached the chancel steps, where their witnesses were waiting. Instead she turned away from him to greet the vicar's sister, who looked absurdly like her brother in a voluminous black dress and high white collar. While the two women fussed over his nephew, Hadrian shook hands with the parish clerk. The vicar took his place and spent a moment leafing through his prayer book.

Once he found the right page, he cleared his throat and launched into the service. "Dearly beloved, we are gathered together here in the sight of God, and in the face of this congregation, to join together this man and this woman in holy matrimony."

Those words took Hadrian back to the last time he'd heard them, in Fort St. George, Madras. He could scarcely imagine a wedding more different from that one than this. He and his first bride had been so eager to wed. The early struggle to make his fortune was behind him, while the tragedy of his past had begun to loosen its grip upon his heart. Margaret's vivacity and contagious high spirits had helped him look to the future with boundless hope.

He'd dreamed of siring a family of fine sons to carry on the Northmore name—lads who would never experience the danger and deprivation he and his brothers had endured. He'd foreseen a lifetime of happiness ahead with a family he would adore. Instead, after only two sweet, fleeting years, he'd lost his wife and infant daughter. And he had learned what a perilous thing hope could be.

An expectant pause wrenched Hadrian back from his painful reverie. Too late, he realized the moment for confessing any impediment to his present marriage had passed. Did the fact that he knew almost nothing about his bride count? Or that he did not much like the lady, let alone *love* her?

The vicar could not have guessed any of that, or he would never have fixed Hadrian with such a benevolent smile and asked, "Wilt thou have this woman to thy wedded wife?"

Wife. Until now, that word had made him think of someone quite unlike Artemis Dearing. It troubled Hadrian to find her so very alluring when she was so different from the wife he'd lost. He held her in a solemn gaze, determined to betray nothing of the wrenching memories this ceremony had revived. "I will."

Next the vicar addressed Lady Artemis. "Wilt thou take this man to thy wedded husband?"

"I will." She focused her attention on her small nephew, as if pledging her love and life to *him* instead of her bridegroom.

Stifling an unexpected pang, Hadrian reminded himself this marriage was entirely for the child's benefit. And he would have it no other way.

Chapter Five

While Reverend Curtis read the words of the marriage ceremony, Artemis struggled to keep her attention fixed upon her nephew, so she would not be so intensely aware of Mr. Northmore's potent presence. His relentless gray gaze seemed to measure her value as a wife and find her lacking in all respects.

The tone in which he spoke his vows made it clear he would just as soon have been marrying the vicar's middle-aged sister as her. Then why had he pressed that unsettling kiss upon her after she'd accepted his proposal? Did he think her a pathetic, lonely spinster who needed an amorous incentive to go through with this wedding?

"Please join hands," the vicar bid them.

"But..." Artemis shrank from the prospect of Hadrian Northmore's touch, though a small, traitorous part of her hankered for it. "My nephew..."

"*Our* nephew," he muttered.

Miss Curtis stepped forward. "I can take him. Surely he will be content to let me hold him for a few moments."

Artemis had her doubts, but she did not want to make a scene by refusing the lady's help. Surrendering Lee to Miss Curtis, she turned quickly back to her bridegroom. She hoped he would not mistake her impatience to get the ceremony over with for eagerness to become his wife.

She willed herself not to flinch when Mr. Northmore's large, powerful hand enveloped her slender, waxen fingers. The heat of his touch surprised her. As he repeated his vows after the vicar, she stared down at their clasped hands, refusing to meet his forbidding gaze. She told herself she did not care if he compared her unfavorably with other women—she had no illusions about her meager charms. Daphne had been the beauty of the family. She was the sensible one, the dutiful one—content to remain in the background while her adored sister captured all hearts.

"Repeat after me," the vicar prompted her, "I, Artemis Caroline, take thee, Hadrian Arthur, to my wedded husband."

Lee had begun to fuss the moment Miss Curtis took him. Now he was wailing so loudly his cries echoed off the old stone walls of the sanctuary.

For once, Artemis welcomed his tearful uproar, which drowned out her insincere promises to love, cherish and obey Hadrian Northmore. She hoped God would understand why she could never love the man, any more than he could love her. The best she could truly promise, for their nephew's sake, was that she would try not to hate him.

"Have you the ring?" the vicar asked Mr. Northmore, raising his voice to carry over Lee's howling.

Artemis could scarcely conceal her amazement when her bridegroom fished in his pocket and pulled one out. Had he purchased it in London while waiting for the license to be issued? She hadn't thought him the sort of man to remember such niceties. Then again, she was not well enough acquainted with Hadrian Northmore to know *what* sort of man he might be.

Once the ring was on her finger, Artemis turned toward the vicar's sister with her arms outstretched. "Let me take Lee again before he deafens us all."

Flushed and flustered, poor Miss Curtis looked relieved to hand over her small, noisy charge. "The child certainly has a healthy set of lungs."

"Hush, now." Artemis spoke in a half-soothing, half-chiding tone as Lee burrowed into her embrace.

"Hush is right." Hadrian Northmore pulled out a handkerchief to wipe Lee's dribbling nose. "Or everyone will think this is your way of objecting to the marriage."

As the vicar and their witnesses chuckled at the quip, Lee tried to avoid his uncle's handkerchief by turning his face toward his aunt. Mr. Northmore refused to give up, slipping his hand between the child's wet face and the bust of Artemis's gown. While he made a thorough job of mopping Lee's nose, the back of his hand brushed repeatedly against her bosom.

Artemis barely stifled a squeak of alarm. Or was it something else? Rather than shrinking from the casual friction of his touch, her nipples thrust out against her muslin bodice as if straining toward his hand, inviting the fevered chill he kindled in her flesh. By the time he drew back, Artemis was left shaken and breathless.

Fortunately no one else seemed to notice, Mr. Northmore least of all.

"That did the trick." He nodded toward Lee, quietly sucking on his thumb. "Now that we can hear ourselves again, what comes next, Vicar? Are we finished yet?"

"Only a little more." The vicar said a brief prayer, then pronounced them man and wife. "Once we have all signed the parish register, you are free to be on your way."

Hard as she tried, Artemis could not keep her hand from trembling when she signed her name. The enormity of what she had just done threatened to overwhelm her. She desperately needed a few minutes to marshal her composure before she was forced to share close quarters in the post chaise with her new husband.

Mr. Northmore did not appear inclined to linger after he had given the vicar and their witnesses each a generous present of money.

"You go ahead." Artemis searched for a plausible delay. "Lee and I will be along in a moment. There is something I would like to say to Miss Curtis."

At the moment she had no idea what, but surely she would think of something.

"As you wish." Mr. Northmore gave a brusque nod. "I'll go tell the post boy to make ready for our journey."

Journey? The word made Artemis even more uneasy. Where were they to go? She'd assumed they would stay at the local inn for tonight, at least, while discussing their plans for the future. Evidently, her new husband felt no need to consult her before making such decisions.

Had she made a grave mistake by placing her future, and Lee's, into Hadrian Northmore's powerful hands?

What sort of woman had he let into his life? Hadrian wondered as he strode out of St. Botolph's. All his instincts assured him his bride had not really wanted to speak with Miss Curtis. How could he have wed a woman who would lie about something so trivial? Even if their marriage was only a convenient arrangement, he should not have rushed into it so blindly.

As he stalked through the churchyard trying to calm his doubts, a pretty young lady with red-gold hair came flying toward him.

"I'm too late, aren't I?" She stopped in front of Hadrian, gasping for breath. "I've missed the wedding?"

"It just got over, I'm afraid. Are you a friend of the bride?"

"You might say that." The girl fanned her flushed face with her hand. "Her sister was my best friend in the world. When I heard from the servants that she was to be married today, I felt I must come. Are you Mr. Northmore?"

"I am." Hadrian gave a stiff, wary bow. "And you are…?"

"Susannah Penrose." She curtsied. "Lady Kingsfold's sister. I am sorry we did not get an opportunity to meet the other day when you called at Hawkesbourne."

"Of course. I see the resemblance now." Had the Dearing sisters looked alike, too? Hadrian found himself suddenly curious about the girl who had been his brother's downfall. "I'm sorry you came all this way for nothing, Miss Penrose. If I'd known you wished to attend the ceremony, I would have asked the vicar to wait."

"That was not my only reason for coming here this morning." Miss Penrose hesitated, as if gathering her courage. "I know you are angry with Ford over what happened to your brother, but please do not blame him! He tried to talk sense to the Dearings, but they refused to listen. That was the day Mama died and Ford had to go all the way to Brighton to fetch Binny and Sidney home. Then—"

"Talk sense to the Dearings about what?" Hadrian demanded as soon as he could squeeze a word in.

"About allowing your brother to court Daphne. Laura told me what happened. Lord Henry was furious with them for interfering and said some beastly rude things."

Her words rocked Hadrian. "Are you saying my brother wanted to court Lady Daphne...to marry her?"

He'd assumed the marquis had called Julian out for refusing to marry the lass after he'd bedded her. Even if that had been the case, Hadrian still considered death far too harsh a penalty. But if Julian had been killed simply because he'd aspired to a lady *above his station...*

Susannah Penrose bit her full lower lip. "I cannot say for certain if he meant to marry her. I do know he admired her a great deal and she was madly in love with him. When we first met your brother, I was quite envious of his interest in Daphne. It is my fault her sister found out she'd gone to meet him in secret. I never meant any harm, I swear! If she'd only confided in me, I would have kept her secret to my grave."

The young lady's pretty features crumpled, making her look like a tearful child. She pulled a handkerchief from her reticule and began to wipe her eyes.

"Do not blame yourself, Miss Penrose." Hadrian struggled to relax his stiff scowl. "It is clear where the responsibility for my brother's death lies. I wish Julian *had* set his sights on you rather than your friend."

Would Julian have known that? A spasm of guilt gripped Hadrian as he recalled the advice he'd asked Ford to convey to his brother, about the sort of wife he should seek. *One with good breeding and useful connections who can help the lad continue his rise in the world.*

Had Julian pursued Lady Daphne in a misguided effort to please *him?*

"Forgive me." Miss Penrose contorted her lips into a feeble smile. "I did not mean to stir up painful memories. I only wanted to say a few words in Ford's defense and beg you to make up your quarrel with him."

Hadrian hated to disappoint the girl, but he was still not convinced Ford had done all he might to avert this tragedy.

Miss Penrose clearly sensed his reluctance. "Surely you can forgive Ford if you could forgive Lady Artemis enough to marry her."

"Our marriage has nothing to do with forgiveness." Especially now that he had a clearer understanding of what had happened. "It is only for the sake of the child."

"I was certain it must be." Susannah Penrose stuffed her damp handkerchief back in her reticule. "It is very good of you to rescue the poor babe from that cold, crumbling old mansion. It grieved me to think of him growing up in such a place. Daphne hated it. She used to say genteel poverty was the worst kind. It must have been a wrench for Lady Artemis to leave, though. She was devoted to the horrid old place."

"Genteel poverty?" Hadrian gave a harsh, mirthless chuckle. "What is that—having only five carriages instead of ten?"

"There may be a dozen carriages at Bramberley," Miss Penrose replied, "but that hardly signifies if they are too old to be of use and there is only a single pair of horses to pull them. Ask Ford if you do not believe me. He says all the Dearings' income goes to keep up appearances and prevent Bramberley from falling into total ruin. Lady Artemis and the child will be far better off with you."

As the girl's words sank in, a fever of rage swept through Hadrian. No wonder Artemis Dearing had been willing to wed him in spite of her obvious aversion. The wretched manipulator, pretending their marriage was for her nephew's sake when she had only been using the child to secure her own comfort! And he had been so gullible, assuming she could have no mercenary motive for wedding him.

His countenance must have betrayed some of the indignation seething inside him, for Miss Penrose backed away, her eyes wide with a mixture of confusion and alarm. "Since I am too late for the wedding, I should be getting home. I hope you will consider what I said about Ford. I know he would be glad to make up your quarrel, though he might not be willing to make the first move."

Hadrian made an effort to better hide his feelings. "I promise you, I will think carefully about everything you have said, Miss Penrose."

His response seemed to satisfy her. "Good day, then, Mr. Northmore. Tell Lady Artemis I wish you both joy."

Joy? The moment Susannah Penrose was out of sight, Hadrian let his features lapse into a bitter sneer. That was the last thing he expected his marriage to bring him.

"Where are we going?" Artemis tightened her hold on her nephew as their post chaise flew past the local inn without even slowing. "I thought we would be staying here for tonight at least."

Since it appeared they would be going farther, she edged over as far as possible on the carriage seat. She did not want to risk getting jostled against Hadrian Northmore, their hips forced into brief contact or her knee brushing against his. Any such friction might excite the disturbing undercurrent of awareness she fought to suppress.

"We are going to Durham," Mr. Northmore announced in a tone that brooked no opposition.

"Durham?" Artemis prayed she had heard him wrong. "But that is hundreds of miles away!"

Hundreds of miles from the safe, familiar countryside where she had lived her whole life. Where her family had lived for generations.

"Three hundred." Mr. Northmore seemed to take grim satisfaction in conveying the information. "That is why I wanted to get on the road as soon as possible."

"On the road?" Artemis hoped that did not mean what she feared it might. "Surely you do not propose we travel all the way to Durham in this carriage. It would be much faster and more comfortable to go by sea."

"I just spent four months on a ship coming from Singapore." He folded his arms across his broad chest. "I do not intend to set foot off dry land again until I go back."

"My comfort and Lee's mean nothing, I suppose." As Artemis contemplated days spent bumping over rough roads and nights trying to sleep in a succession of unfamiliar beds, her lip threatened to quiver. She bit down on it hard, determined not to give Hadrian Northmore the satisfaction of knowing how his imperious plans dismayed her.

His lip curled. "Your comfort is very important to you, isn't it?"

"What do you mean by that?"

"You don't understand me?" His sneer darkened into a scowl. "Then I had better make myself plain, hadn't I? You lured me into marriage to help yourself to my fortune and you used that child to do it! I wonder if your sister meant to do the same thing to Julian?"

If he had struck her a bruising blow with the back of his hand, Artemis could not have been more shocked or outraged. "How dare you?"

"You've said that to me quite often in the past few days. How dare I do this, how dare I say that, as though I have no business questioning anything you do?"

Unfolding his arms, he leaned toward her until they were almost nose to nose. Under other circumstances, Artemis might have thought he intended to kiss her.

Instead he dropped his voice to a low, menacing rumble. "I dare say it because it's true and your fine title doesn't change that. You put on a good show the other day when you came to see me. Dressed to the nines with your carriage and your servant. Pretending you were conferring a great favor upon me by accepting my proposal. But it was only a show, wasn't it? Your proud family has no fortune, just a big, old house that's crumbling away and a name that once meant something."

How had he found that out? Much as it galled Artemis to hear him say such things about her family, she could not deny them.

He drew back abruptly, leaving Artemis with the bewildering sense that something had been ripped away from her.

Shaking his head in disgust, he muttered, "Who would suspect a marquis's daughter of being no better than a common fortune hunter?"

She longed to fire back an indignant retort, but indignation was the privilege of innocent people who had been wrongly accused. "I…regret misleading you about my family's circumstances. I was afraid if you knew the truth, you would exploit my position to take Lee away from me. I could not let that happen."

She braved his direct gaze, hoping he might see she was telling the truth. Instead, a volatile awareness crackled between them.

"You must believe me." She felt exposed and vulnerable, overwhelmed by the potent hostility that radiated from him. "I had no intention of deceiving you for mercenary reasons. I want nothing from you except to be able to raise my…*our* nephew."

"Why *must* I believe you?" he growled. "Because you order me to?"

"Of course not. It is only a manner of speaking." Now that he had this one misdeed to hold against her, he seemed determined to cast everything she said or did in the wrong. "What I mean is I hope you will believe me because I am telling the truth. I may have misrepresented the urgency of my situation, but I never told you an outright falsehood."

It was clear from his dubious look that Mr. Northmore did not believe a word she'd uttered. Artemis told herself she did not care what he thought of her, but she could not bear to have him speak ill of Daphne.

"You cast an ugly slur upon my sister by implying she let herself get with child to snare your brother. I assure you, that was not the case. Daphne may have been naive and impulsive, but she was *never* mercenary. She would not have…lain with your brother if she had not fancied herself in love with him and believed he loved her."

"You reckon she only *fancied* herself in love with him. Why is that? Because his blood was not blue enough to mingle with the likes of a Dearing?"

"Because they hardly knew each other."

"Whose fault was that?" His eyes flashed with fury. "Your family would not receive him. They forbade your sister to see him, even after Lord Kingsfold tried to intervene."

"It was none of Lord Kingsfold's business!" Artemis protested. "He had no right to question my family's decisions. Swaggering back into the neighborhood with his new-made fortune and his *progressive* ideas, thinking his money gave him the right to dictate what everyone else should do."

"Which did you resent more?" asked Hadrian. "That he meddled in your family's private affairs or that he made a success of himself and that estate of his? Or was it the greatest sin of all—that he was right? Did you ever think that if you'd heeded him, three young lives might have been spared?"

"Did I ever think?" The question jolted Artemis out of her accustomed reticence. "Only every night, the moment I lay my head on the pillow. That and everything else I might have done to contribute to my brother and sister's deaths."

Desperate to escape this painful subject before she betrayed any more of her secret shame, she abruptly changed tack. "May I ask why you propose to drag Lee and me all the way to Durham?"

Throughout their confrontation, Lee had remained unusually quiet, looking around the carriage box and at the swiftly changing panorama visible through the windows. Artemis knew better than to suppose he would remain so contented for the next three hundred miles.

"A few years ago I had a house purchased up there for Julian to use. While I was in London, I sent a message for the servants to make the place ready for us. I want my brother's son brought up there." A severe, brooding expression clenched Hadrian's features. "Away from the softness and bad influences of the south. I want my nephew to know where he comes from and what he's meant to do with his life. I don't want to repeat the mistakes I made with his father."

The man was not only taking them to that strange, distant place—he meant to make them stay there! A wave of nausea rocked Artemis's stomach. What had possessed her to wed a man she had every reason to mistrust? Had she fallen under the spell of his compelling looks, dynamic presence and stirring kiss? How many times must she let herself be deceived before she learned her lesson?

The anger she had sought to suppress for the past several days came boiling to the surface. A lifetime of aloof restraint was no match for it. "So you admit you made mistakes with your brother? You are responsible for turning him into an incorrigible rake who ruined my innocent sister!"

"No!" he thundered, as if she had accused him of the most monstrous crime imaginable. The instant that word erupted from his lips, he immediately moderated his tone. "I only meant that, with the benefit of hindsight, there are things I will do differently this time. Having the lad raised up north is one of them."

His outburst made Artemis shrink back in her seat. But Lee chortled as if his uncle were Punch, in a puppet show, flailing the hapless Judy with a stick. Was that the sort of relentless conflict she must endure for the next eight months?

Artemis prayed the time would pass as quickly as the past few days had flown by. She could hardly wait for Hadrian Northmore to sail out of her life!

Chapter Six

He *had* made a mistake, Hadrian fumed as the post chaise headed northward through Surrey. An error much more grievous than any he might have committed in his brother's upbringing.

When he'd departed for the Indies, seventeen years ago, he had been only a lad himself. One who'd never been to Newcastle or York, let alone London. How could he have known what trials and temptations awaited young Julian in the south?

But he was a man of the world now. He should have known better than to rush into marriage with Lady Artemis Dearing. During his years abroad, he'd seen plenty of designing women at work, including Simon Grimshaw's unlamented late wife. He should have been on his guard, rather than taking the lady's word that she despised his vulgar fortune. Her sudden turnabout from abuse and insults to a suggestion of marriage ought to have roused his suspicion, as should her insistence on a hasty wedding.

But he'd been blinded by his damnable fascination with her. She was so different from any other woman he'd ever met—so self-contained, so indomitable. Those qualities, together with her subtle, elusive beauty, had piqued his interest. Now that he understood her mercenary motives, he must nip his dangerous fancy in the bud.

For the next several hours, they sat side by side on the narrow seat of the post chaise with a barrier of hostile silence bristling between them. Their nephew was as good as gold for a while, content to nestle on his aunt's lap. He watched the countryside roll by, crowing with delight whenever he spotted a herd of cows or sheep. In time that diversion lost its charm and he grew fussy.

"Are we going to stop for the night?" asked Lady Artemis as she strove to quiet the child. "Or must we race straight on to Durham like the mail coach, only pausing long enough to change horses and bolt a cold lunch?"

"Of course we're going to stop." Hadrian bridled. What sort of brute did she take him for? "I wanted to get through London today. But if you'd rather, we can put up at the next inn we come to."

"I'm sure we would not want to interfere with your plans." She lifted the little boy to her shoulder. "Hush, now. London is not much farther. When we get there you will see plenty of novel sights—bridges, tall buildings, boats on the river."

Hard as he tried, Hadrian could not deny the note of playful warmth that crept into her voice when she spoke to the fretful child.

She managed to keep him quiet until they'd crossed the Thames and stopped at a large coaching inn near the start of the Great North Road.

"You see? That was not so bad." Hadrian spoke in a hearty tone as he helped her from the carriage. Her mention of him *dragging* them off to Durham had troubled his conscience. But he was not about to let his bride dictate his actions from the very first day of their marriage. "Traveling by ship might be faster, but spring storms can stir up rough seas. I would prefer a full day's carriage drive to a single hour of seasickness."

He ruffled his nephew's fair hair. "Besides, I do not want to take any chances with this young gentleman's safety."

"Nor do I!" Lady Artemis shot him an offended yet defiant look. "Lee behaved much better than I expected today. I doubt he will be so obliging for the entire journey."

Dismissing her warning, Hadrian strode off to arrange their accommodations. He returned shortly to announce, "I booked us a pair of rooms with a private dining parlor in between. I hope that will suit you."

Lady Artemis replied with a strained nod, "I would sleep over the stables as long as I have a place to feed Lee, change his linen and put him to bed."

Half an hour later, while Hadrian was washing for dinner, an impatient knock summoned him to the door between his bedchamber and the parlor.

The instant he opened it, Lady Artemis thrust his squirming nephew into his arms. "He will not sit still in a chair to be fed. When I try to hold him on my lap, he wriggles about so much that I spill half the food before I can get any into his mouth."

One glance at her gown confirmed that. The pale blue muslin was spattered in several places, including one bright yellow blotch on the bodice.

"What do you expect me to do?" Hadrian gripped the child firmly under the arms to keep from dropping him. "Tie him down?"

"No." She heaved an exasperated sigh. "I expect you to hold him on your knee while I spoon food into his mouth. You claim such excessive concern for his welfare, I should think you'd want to make certain he is properly nourished."

"Of course I do." Hadrian resented any suggestion to the contrary.

Marching past her into the parlor, he sank onto a chair. Holding his nephew in a secure grip, he looked the child in the eye and spoke in a firm tone. "Now sit still and eat up your supper like a good lad."

With that, he perched the child on his knees to face Lady Artemis.

She flung herself on to a chair opposite them and picked up a bowl of soft-boiled eggs. "There was no need to frighten him by taking that tone."

"I don't hear him wailing, do you? I reckon it would take more than a sharp word from me to give this young master a fright. He doesn't seem to be afraid of anything." Hadrian could not help taking pride in that. "If you ask me, it wouldn't hurt him to learn a bit of caution and to mind his elders."

She hadn't *asked* his opinion on child-rearing. Hadrian sensed her unspoken thought. But she could not deny their young nephew was tucking into his supper now, eating all his egg before starting on a dish of stewed fowl.

"Lee will have plenty of time to learn all that," she insisted. "At this age, surely it is more important for him to be happy and know he is loved."

Those hardly sounded like the words of a woman who'd used the child to snare a wealthy husband. Much as Hadrian wanted to despise her as a fortune hunter, reason suggested otherwise. After all, she could not possibly have anticipated his return to England. It was daft to suppose she'd cared for the lad all these months in the hope that such an opportunity might present itself.

If not that, what *had* made her keep a child she could easily have cast off after her sister's death? "Did your uncles approve of you raising an illegitimate child?"

"Hardly. They wanted me to give him to one of our tenants to raise or—" Jamming her lips together to stop the indignant flow of words, she thrust the spoon into her nephew's mouth.

"Or what?" The words popped out before Hadrian could contain them.

Curiosity betrayed a level of interest he did not want to feel. But he reminded himself it was his flesh and blood they were discussing. He had a right to know.

Lady Artemis did not seem inclined to answer. Instead she busied herself wiping the child's mouth before taking up a bowl of milk pudding.

After the boy had swallowed several large spoonfuls, she murmured, "If I'd insisted on keeping Lee, Uncle Henry would have cast us out of Bramberley."

Having avoided looking at Hadrian all the while she fed their nephew, she suddenly glanced up, impaling him with her blue-violet gaze. "That is why I agreed to marry you, Mr. Northmore—because I had no better choice. I would have wed the devil to keep from losing Lee."

She sounded sincere, all the more because her remark was so unflattering. Yet Hadrian sensed she was not telling him everything. While she finished feeding his nephew, he found himself drinking in her delicate beauty. Hard as he tried to divert his thoughts, he could not help wondering whether her dark hair would be as soft to touch as he imagined. She was not tempting in the blatant way of some women. Yet everything about her seemed to whisper a subtle challenge that no ordinary man had a hope of making her his.

"There." She set aside the empty pudding bowl. "Now I must put Lee to bed."

With a mixture of relief and regret, Hadrian handed the child back to her. It had been a perilous pleasure holding the wee lad on his knee. Not to mention gazing at his tempting bride. "While you're doing that, I will order our dinner."

Lady Artemis bobbed a nod and bore the child off to her bedchamber.

He did *not* owe her an apology, Hadrian insisted to himself once she'd gone. The woman had deliberately misled him. He would challenge any man in his situation *not* to believe she must be after his money. But if she was entirely in the wrong and he was not the least to blame, why did he feel a nagging need to make amends? Refusing to examine his motives too closely, he ordered the best dinner the inn could provide.

When it had arrived, he knocked on her door, prompting a loud squall from his nephew.

An instant later, the door jerked open to reveal a disheveled Lady Artemis. "He had just nodded off, finally. What do you want?"

"I didn't mean to wake him." Hadrian gestured toward the table, spread with an array of covered dishes. "I thought you'd want to eat."

"I will once I get him settled. Heaven knows when that will be now." Casting a glance at Hadrian's face and another at the table, she moderated her tone. "Thank you for ordering the food. Do not feel obliged to wait for me."

She shut the door before he could reply. A moment later, the child quieted.

Returning to the table, Hadrian poured himself a glass of wine. He *would* wait for her—a little while at least. Surely the lad would not take long to nod off.

The first glass of wine tasted so pleasant, Hadrian followed it with a second. He hoped the drink might help him forget this was his wedding night. Instead, it made him forget everything else. Thoughts he had no business thinking ran rampant through his mind, unfettered by his usual strict control. His eyelids began to feel heavy.

Surely Mr. Northmore must have finished eating and gone to bed by now. Hungry as she was, Artemis had no inclination to dine alone with her new husband. What if he raised the subject of her deception again?

She told herself she did not care if *that man* had a bad opinion of her. She was satisfied her actions had been justified. Yet she could not help wondering what her honorable Dearing ancestors would think of her intentionally deceiving Mr. Northmore. She did not need him stirring up the stew of shame that roiled in her belly.

The thought of stew made her mouth water. Perhaps if she had something to eat, her stomach would settle. Gingerly, Artemis rose from the bed and crept to the door. She eased it open, cringing when the hinges gave a faint squeal. But Lee did not stir at the noise. All was still in the parlor as well. Breathing a sigh of relief, she tiptoed in and closed the door softly behind her.

A squeak of alarm rose in her throat when she glanced toward the table and saw Hadrian Northmore sitting there. It died away again when she noticed he was leaning back in the chair with his eyes closed and his head tilted to one side. A wine bottle stood half-empty beside his clean dinner plate. He must have taken a drink or two while waiting for her to join him, and fallen asleep. Clearly he had not exaggerated when he said a Northmore could sleep anywhere. Artemis envied him that ability.

Just then her stomach gave a great yawning growl. As quietly as she had slipped away from her nephew, Artemis now approached his uncle. Sliding onto the empty chair opposite him, she carefully lifted the cover off the nearest dish. It released a whiff of warm, moist air that smelled good enough to eat.

Artemis inhaled greedily. Pigeon pie—one of her favorites! How long had it been since she'd had a taste of it—Lord and Lady Kingsfold's wedding breakfast, perhaps? She helped herself to a generous wedge and ate it as quietly as she could, relishing every bite. Then, thirsty from eating the pie, she drank a glass of wine.

While Mr. Northmore slumped in his chair, his breath coming in slow, deep waves, Artemis consumed a hearty meal. She kept a wary eye on him as she ate and drank, hoping he would not wake before she had finished. But as he continued to sleep, her wariness gradually changed to something else.

How could she have thought his dark, powerful features unappealing when she'd first glimpsed them? She now found his proud, jutting chin, fierce Roman nose and sweeping raven brows far *too* attractive for her peace of mind. With his piercing gray eyes closed and the stern line of his mouth relaxed in sleep, she caught a glimpse of a very different man than the one she'd clashed with these past few days.

Catching herself gaping at him, she forced her attention back to her plate, only to discover it was empty and she could not eat another bite. Artemis congratulated herself on managing to get a good supper without having to make awkward conversation with her new husband. Then she rose from her chair and prepared to steal away to bed.

But something stopped her.

Perhaps it was Hadrian Northmore's air of innocent tranquility. Or perhaps it was the unlikely sense that this powerful man needed her, if only for the trivial task of waking him. Left to his own devices, he might sleep all night in that chair, to wake in the morning stiff and starving. It was partly her fault he'd fallen asleep there. If she had not delayed, hoping he would dine without her, he'd be in bed now, resting comfortably on a full stomach.

Artemis stifled a groan. Though she knew what she must do, she was not happy about it. Hadrian Northmore struck her as the kind of man who would be very gruff when woken from a sound sleep, even if it was for his own good.

"Mr. Northmore," she whispered, hesitant to touch him. "Wake up!"

Her words had no effect. His eyes remained shut, though they seemed to move restlessly behind his closed lids. Some tension crept back into his loose limbs. His lips moved, but no words came out.

"Hadrian!" She spoke louder and tried his given name, hoping it might better penetrate his slumber. "Come now, it's time to wake up."

Still he gave no sign of having heard her.

Caution urged Artemis to keep her distance, but something stronger drew her toward him. She grasped his shoulder and shook it. At the same time, she brought her lips close to his ear and spoke in an urgent whisper. "Hadrian, please, you *must* wake up!"

His head rolled on to the shoulder where her hand rested, trapping it against his face. Before she could pull away, he made a subtle movement, caressing her hand with his cheek. The warm, rugged friction was such an unexpected and pleasant sensation, Artemis could not summon the will to do anything but soak it in with every nerve.

Then he turned his head farther, searching out her fingers with his lips. He did not press the usual sort of kiss upon them that a gentleman might when bowing over a lady's hand. Instead, with slightly parted lips and the velvet flick of his tongue, he bestowed a languid caress over each one, sending ripples of desire through her flesh.

As she hovered near him, her mouth flooded with hot moisture, as it had when she smelled the pigeon pie. The secret crevice between her legs moistened, too, hungry for something she could not name.

Then his arms stirred, twining around her with gentle but irresistible strength, easing her onto his lap to be kissed and fondled. When his lips closed over hers, a cascade of sensations overwhelmed her, leaving her dazed and yielding. His mouth tasted of wine. Yet the primal, rhythmic caress of his tongue made *her* light-headed and prey to raw urges she had always kept under tight control.

Before she could rally the will to restrain them, he reached up to touch her breast, rubbing in slow circles, then gently kneading. That morning in church, the casual brush of his hand had unsettled her. That had been nothing compared to this. Sparks of fierce, sweet fire crackled through her, making her breath and pulse race.

She raised her hand with the vague intention of pushing him away, but when her fingers came in contact with his powerful shoulder, they clung to it instead. How could she, who flinched from the most casual contact with strangers, welcome such intimate attentions from a man she neither liked nor respected and certainly did not love?

The intense, foreign urges he awakened in her body baffled and disturbed her. If she gave in to them, they would only make her vulnerable to a man she dared not give any more power over her.

"Hadrian." A woman's voice reached him through the heavy haze of sleep. "It's time to wake up."

Her soft hand rested upon his shoulder. "Hadrian, please! You *must* wake up!"

It had been so long since he'd held a woman in his arms, sating his senses on her warm, fragrant softness. He pressed his cheek against her fingers. Then he nibbled them with his lips and tongue as if feasting on morsels of the most delicate, delicious tropical fruit. Kissing her fingers was such a sweet, wanton pleasure that he could not wait to taste her lips!

He reached up to enfold her and draw her closer. She slipped into his embrace with only the briefest hesitation, filling arms that had been empty for far too long. When he kissed her, she tasted like a banquet, mingling many delectable flavors with one that was altogether hers. The moist, yielding warmth of her mouth roused his long-suppressed desire. He cupped her breast and began to fondle the firm, gently rounded flesh through the bodice of her gown.

"Margaret," he whispered.

The word seemed to act like an evil incantation, turning the willing woman in his arms into a fierce, writhing tigress.

"Let me go, damn you!" The palm of her hand struck his cheek a stinging blow that shocked Hadrian fully awake.

His eyelids flew open, followed by his mouth, when he encountered the blazing amethyst glare of Lady Artemis Dearing.

"What in Go—? Bloody he—!" He bit off a spew of curses.

The taste of her kiss still lingered on his tongue and the desire it had ignited in his loins would not be quenched.

Artemis strained to break free of his arms at the very instant Hadrian let her go. Stumbling backward, she slammed against the wall, making the window rattle and the candle flame in the wall sconce dance wildly.

"I thought we agreed," she gasped. "This arrangement between us was to be a marriage in name only."

Shock and fright gripped her delicate features, calling forth all manner of protective urges in him. He glimpsed something else he could not so readily identify. Was it disgust...or longing?

Hadrian struggled to master his astonishment at the situation in which he found himself. He could not bear to have his cool, disapproving bride see him at the mercy of so many conflicting emotions beyond his control.

"I do not recall us ever having a proper discussion of the matter." It took every crumb of poise he could muster to pretend he had not been stimulated by the tempting taste of her favors he'd just stolen.

Lady Artemis pressed her back to the wall, with the enticing result of lifting her slender, perfectly shaped breasts. Hadrian's hand tingled with the memory of fondling them and itched with the urge to do it again.

"If that was what you wanted…" she wiped her mouth with the back of her hand, as if she had just spat out something revolting "…you should have made your expectations clear from the beginning."

Her obvious aversion vexed and puzzled him in equal measure. He could have sworn she'd come to him willingly and responded to his kiss. Or had that only been wishful dreaming?

"Would it have changed your answer to my proposal, if I had?" He was still not convinced she had no designs on his fortune. Would she have bartered for a rich husband with the usual currency of such unscrupulous women?

Lady Artemis gave his question careful thought before answering, her kissable lips drawn in a tight, suspicious line. "No, I suppose it would not."

"Then what is there to fret about?" Hadrian sought to make light of their highly charged encounter. "You were mistaken if you thought I meant to…claim my marital rights just now. I was in the middle of a dream when you tried to wake me."

When she cast him a doubtful look, he continued. "Surely you've heard of people walking and talking in their sleep. Why not kissing?"

"So it was all a mistake and you have no desire to consummate our marriage?" It was clear she felt sullied by the touch of a man so far beneath her and the common, carnal desires he had provoked.

"Not unless you do. I am always happy to oblige a lady."

She pulled herself up to her full willowy height and spoke in a tone of scathing disdain. "That will not be necessary."

"Please yourself." He affected a careless shrug. "But just so you know, it is not such a terrible ordeal—being bedded by a man who is patient and knows what he's about. You might enjoy the experience if you give it a try."

Her pretty mouth puckered in distaste, but her eyes darted restlessly. "I doubt that very much."

He could not let such an insult pass unchallenged. "Any woman I've ever taken to my bed has declared herself well pleased with my attentions."

Lady Artemis gave a derisive sniff. "I suppose some women will say anything if they are well enough paid."

"I wouldn't know," Hadrian snapped, stung by the contempt he heard in her voice. "And you are a fine one to talk of what a woman will do for money."

She ignored that jibe, but inched closer to the door, clearly eager to escape from him. "You have had many paramours, then? If you wish to gratify your desires in future, I suggest you find some such strumpet who will be eager to oblige you."

"With pleasure," Hadrian lied—rather convincingly he thought, given the vexing desire she had roused in him.

When Artemis spun around to wrench open the door, his smarting pride made him call out, "Do let me know if you change your mind."

She did not bother to glance back at him, but hurled her contemptuous retort over her shoulder. "You would have to wait a good deal longer than eight months for that!"

Hadrian Northmore certainly would have to wait more than eight months for her to come begging him to take her into his bed. The infuriating man would have to wait for hell to freeze! As Artemis marched away with her head high, only the fear of waking Lee kept her from slamming the door behind her.

The instant it shut, her knees gave way beneath her. She slid to the floor with her back pressed against the door. Wrapping her arms around her bent knees, she rested her forehead against them. As she expelled breath after shaky breath, Artemis strove to quell the tempest Hadrian Northmore had whipped up inside her.

First, the unexpected delight of his sensual touch and kisses. Such ravenous pleasure they'd unleashed before she came to her senses. Then the sickening humiliation to discover his delicious seduction had never been meant for her at all. She'd been nothing more to her husband than an inferior substitute for the woman of his dreams.

How could she have been so foolish as think otherwise for even an instant? Daphne had been the beauty of the family—everyone had said so. Everyone also said how opposite the Dearing sisters were in every way. If two decades of such remarks had left Artemis with any stubborn illusions that she was attractive or desirable, her first and only suitor had disabused her of them in the cruelest terms. Hadrian Northmore had only seconded his opinion.

Artemis would never forget the look of horror in his eyes when he'd opened them to discover her in his arms. As if that had not been degrading enough, he'd mocked her with repeated offers to bed her. She could not decide which sickened her most—that he was prepared to use her body to satisfy the lusts his dream siren had roused or the possibility that he had taken pity on his dowdy, love-starved bride to offer her a taste of the carnal delights she'd been missing?

Artemis fought back a sob of humiliated rage.

She'd refused his patronizing offers of seduction even though they secretly tempted her. Then the rogue had dared to boast of all the other women he'd dallied with. He had taunted her with his gloating certainty that she would one day beg him to take her into his bed.

How could she have deluded herself into thinking eight months of Hadrian Northmore's company would be bearable? Artemis wallowed in self-recrimination, hoping it might distract her from memories of the yearning passion he had kindled. Would she have felt such intense hostility toward him, her conscience whispered, if she had not enjoyed his amorous attentions so much?

Chapter Seven

Had Daphne Dearing bewitched young Julian the way her sister threatened to bewitch him? That question preoccupied Hadrian late the next afternoon as he stared out the carriage window on the second day of their journey. Had the fine lady enticed his brother with protests of reluctance, while an arch of her lips or an ember in her gaze challenged and lured him to his doom?

Outside, spring rain pattered down on the green pastures of Cambridgeshire. Hadrian's head ached fiercely, as it often did in damp weather. It did not help that his nephew had been wailing ever since they'd paused at the last tollgate.

"What ails the lad?" Hadrian growled. "Is he going to bawl all the way to Huntingdon?"

Artemis cradled the child in a protective embrace as if she feared his uncle might strike him. But when she spoke, it was in a tone of exaggerated politeness that set Hadrian's teeth on edge.

"Children are apt to fuss when they feel unwell. I expect Lee is cold and hungry, and his digestion is upset from all the jostling. He has been taken away from his familiar surroundings and he is too young to understand why. On top of all that, he has been cooped up in this carriage with nothing of interest to see or do. I am amazed he has been in such good temper until now."

Was she talking about their nephew or herself? Hadrian bristled.

"We should reach Huntingdon in half an hour. We can put up there for the night. Will it be too much trouble for you to keep the child quiet until then?"

"*The child* has a name." Artemis shot him a scathing glare, entirely at odds with her measured tone.

"So he does." Hadrian resented the unwelcome excitement that sizzled through him when their eyes met. "I meant to ask you about it. What sort of name is *Lee?* It hardly sounds grand enough for a descendent of the Dearings."

"It is short for Leander, of course." She looked away, focusing her attention on the child, who seemed to be growing calmer. "After his uncle."

Hadrian could scarcely believe his ears. "Named after the man who killed his father? That is obscene!"

His outburst made the child cry harder.

Artemis heaved an indignant sigh. "Now look what you've done."

"Me?" cried Hadrian. "He's likely blubbering over that fool name."

"It is a fine name. Leander was a Greek hero who swam the Hellespont."

"Every night until he drowned—the fool." Hadrian raised his voice to carry over his nephew's howls. "If he'd had any sense, he would have got his hands on a boat. Or better yet, stayed clear of a woman he had no business with!"

"Like your brother?" Artemis snapped. "Is that what you would have advised him when he took up with my sister? Yet you condemn *my* family for discouraging Daphne from keeping company with him."

She had a point, much as Hadrian hated to admit it. But he hadn't been thinking of Julian and Lady Daphne. It was his marriage to Artemis that he'd assumed would be an easy paddle in a calm, shallow lagoon. Too late he'd discovered the water was deeper than he'd reckoned, with treacherous currents flowing beneath the surface.

Their hostile exchange did nothing to soothe the child. His face was so red that his plump cheeks looked like a pair of ripe apples. His shrieks pierced his uncle's skull.

"Can you do nothing with him?" Hadrian demanded, furious with himself when the words came out sounding like a desperate plea.

Five more minutes of this and his brains would come pouring out of his ears!

"I?" The lady's nostril's flared and two livid spots flamed in her pale cheeks. "*You* are the one responsible for the poor little creature's suffering, yet you expect me to quiet him so that you are not disturbed?"

She made him sound like an ogre. Was that how she saw him? His words and actions from the previous night rushed through Hadrian's mind. Each memory struck his throbbing head a savage blow. He had taken shocking liberties. She might have excused those on account of his sleep-befuddled state. But he'd been wide awake when he made those impudent suggestions no gentleman should make to a lady.

While Hadrian struggled to think of something to say that might satisfy her, Artemis bundled his wailing nephew onto his lap. "See what *you* can do with him."

She crossed her arms and angled her body away as best she could in the close space of the carriage box.

Her abrupt action shocked both Hadrian and Lee silent for a moment. In the boy's case, it did not last. He gulped down several shuddering, tearful breaths to fuel a fresh bout of bawling, more earsplitting than before.

Not knowing what else to do, Hadrian looked the little fellow in the eye and spoke firmly. "That's enough out of you, sir. Quiet down before you spook the horses."

A firm approach had worked with the child last night. Today it only made matters worse. Lee's cries took on a shrill, frenzied note.

Hadrian cast a pleading look toward Artemis, ready to promise her anything if she would pacify Lee. But all that met his gaze was a tight knot of rich, dark hair and his wife's slender neck rising from the collar of her jacket. Several wispy curls had escaped from the severe upsweep to cluster at her nape. For a blissful instant, he could think of nothing but how he would like to graze his lips over her neck, nuzzle his cheek against it and inhale her scent until it made him dizzy.

Those delightful fancies blocked out the pounding pain in his head and his nephew's deafening shrieks. He came back to his senses to find the child sniffling and hiccoughing, but otherwise blessedly quiet.

Artemis spun about to stare at them both. "How did you make him stop?"

The anxious set of her features told Hadrian she feared he might have strangled Lee while her back was turned.

"Nothing," Hadrian muttered. "That is…I don't know."

"Perhaps it was your face." She pulled a calf-eyed gawk. Was that how *he* looked?

Lee glanced at his aunt and heaved a deep, wet gurgle, followed by another. Was the child…laughing?

"Make another face," Hadrian urged her when the momentary distraction appeared to be wearing off.

"You make one," Artemis snapped. "You were so anxious to stop him crying."

No doubt she considered such larking about beneath her dignity. Though he had his share of pride, Hadrian was willing to play the fool if it promised to spare his throbbing head. Clicking his tongue to get his nephew's attention, he thrust out his lower lip and crossed his eyes.

The lad responded with a hearty chortle. That encouraged Hadrian to screw up his mouth and waggle his eyebrows. Lee clapped his hands and laughed harder. It was such an infectious sound Hadrian could not resist joining in. Next he rolled his eyes while making a rude noise with his tongue. His nephew squealed with glee. The lingering film of tears in his eyes made them twinkle with quick-silver delight.

That egged Hadrian on to new heights of comical invention. Before long, they were both laughing so hard they could scarcely catch their breath. At some point, Hadrian noticed another thrill of laughter harmonizing with theirs.

While making another droll face, he stole a fleeting glance at Artemis. Her fine features were more animated than he had ever seen them. Her shapely lips were relaxed into an unforced smile. Her beguiling eyes sparkled with unexpected merriment. He had admired her sculpted alabaster beauty from the moment he'd first set eyes on her. But the way she looked now, her face alight with laughter, took his breath away.

At that moment the post chaise slowed to a stop.

"I wonder what's the matter?" Hadrian handed his nephew back to Artemis, who reached out immediately to take him.

Peering out the carriage window, she answered in a tone of disbelief. "We've stopped at an inn. Can this be Huntingdon… already?"

He shook his head. "Not so soon, surely."

But it was. Hadrian marveled how swiftly the last hour of their journey had flown by. To his further amazement, he realized the pain in his head had disappeared completely. As he arranged their accommodations for the night, he fancied himself afloat on a warm cloud of relief.

"Shall I hold this young fellow again tonight while you feed him supper?" he asked Artemis as they climbed the stairs to their rooms.

"Why…yes." She looked astonished by his spontaneous offer of assistance. "I would appreciate it. Thank you."

"Will you dine with me tonight?" he ventured, less certain of her answer. "I promise I will not fall asleep at the table, no matter how long you take putting this young gentleman to bed."

"I could." A flicker of uncertainty crossed her face. "If you wish."

"I do." He would drink coffee and not sit down until she arrived. That should prevent any repeat of last night's unfortunate events. "We need to talk, you and I, without a certain small but vocal audience. Clear the air and all."

Though Artemis gave a judicious nod of agreement, Hadrian pictured her donning invisible armor to protect herself against whatever he might try to inflict upon her.

Was there any hope his indomitable adversary might agree to a truce?

"Who would have thought your uncle could be so comical?" Artemis murmured as she lay beside Lee, stroking his hair to soothe him to sleep. "Or so knowledgeable about the classics. I was amazed that he knew the legend of Hero and Leander."

She'd been affronted when Hadrian had used his knowledge to scoff at Leander's gallant deed of swimming the treacherous waters of the Hellespont repeatedly to tryst with his beloved. But on reflection she could not deny the young man had behaved foolishly, tempting Fate again and again until it turned against him.

Something else she could not deny—there was a great deal more to Hadrian Northmore than she'd first thought. That did not mean she could let down her guard around him—quite the contrary.

With a shudder, she stirred from her troubled thoughts to find Lee fast asleep. Now she had no excuse to delay her dinner with his uncle. Since Hadrian had vowed to stay awake until she arrived, she might as well get it over with as soon as possible.

Pressing a soft kiss on her nephew's brow, she reminded herself that she was doing all this for his sake—so they could remain together and so his future would be secure. It was what she wanted most in the world. Perhaps it was only fitting that such a precious boon should come at a high cost. Hadrian Northmore had not become a successful man of business by driving easy bargains.

When Artemis slipped into the parlor a moment later, she found Hadrian standing at the window with his hands clasped behind his back, staring down at the stable yard below. He turned toward her with a startled look, as if she had roused him from some deep, private thoughts. Thoughts about the woman of his dreams, perhaps?

He recovered his composure swiftly, arranging his features to look as if he was pleased to see her. Artemis knew better. He was only making faces, as he had at Lee this afternoon in the carriage.

"That was quick." He nodded toward the room next door where their nephew lay sleeping.

Artemis nodded. "I thought it would take him much longer to settle after the state he was in this afternoon. Perhaps he tired himself out by crying and laughing so hard. I fear strong emotions have quite the opposite effect on me."

She had only meant to *think* that, not say it aloud—especially not to Hadrian Northmore. After the dangerously intense feelings he'd provoked in her last night, she had hardly slept a wink. That might be why she could not mind her tongue properly now. As she moved toward the table, Artemis vowed to say as little as possible this evening.

"I, on the other hand, am like our nephew." Hadrian sprang forward to pull a chair out for her. "I find strong emotions tiring. When my feelings are stirred up, I am more apt to…react excessively to the most trivial incidents."

Once Artemis was settled at the table, he rang the bell to summon a servant. Then he took a seat across from her. "Has that ever happened to you?"

His question startled her almost as much as his bewildering kiss the previous evening, and for almost the same reason. It was such a private subject—one might say *intimate*—to speak of one's deepest feelings. She had seldom discussed such matters with anyone, not even her sister, who'd been her closest confidante.

However, like his kiss, Hadrian's candor had a seductive effect that lured her to respond in kind. "I never thought of it in that way. But since you mention it, I suppose it has."

"I believe you will agree we've both had our feelings wrought up of late."

The corner of her lips arched, quite against her will. "That is a masterpiece of understatement."

His features crinkled into a wry, reluctant-looking grin that might have mirrored hers. "So we have found a bit of common ground at last."

Before she could decide how to reply, the waiter arrived, carrying a large tray laden with covered dishes. Artemis was grateful for the interruption as well as the food. Overwrought emotions might play havoc with her sleep, but they did not spoil her appetite.

The waiter set all the dishes on the table, then whisked off the covers, releasing succulent aromas to waft through the small parlor.

"Our compliments to the kitchen," said Hadrian. "This all smells very good. I will ring if there is anything else we need."

Artemis could not decide whether she was sorry or glad he had dismissed the servant. This meal would be awkward enough without an audience. On the other hand, having someone else present might keep Hadrian from delving into private matters.

Once the waiter had gone, Hadrian reached for the nearest dish. "Will you have some loin of pork?"

"Please." Artemis held out her plate, relieved to be talking about something as harmless as the food.

He helped her to a generous portion of meat. "Veal pie? Asparagus? Batter pudding?"

"A little of everything, if you please."

He filled her plate. While his hands and part of his attention were occupied with the task, he spoke in an offhand way, as if making polite table talk. "I had no idea traveling with a young child could be such an ordeal."

"I tried to warn you." Artemis could not resist the urge to remind him.

"So you did." He gave a rueful shrug. "But you'll soon discover I do not make a habit of heeding naysayers. If I had avoided every undertaking someone warned me might be difficult, I would never have made my fortune."

Though she still wished he had heeded her in this instance, Artemis could not suppress a grudging flicker of admiration for his tenacity and strength of will. All her life she had let her actions be guided by the wishes of others. Wedding Hadrian Northmore over her uncles' objections had been her first real act of rebellion and she was not convinced she had done the right thing.

Hadrian handed Artemis her well-laden dinner plate, then proceeded to fill his. "If the rest of our journey is as bad as today, heaven help us all."

Artemis nodded as she took a bite of succulent roast pork. One benefit of traveling with Hadrian Northmore—she had not eaten so well in months.

"Do you reckon we can put our differences aside for a few days?" he asked. "Can we work together to keep young Lee in good humor for the rest of our journey?"

Part of her wanted to point out that he was responsible for this situation, and to ask why she should share the consequences. But blaming Hadrian would not keep Lee from screaming all the way to Durham. "A short while ago you said we had a bit of common ground and you were right. Our nephew's welfare should be our greatest mutual concern. I fear I have been guilty of forgetting that."

"Something else we have in common." Hadrian paused in the act of filling her wineglass. "If we keep on at this rate, it may soon be hard to tell us apart."

"I am certain there will always be plenty of differences between us." Was that such a bad thing, though? She and Daphne had been as different as could be yet they had always got on well together. "For instance, I am prepared to admit when I'm wrong."

As soon as those words slipped out, Artemis wished she could recall them. Not because they weren't true, but because she did not want to spoil this fragile harmony.

But instead of firing back a scathing retort, Hadrian chuckled. "So you are, and I reckon it is a good quality in others. I do not mean to boast when I say I am seldom wrong…in matters of business at least. I would not have succeeded if I'd made a great many mistakes or spent a lot of time doubting myself."

"No." Artemis took a sip of her wine. "I don't suppose you would."

"I hope you will pardon me for talking in terms of commerce, but it is what I know best. It seems to me that virtues and vices are all head and tail of the same coin."

Artemis mulled the notion over for a moment. "I believe I see what you mean. Someone who is courageous might also be foolhardy at times. Or someone who is confident might be too proud."

"Just so." He seemed pleased that she'd grasped his point so readily. "I reckon the tail side of being right so often is that I have trouble admitting my occasional mistakes."

A bubble of laughter gushed up from somewhere inside Artemis. "You even have trouble admitting that you have trouble admitting you are sometimes wrong."

He took a deep draught of wine, as if fortifying himself for a challenging task. "It is a bit of an effort, yes."

"Then may I assume this entire conversation is a very roundabout way of offering an apology?" Artemis scarcely recognized the note of banter in her voice. She sometimes thought such things for her own amusement, but she'd never dared say them out loud, especially to a man like Hadrian Northmore.

To her amazement, he did not take offense, but flashed her a shamefaced grin. "You might take it that way if you were minded to. Especially if it would persuade you to accept my proposition."

"Proposition?" The word took Artemis aback, reviving memories of the previous night, when he had offered to *oblige* her by consummating their marriage.

"About working together to make the rest of our journey to Durham as painless as possible for young Lee. And for our ears. Remember?"

"Of course." She felt foolish for allowing her thoughts to leap so quickly to that other matter. "I am willing to do whatever is necessary."

"Capital!" Hadrian reached across the table, offering her his hand. "Then let us seal our agreement as I am accustomed to in business."

As she extended her fingers, Artemis marveled at the turnabout that had taken place between them in the past twenty-four hours. Did Hadrian regret the things he'd said to her last night? Was his sudden show of cordiality another attempt to signify he was sorry, without admitting he'd been wrong? Or was it only a measure of his desperation to keep Lee pacified for the remainder of their journey?

They clasped hands for a fleeting instant before she pulled away. Even his most innocent touch flustered her.

Given the reluctant manner in which Artemis shook his hand to seal their agreement, Hadrian feared she might not keep up her end of the bargain. But as their post chaise rolled toward the market town of Stamford the next morning, he was forced to admit he'd been mistaken.

Yesterday's rain had ended, leaving the spring air fresh and the sky a cheerful blue, dotted with tufts of cloud. All along their route the meadows were full of cows and sheep grazing. Artemis pointed them out to Lee, along with other sights of interest—a flock of geese, boats on the River Nene and the spire of Peterborough Cathedral.

When Hadrian sensed his nephew was beginning to tire of

viewing the sights, he took his turn entertaining the lad. Once again, he proceeded to pull faces and to make comical noises. Lee rewarded his efforts with peal after peal of merry laughter, in which Hadrian and Artemis could not resist joining.

Now and then their eyes met, igniting the spark of desire he had come to expect but never quite got used to. Something else seemed to arc between them as well—a flicker of camaraderie that was even harder to resist.

Once again the time flew by. Before he knew it, they were stopping in Stamford for a change of horses and a bite to eat.

Afterward he suggested a stroll around the town before they set off again. "I reckon we'll all be the better for a bit of air and a chance to stretch our legs."

Their walk seemed to agree with the lad, for he began to nod and yawn not long after they got back on the road. Artemis rocked him in her arms, crooning a little tune until he fell asleep. A strange, tender warmth kindled in Hadrian's chest as his gaze lingered upon the woman and child.

"Perhaps this long coach ride was not my best idea," he admitted in a rueful murmur when Artemis stopped singing. "Once we reach Durham, though, I promise there will be no more gadding about."

He feared she might seize the opportunity to remind him that she'd told him so.

To his surprise, she generously refrained. "A journey of a few hundred miles must seem nothing to you after traveling halfway around the world and back. This is the farthest I have ever been from Bramberley. Could I trouble you to tell me about your travels? It would help pass the time while Lee is sleeping."

"It's no trouble. I must warn you, though, I am better at making faces than I am at spinning tales." He thought for a moment, searching for a story that might hold her interest. "I could start by telling you how Stamford Raffles defied the Governor of Calcutta and risked war with the Dutch to establish a trading post at Singapore."

He began a bit awkwardly, stumbling over his words, sometimes mixing up the sequence of events. But as he continued, Artemis's rapt expression and penetrating questions loosened his tongue. He offered up each reminiscence reluctantly at first, expecting her to scorn them. But Artemis surprised him, as she had so often in their brief acquaintance, her eyes wide and sparkling like a pair of matched amethysts.

There was something irresistibly flattering about engaging the interest of a woman so refined and well educated. Though caution warned him not to make too much of it, he could not help relishing his appreciative audience.

In the middle of his story about a plague of rats that had afflicted the colony in its early days, young Lee woke from his nap. But the lad seemed to take his cue from Artemis, sitting quietly in her arms, listening as if he understood every word out of his uncle's mouth.

"After an orgy of rat killing," Hadrian concluded with a rather theatrical flourish, "and all the money *Tuan* Farquhar had paid out for bounty, we were finally rid of the bloody nuisances. A few days later we were overrun by centipedes! Grimshaw said it was like the plagues of Moses, but I reckoned the rats must have been eating the centipedes. With the rats gone, there was nothing to stop them multiplying."

Artemis shuddered. "What did you do about the centipedes?"

"Farquhar put a bounty on them next, and it was not long until they went the way of the rats. Luckily, whatever the centipedes had been feeding off did not give us any trouble. Now I have done my part. It is time you took a turn at storytelling." He flashed his nephew a grin. "Don't you agree, lad?"

Lee bobbed his head and giggled.

"You see?" said Hadrian. "He's all for it."

"But I have not led the sort of adventurous life you have." Artemis shrank back into the corner of the seat, as if she wanted to disappear. "My sister often complained we never went anywhere or did anything."

She would not need any great adventure to hold his attention, Hadrian reflected. He was curious about *her*—the intriguing woman behind her cool, polite facade. The woman of whom he'd caught such tantalizing glimpses. It would be a challenge to cultivate an acquaintance with her and discover why she kept herself hidden away.

To Hadrian Northmore, who had spent most of his life proving his worth, such a challenge was impossible to resist.

Chapter Eight

She was not up to the challenge of following Hadrian's enthralling stories of the Orient. The afternoon had flown by on the wings of his tales. At times Artemis felt as if she'd been transported out of the rattling post chaise to the rail of a great ship rounding the Cape of Good Hope or a merchant's *godown* listening to the patter of rain on the palm-frond roof. She fancied she could smell the tang of fresh cinnamon bark and *gambier* pepper, taste the elusive sweetness of a mangosteen.

Until today the thought of travel had not appealed to her in the least. She preferred familiar surroundings and experiences to novel ones, especially anything exotic. In her, familiarity had never bred contempt but rather a sense of order, continuity and safety. Anything foreign carried a whiff of danger.

Hadrian Northmore was unlike any man she'd ever met before and this marriage of theirs was foreign territory to her. She never knew what to expect. At every turn, she found her safe, familiar assumptions challenged. It kept her in an unwelcome state of turmoil. And yet she could not deny there was something curiously exhilarating about it, all the same.

Worried that his penetrating stare might probe her thoughts, she scrambled to divert him. "If you wish to be lulled to sleep, I can tell you how I have spent the past twenty years—caring for my brother and sister, doing needlework, playing the pianoforte, reading books, going to church. The only remotely exciting thing I've ever done was go up to London two summers ago for the coronation."

"There you are, then," said Hadrian. "A spectator of history. That is a story you can tell your grandchildren…I mean Lee's children. Let us hear every grand detail."

Was he mocking her? Artemis feared so, but she could not be certain. "It *was* a magnificent affair. His Majesty never does anything on less than a grand scale."

When Hadrian continued to watch her expectantly, Artemis plundered her memory for something to tell him. "It was a very hot day. The Abbey was like a huge stone oven. The whole place was buzzing with rumors that Queen Caroline meant to force her way into the Abbey to be crowned, but she never did get in. Daphne and I were so proud to see our brother walking in the procession with the other peers."

Her voice trailed off. She was making a miserable hash of it. When Hadrian had given an account of getting to shore through the roaring surf of India's Coromandel Coast, she'd hung on his every word. But when she tried to relate the events of a splendid royal coronation, she made it sound so commonplace.

"Go on." Hadrian seemed more interested than her story warranted. "There must have been more to it than that."

"There was a banquet afterward. I never smelled so much delicious food in my life."

"How did it taste?"

Artemis gave a sour chuckle. "You would have to ask one of the *gentlemen* who fell on it like a herd of starving swine, while we famished ladies could only watch from the balconies. Between the heat, fatigue and hunger, I was afraid poor Daphne would swoon."

"What about you?" Hadrian demanded. "Were *you* not tired, hot and hungry, too?"

It was clear he considered her sister a pampered little tyrant, the way some people accused Lee of being spoilt. Could nobody understand how much she loved them both? She'd tried so hard to make up for the great losses in their lives, always afraid she would fail them.

"Those were minor deprivations I could easily bear. My sister felt things more keenly, both good and bad. After all that has happened, I know you must think very ill of my sister. But if you'd ever met her, I do not believe you could have resisted her charm." Artemis nuzzled her cheek against Lee's tousled curls as she held Hadrian's remorseless gray gaze, willing him to relent. "Any more than you can resist your nephew's. He has her smile, her laugh, her eagerness."

"And his penchant for trouble?" The granite severity in Hadrian's eyes softened. "Did he inherit that from his mother, too?"

Part of Artemis wanted to rap out a defensive reply, but somehow she did not feel the need to protect her sister and brother so fiercely from Hadrian. She only wanted to make him understand.

"I must admit Lee comes by his recklessness honestly. But not from his mother alone. I believe he inherited an ample measure from my brother...and yours."

For the first time in many months, Artemis thought of Julian Northmore with something other than soul-gnawing revulsion. How could she continue to hate the young man when his blood ran in her beloved Lee?

Was Hadrian entertaining the same sort of thoughts about Daphne? With all her heart, Artemis hoped so.

Part of Hadrian wished he could continue to despise the young woman whose thoughtlessness had nearly put an end to his family. But, as Artemis had reminded him, it was thanks to her sister he still had his nephew to carry on the Northmore name and see through his plans for the future.

And if he could not hate Daphne, how could he bear any ill

will toward Artemis? She was guilty of nothing more than loyalty and devotion to her family, virtues he'd long held in the highest regard.

For the next two days, as they journeyed north through the Vale of York and into his native County Durham, those thoughts did battle with Hadrian's anger and pride. In spite of his conflicted feelings, he took great pains to be agreeable to Artemis, and he sensed she was doing the same. Were her efforts *all* for the child's sake or was she also trying to make amends for deceiving and insulting him?

Whatever her reasons, the result was the same—Lee remained cheerful and content, delighting in their efforts to entertain him. Artemis prevailed upon Hadrian to tell more stories of his experiences abroad, while he managed to coax forth a few recollections about her life at Bramberley. Those accounts usually featured her late brother and sister, with Artemis an admiring observer in the background. To Hadrian's ears, her every word rang with abiding love for Leander and Daphne.

Whoever was to blame for the tragic strife between their families, Hadrian could not deny her loss had been heavier than his. And not only because she'd lost two family members to his one. She grieved a brother and sister she'd known and loved well. Part of him *wished* he could mourn his brother that way, but it had been a great many years since he'd last set eyes on Julian. Apart from their ties of blood, his departed brother had been little better than a stranger.

On learning of Julian's death, Hadrian had feared the extinction of his family, lamented the failure of a vow and mourned the end of a dream. But he had not been ravaged by the intense, personal bereavement he'd experienced twice before and had sworn never to suffer again.

Artemis had.

Was it any wonder she'd been wary and hostile toward him? Or that she'd been willing to do anything to hold on to the child who bore her brother's name and her sister's likeness?

That child now nestled on her lap. The rhythmic buzz of his slumbering breath filled the silence inside the darkened carriage as it sped through the moonlit countryside. This was the first night they'd driven on after stopping to eat dinner and change horses. Hadrian was determined to sleep under his own roof tonight, free from the prospect of more miles to travel the next morning.

"Have we much farther to go?" Artemis echoed his thoughts in a voice faint with weariness.

A pang of guilt struck Hadrian as he remembered what she'd said at the beginning of her journey about Lee being cold, tired, cramped and bored. Had she suffered all those vexations, but been too proud to complain on her own account? Or had she thought he would not care?

Glancing out the window, he recognized the shape of old St. Oswin's church. An unexpected embrace of homecoming swiftly vanished into a bottomless pit of loss. "Only another mile."

After a moment's hesitation, he continued. "Before we get there, I have something to say."

His sense of fairness demanded he speak. And he must do it now, while the darkness veiled her reproachful gaze.

Though Artemis made no reply, he sensed a guarded stiffness in her posture as if she expected his words to be disagreeable. After the way he'd behaved, could he blame her?

"I reckon we got off on the wrong foot, you and me." Those words were hard to say. Yet each one he forced out seemed to lift a heavy stone from his chest. "I don't know if you can understand. I came home from Singapore a week ago, expecting to see my brother again after a long separation. Instead I was told he'd been dead for more than a year. To you and everyone else, it must have seemed like ancient history. But to me it was as if Julian had just been killed that day. And the people responsible were beyond my power to reckon with. All except you…and me. I see now that I took out my anger on the wrong one of us."

"I understand better than you suppose." The voice issuing from the shadows scarcely sounded like hers. "You had too little time to come to terms with what had happened. I had too much. For months, I'd been so anxious and angry, with no one on whom I dared vent those feelings. When you came along, threatening to take Lee away from me, I felt justified in heaping accusations and insults upon you, regardless of whether there was any truth in them."

Her admission staggered Hadrian. He thought she'd had plenty of time to accept what had happened and carry on with her life. Recalling his past experiences with grief, he realized that had been a heartless assumption.

"Do you reckon we can put all that behind us and begin our acquaintance again with a clean slate?"

"Perhaps." She sounded doubtful. "Does that mean you no longer believe I used Lee to secure my own comfort? I know I was wrong to mislead you about my family's circumstances, but I swear I did not wed you for your fortune. All I've ever wanted is to care for Lee and keep him with me. Hold me responsible for Julian's death if you must, but I cannot bear to have you doubt my affection for his son!"

She fairly radiated passionate maternal devotion. Hadrian might have congratulated himself for breaking through her secretive reserve, except that it made Artemis even more dangerously appealing.

"I do *not* doubt it," he muttered, galled to admit he'd been wrong yet again. "Not anymore. I've watched you with the lad ever since we set out on this journey. I've seen the way you hold him and talk to him, the way you know what he wants even though he cannot tell you. And I've seen how he responds to you. Those are not things that can be playacted."

"Indeed they cannot," replied Artemis in a voice choked with relief. A featherlight touch on his sleeve trailed downward until her hand came to rest upon his. "Thank you for being willing to keep an open mind about me."

"You needn't sound so surprised. I'm a fair man and I treat people as I find them." Hadrian fought the urge to raise her hand to his lips, fearing she might misunderstand the gesture. "Is it too much to ask that you keep an open mind about me, as well? Or are you someone who trusts their first impressions absolutely and refuses to alter them on any account?"

She pulled her hand back, as if his touch scalded her fingers. "If I did that, I would be very foolish indeed. Even with someone I thought I knew well, I have been deceived."

Who had deceived her—a man she'd cared for? Hadrian was not prepared for the flare of protective indignation that blazed within him. Was that part of the reason she'd resented and mistrusted him? Not only because of the tragic conflict between their families and the way he'd treated her?

His desire to know her better intensified. Next winter he would return to Singapore, leaving her to raise the child on whom all his future hopes depended. He needed to be certain he could trust her.

Where was she?

Artemis woke with a violent start the next morning from a dream-riddled sleep. The moment she felt Lee's warm, sturdy little body beside her, the worst of her alarm faded. As long as he was nearby, safe and happy, it did not matter much where they were.

As that thought calmed her, memories of the previous night flooded back. Their late arrival—servants scrambling about in their nightclothes fetching baggage, lighting candles, warming beds. Someone had tried to take Lee, but Artemis insisted on keeping him with her for the first night in a strange place. As much for her sake as for his.

Then another memory ambushed her. It felt more imagined than real—words swirling around in the darkness, then one brief but significant touch. Yet she could not dismiss it as a dream. She had spoken to Hadrian of the most painful humiliation of her life. It had been only a passing reference, but that was more than she'd ever confided in anyone else, even her dearest Daphne. What had possessed her to speak of it to Hadrian Northmore?

He might be her husband in name, but in fact he was a virtual stranger she'd known for barely a week. A man who had uprooted her from everything familiar to drag her the length of England. She had promised to make a fresh start on their acquaintance, but that did not mean she was prepared to tell him her most intimate secrets.

To divert herself from those distressing thoughts, Artemis nuzzled her nephew's ear. "What do you think of this place, Lee?"

She swept a glance around the spacious, handsomely appointed bedchamber. "It is a far cry from the little seaside cottage I had in mind for us. I miss Bramberley's fine old wood paneling, but I must admit this flower-sprigged wallpaper is quite cheerful to wake up to. Don't tell anyone I said so, will you?"

Lee chuckled as if he understood.

Artemis sat up and stretched. "Are you as hungry as I am? I believe I smell coffee and bacon. Let's get dressed and go find some breakfast."

As she rifled through her trunk in search of clean clothes for them both, her hand passed over the smooth old wood-and-brass fittings in a homesick caress. Once she and Lee were decently attired, she took him by the hand and ventured forth into the strange house that was to be their home.

It did not take long to locate the wide main staircase and descend to the lower floor. As Artemis peeped into a large room near the entry hall, a middle-aged woman standing inside turned toward her.

"Good morning, ma'am." The woman made an impeccable curtsy, but her dark eyes flicked over Artemis and Lee with cool disapproval. "We met for a moment last night when you arrived. I am the housekeeper, Mrs. Matlock. I trust your quarters met with your satisfaction?"

"Indeed they did," replied Artemis, acutely conscious that the housekeeper was better dressed than she. "Is Mr. Northmore up yet?"

"For hours." It was clear from her tone that the housekeeper approved of early risers. "He wanted to make certain the house was in good order for you and the child."

Something about the way Mrs. Matlock said "the child" affronted Artemis. Did the woman disapprove of Lee's illegitimate birth? It was not something the poor little creature could help.

Hoisting him into her arms, she answered in a tone of icy courtesy. "Everything I've seen so far has been quite satisfactory. Now, if you will excuse us we are in rather urgent need of some breakfast."

"I will not detain you any longer, ma'am." The housekeeper beckoned a young maidservant. "Mr. Northmore instructed me to engage a nursery staff for the child. In the meantime, Cassie can take charge of him. She is the eldest of a large family and has a great deal of experience minding young children."

"But—"

Before Artemis could protest, the girl gathered Lee from her arms. "Isn't he a handsome wee lad? How old is he, then?"

Artemis could not resist sincere words of praise for her darling boy. "He turned a year not long ago."

"He's a fine size for his age. Our Isaac is three months older and not near so big. Can he walk yet?"

"Cassie—" Mrs. Matlock interrupted before Artemis could reply "—the mistress wants her breakfast. She hasn't time to listen to tattle about your family. Fetch the child to the nursery and feed him."

"Yes, ma'am." The girl whisked Lee away, cooing over him, while he did not make a speck of fuss at being separated from his aunt.

Mrs. Matlock turned to address Artemis. "After you've eaten, the local seamstress will be coming to measure you for some new clothes."

"I have a perfectly adequate wardrobe, thank you." Artemis strove to maintain her dignity.

Was this how she would be treated while she lived under Hadrian's roof, as a mere cipher in her nephew's life? That was not the bargain she'd intended to make.

"Master's orders," replied the housekeeper as if that were the final word on the subject.

Artemis was determined it would not be. "Where can I find *my husband,* pray? There are some matters I wish to discuss with him."

His decree that she must have new clothes, to begin with. And the notion of Lee being brought up by a nursery staff. If he no longer believed she was a fortune hunter, as he'd claimed, why did he insist on treating her like one?

"The master has gone out." Mrs. Matlock no longer sounded quite so certain of herself.

"Did he say where?"

"He did not, but I saw him walking down the lane. He may have wanted a bit of fresh air after your long journey."

"I could do with a breath of air myself." And a little privacy. If she was going to raise her objections to their domestic arrangements, Artemis preferred not to have the servants overhear. "Kindly have someone fetch my wrap and bonnet."

"But your breakfast, ma'am?"

Though the savory aroma of fried bacon made her mouth water, Artemis reminded herself there were more important things than food. "I will eat when I return. A bit of exercise will whet my appetite."

A short while later, as she headed down the winding, tree-lined lane, Artemis struggled to reconcile her present mood with the promise she had made Hadrian last night. Was she putting the past behind them and endeavoring to make a fresh start?

This had nothing to do with Julian, Daphne and Leander, she told herself. The problem was Hadrian's forceful, managing manner, which he'd demonstrated so often since they'd met—arranging everything to suit himself without a thought for anyone else. His ambition and industry made a welcome change from her indolent uncles, but could he not have consulted her before making plans that affected her and Lee?

Coming to the end of the lane, where it opened onto a narrow road, Artemis scanned the vicinity for a glimpse of Hadrian. All she saw was a boot print in the damp earth heading southward. Her growling stomach urged her to return to the house but she could not bear to face Hadrian's housekeeper without having spoken to him.

A brisk ten-minute walk brought her to a squat stone church that looked even older than the one back in Sussex where she and Hadrian had been married. Having seen no further sign of Hadrian, she was about to turn back when she heard the deep rumble of his voice from behind an old yew tree in a churchyard.

Was he talking to the local vicar, perhaps about having Lee christened with a new name that he would find less objectionable? It was just the sort of high-handed behavior Artemis had come to expect from him.

As she drew nearer, preparing to confront Hadrian, she was able to make out his words.

"What were you thinking," he asked, "landing yourself in that kind of trouble? Did I not tell you often enough we owed a duty to the others? Everything else should have come second to that. I worked my heart out to keep up my end, but you threw it all away."

Artemis could see him now, standing among the gravestones

with his back to her. But she could not see the person he was talking to. Baffled, she stumbled to a stop.

Hadrian must not have heard her approach, for he kept talking. "Was that my fault? Did I ruin your character with too much money and too little attention, like Artemis said?"

It brought her the most ridiculous jolt of pleasure to hear Hadrian speak her name. Then she realized he must be speaking to his dead brother.

"Perhaps I should have brought you out to India where I could have kept an eye on you. But I'd made a fresh start and I didn't want you there to remind me of the past."

His voice sounded so different. Not stern and masterful, but laden with anguished regret. It was the voice of a man who might need a woman's comfort and support. It called forth something fundamental to her nature.

Yet Artemis knew she should not be there. She was trespassing on Hadrian's most intimate thoughts. She could not have borne it if he'd overheard some of the words she'd spoken over Leander and Daphne's graves. Things she had never been able to say to her brother and sister while they were alive.

As she took one quiet step backward then another, Artemis tried to block out what Hadrian was saying.

"Pa, I hope you can forgive me for failing Julian and you and the lads. I have one more chance to make it right and I won't fail you again, I swear it."

In her haste to steal away, Artemis brought her foot down on a fallen twig. It snapped with a report that rang out like a pistol shot.

Hadrian spun about to confront whoever had dared intrude upon this deeply private moment. His eyes blazed when they fell upon her. "What are you doing here? Did you come to spy on me? Did you think you might hear something to your advantage?"

"No!" Caution urged her not to get too close to Hadrian, but something stronger drew her toward him. "Please, I didn't mean to…"

As she moved toward him, her gaze fell upon the inscription carved on the gravestone before which he stood.

Killed in the Fellbank Colliery Explosion
24th May 1808
William Northmore ae 39 yrs
Augustus Northmore ae 14 yrs
Marcus Northmore ae 11 yrs
Titus Northmore ae 9 yrs
Quentin Northmore ae 8 yrs

"Is this—" the question was wrenched out of her, though she had no doubt of the answer "—*was* this your family?"

Chapter Nine

For a moment Hadrian was too stunned by his wife's sudden appearance to answer her question.

The crack of that twig under her foot might have been the sound of a pistol cocking for the spasm of panic it sent through him. But when he spun around to confront the person listening in on his most guarded thoughts, the sight of Artemis had unnerved him in a different way altogether.

The robust Durham wind had blown her bonnet back, exposing her hair to its impatient caress. It whipped dark tendrils about her face and teased a rosy glow into her cheeks. It pushed her skirts tight against her slender legs, plucking up the hem to taunt him with a glimpse of her dainty ankles. Hadrian did not trust himself to watch the wind have its lusty way with her, as he could not.

The anxious, furtive set of her features drove out those bedeviling thoughts, reminding him of what she must have overheard. He felt naked. Exposed. Vulnerable.

Then she asked the question he could scarcely bear to answer. "Of course they're my family. Why else would I be here?"

"And they all…died…in a colliery explosion?" The horror and pity in her voice threatened to break through a barrier he had erected around that part of his life.

He had no choice but to respond to that threat. "All except me and Julian. He was too young to work when it happened. He's with them now, though. Your brother saw to that."

Artemis swayed, as if she was being buffeted by something stronger than the upland wind. But she managed to stay on her feet. "Why did you not tell me what happened to your father and brothers?"

"Why *should* I have told you? Someone like you could not begin to understand!"

The moment those words were out of his mouth, Hadrian knew he should not have spoken them. After all, he'd been the one who wanted to put the past behind them. Now he wondered if there were some parts of his past that he could never escape—things that would haunt him until his dying day, no matter how far he ran or how deep he tried to bury them.

But what else *could* he say? Admit that it troubled him to tell her what he'd never been able to tell his partners or even his beloved first wife? That was something he truly could not expect her to understand, for he could not quite fathom it himself.

Artemis flinched from his bitter outburst, but her reply surprised him. "Perhaps you were right. I do not understand how your father came to be in a coal mine with four of your brothers, all so young. But I want to know, if you will tell me."

He'd expected her to storm away or hurl an angry retort that would give him an excuse to break off this disturbing encounter. He was not prepared for her concern.

It slipped past his defenses. "My father wasn't always a miner. He had a farm once, not far from here, land Northmores had worked for as long as anyone could remember. If only he could have held on to it until me and my brothers grew big enough to help him. But he got hit with a string of bad harvests and had to borrow money he couldn't repay. There was nothing for it but to go to Fellbank and take work in the colliery."

"But your brothers?" Artemis's dark brows knit together in a baffled frown. "The youngest was only eight. *That* is what I cannot understand."

"I knew you wouldn't," he muttered, vexed that she would not leave it alone. "You and your *genteel poverty*. One miner's wages would not keep a family of four, let alone eight. Around here, all the lads go to work by the age of eight if they can get a place. Lasses, too, when there's work enough for them."

"That is monstrous!" Her striking eyes flashed with passionate indignation. "It is one thing for children to help out on farms, gathering eggs or herding sheep. But underground in a mine? Such practices should not be permitted in a civilized country!"

"No, they should not." Hadrian heaved a deep, frustrated sigh. "What do you reckon I've worked for all these years? To raise up my family so they never again have to fear being wiped off the earth. But more than that—to keep lads and lasses out of the mines so they have a chance to go to school and learn enough to do something else with their lives, if they choose to."

Was Artemis beginning to understand now?

In case not, he continued. "Nobody with the power to change things is going to listen to a bunch of sooty, ignorant miners who talk too broad for them to understand. That was why I sent Julian down south to the best schools. That is why I wanted him to stand for Parliament. So he could speak for lads like our brothers in a way the high and mighty *could* understand."

If his fierce indignation had been a bludgeon and every word struck a blow, Artemis could not have looked more stricken. Though Hadrian knew none of this was her fault, too many painful memories had been roused—too much impotent anger and gnawing guilt let loose. He could not rein it in.

"Now do you understand?" he demanded. "Do you see what your family has done?"

Intense, contradictory feelings overwhelmed Hadrian at that moment—a tidal wave of liberating release and a paralyzing undercurrent of shame. He wished Artemis would strike back, as she had when they'd first met, with regal disdain and bitter hostility.

Instead she gave a jerky nod, as if she were a puppet in the hands of an unskilled master. Her icy facade seemed dangerously brittle.

"Now I understand—" her whispered words tore into Hadrian like tiny shards of glass "—why you hate me."

Hate her? He wanted to deny it, but his throat was too constricted with guilt to speak.

Artemis would not have heard him anyway, for she had turned and fled from him as if in terror for her life.

Artemis ran from the churchyard, desperate to escape the memory of that headstone with its heartbreaking list of Hadrian's dead brothers. Her imagination conjured up images of those boys, all looking like Lee might when he turned eight…nine…eleven years old. How would she feel if she'd lost her precious boy five times over, along with the father she'd bashfully revered, all in one calamitous day?

Would she have had the strength to go on as Hadrian had? Somehow he'd found the courage to venture halfway around the world and make his fortune from nothing so he could provide for his one remaining brother. But he had not stopped there. He'd striven to protect other children from suffering the same fate as his brothers. Her heart swelled with pity and admiration.

"Artemis!" His voice pursued her, hoarse with urgency. "Wait… please!"

Part of her wanted to run faster so she would not have to face him. Another part insisted she owed him a hearing…and so much more that she could never hope to redress. Gasping for breath, she staggered to a halt and waited for Hadrian. However harshly he denounced her, it could not be worse than the tribunal of her own conscience. She stared at the ground, unable to look him in the face.

"Artemis." His footsteps slowed as he approached her. His voice sounded a little winded, too. "I'm sorry for what I said just now. For a long time, I've refused to let myself think about what happened to my father and brothers. All of a sudden it overpowered me, but that was no excuse for lashing out at you the way I did. I don't blame *you* for what happened to Julian, I swear. And I most certainly do not hate you."

Those were the last words she'd expected to hear from him. They should have eased her guilt, but they did not.

"You…should blame me." She pressed a hand to her chest to keep her heavy heart from battering its way out. "I blame myself. I tried so hard to shift the responsibility for what happened on to Julian and Lord Kingsfold and you so I could absolve Leander and Daphne…and me. Now I can no longer deny what I've done."

Having acknowledged her guilt gave Artemis the nerve to look Hadrian in the face. But the condemnation she'd expected to find was absent from his gaze. She could not make out whatever was there in its place.

"What is it you reckon you've done?" he asked in a husky murmur.

Must she confess aloud the things she'd been reluctant to examine too closely, even in the privacy of her own thoughts? That was the very least she owed Hadrian and his family, surely.

"Is it not obvious? I was the one who brought up Leander and Daphne after our parents died. They were both so different than me—so sociable and high-spirited. Because I envied them those qualities, I encouraged their gregarious ways. Because I wanted to make up for the loss of our parents, I indulged them and made excuses for their behavior."

Hadrian began walking slowly in the direction of his house. He beckoned Artemis to join him. "None of that sounds so terrible to me."

"Don't you see?" She fell in step beside him. "I raised my brother and sister to be amiable and outgoing. But, as you told me, vices are the tail side of virtues. Leander and Daphne could also be impulsive, willful and reckless."

Not long ago, she would have cut to the quick anyone who dared say such a thing about her adored brother and sister. To say it herself made Artemis feel treacherously disloyal to their memories. But it was true, and Hadrian deserved to hear the truth.

His dark, dynamic features creased in a pensive frown as he pondered her words. Then he shook his head. "You are not responsible for your brother and sister's actions. I'm certain, if you'd had your way, Daphne would never have lain with my brother and Leander would never have called him out."

"Perhaps." She could not excuse herself so easily. "But what I did was just as bad. How could I have expected Daphne to stay away from your brother when I'd spent eighteen years doing my best to give her whatever she fancied? How could I expect Leander to put reason and caution before pride, when I'd filled his head with notions of family honor and tales of our illustrious ancestors?"

Hadrian's frown deepened. Perhaps he had begun to grasp how deeply she was at fault.

In case he did not, Artemis summed it up. "Because of me, you lost the last remnant of your family. And countless children, little older than Lee, lost the man who might have been their champion."

It was all she could do to contain the sob that ached in her throat and hold back the tears that might cool her stinging eyes. She did not want Hadrian's false reassurances of pardon because he felt sorry for her. She did not deserve his pity.

As they walked on in silence, Artemis shored up her composure in preparation for whatever recriminations Hadrian might heap upon her. If only she had not let herself begin to think well of him, she would be so much better able to bear his disdain.

As they rounded a bend in the tree-shaded lane, his house appeared in view. Its golden-brown stones glowed faintly in the spring sunshine, while stray sunbeams glinted off its many windows.

"I'm afraid it will not do," said Hadrian, "you trying to take all the blame on yourself. I reckon there are many people to divide it amongst. So many that no one can claim the lion's share and none is in any position to cast stones at another. Least of all me at you. How old were you when you had to take over the upbringing of your brother and sister?"

She was so astonished by his forbearance and the unexpected question that she answered without stopping to think if it was something she wanted to reveal. "Ten years old when my mother died. Daphne was not much older than Lee is now and Leander had just turned four. Three years later, we lost our father."

"So you were no more than a child yourself." A sigh escaped Hadrian's lips. "Did you have no one to help you raise your brother and sister?"

"There were servants, of course, for their day-to-day care—a few at least. And my father's uncles were our guardians, but they knew nothing about raising small children...and cared even less."

Those last words slipped out in spite of her. Dearings did not criticize members of the family to outsiders. At the moment, though, Hadrian did not feel like an outsider. Though his loss and his struggles had been so much worse than hers, they forged a bond with her that Artemis could not deny.

"Don't be so hard on yourself." As they walked, Hadrian edged closer to her until they were almost touching. "It's not an easy job to raise a child. Even in the best of circumstances and with the best of intentions, people make mistakes. I cannot see that you have anything to reproach yourself for. If I once claimed otherwise, it was only because *I* did not understand."

Was this how Papists felt when they made their confession and were shriven of their sins? Though Artemis could not surrender her whole burden of guilt, she did feel lighter somehow—less tightly bound. But there was one further step in the search for absolution.

Penance.

"Do the Durham mines still employ children as young as your brothers were?"

"I'm sure they do," replied Hadrian. "Not only here, but throughout the country. Why would the owners quit a practice that saves them money? Now that I am in business, I can see their side of it, though I still believe it is wrong. Nothing less than an Act of Parliament will stop collieries from employing young lads and lasses in the pits."

Artemis tugged on Hadrian's sleeve to make him stop for a moment. "You thought I would not understand or care what happened to your family and you were half right. I cannot imagine how such things are permitted in a country that claims to be civilized. But now that I know about them, I care a great deal. What can I do to help?"

Hadrian studied her face, perhaps searching for proof of her sincerity. "Without Julian to lead the campaign for reform, we will have to wait for his son to come of age. The best way you can help is to make a better job of raising our nephew than I did of raising his father."

"I beg your pardon?" Could Hadrian mean what she thought he meant?

He gave a rueful shrug. "You said yourself, I ruined Julian's character with too much money and too little attention. For years, I sent back every penny I could spare so he'd have the best of everything. I told myself that rubbing shoulders with young gentlemen of consequence would help him become a better advocate for children working in the mines. Now I wonder if I was only trying to keep him from harm and make up for what he'd lost. Showering him with money was the wrong way to go about it. I reckon you will strike a better balance with Lee."

The full implication of his words sent Artemis reeling. "Are you saying that your only reason for wanting custody of Lee, for marrying me, for bringing us here, is so he can be molded into an instrument to further your plans?"

"What's wrong with my plans?" Hadrian looked as taken aback by her response as she was by his. "I am not proposing we send the lad down to work in the mines. Only that we prepare him to lead the fight for reform one day."

Did Hadrian not see? He was asking for the one thing she could not give up—her nephew's freedom and happiness. "What if he does not want that responsibility? Is he to be raised with no say at all in his own future? I'm sorry, Hadrian. I truly want to help you, but I cannot agree to that."

Could Artemis mean what she'd just said? Mouth agape in disbelief, Hadrian stared after his bride as she turned her back on him and walked away for the second time in an hour.

But so much had happened in that hour. So much had changed between them...at least he'd thought it had. Could that shift have been entirely on his part, while Artemis continued to regard him the same way she had from their unfavorable first meeting?

No. He could not accept that the things she'd told him about herself, and the flashes of intense emotion she'd betrayed, were less than sincere.

Reason warned him to let the matter rest for a while, not to press Artemis now, when feelings on both sides were running dangerously high. But pride refused to heed that sensible warning. How could he let her raze his cherished plans to smoking rubble, then march away victorious?

"Artemis!" For the second time in an hour, he followed her. Not as a regretful supplicant this time, to beg her pardon, but charged with iron purpose, determined to have his way.

He caught up to her on the wide landing of the main staircase. "Stay and listen to me, will you?"

When she did not deign to reply, he caught her by the arm and spun her about. He judged his grip carefully. He did not want to hurt or intimidate her, only get her attention. And perhaps he just needed to touch her. "This matter is not resolved."

She glared at him—for daring to lay hands on her, no doubt. If only she knew how he longed to lay hands and lips on her again, the way he had on their wedding night. Not in a fumbling, half-awake daze, but in full possession of his senses and abilities. Somehow, her challenge to his authority whipped up that suppressed desire, like a rogue breeze over the embers of a bonfire.

Hadrian fought to quench the flames. He did not want unwelcome desire to cloud his judgment or give Artemis an unfair advantage over him. But the sight of her did nothing to quell his unruly urges. She'd removed her bonnet upon entering the house, letting her wind-blown hair tumble over her shoulders. Her lips looked fuller and softer. Her eyes glittered with a dozen shades of purple—a different one for every emotion he glimpsed, but could not readily identify.

"Is it not resolved? Well, I am." She made no attempt to shake off his hand. Was it because his touch had no effect upon her...or quite the opposite? "I cannot raise our nephew to be a slave to your plans, no matter how well intentioned."

Did she mean that backhanded compliment to appease him? It would take more than that from her to make him abandon the purpose to which he'd dedicated his life.

"You took a vow to obey me, remember?" He tried to release her arm, but his fingers froze around it, unable to let go. "It is not one I mean to impose upon, given the circumstances of our marriage. Indeed, there is only one thing I will ever ask of you as a husband."

There was something else he would have liked to ask, but Artemis had made it clear that was out of the question.

With his free hand, Hadrian gestured around. "As the man who will provide you with a house that is not centuries old and crumbling around your ears, servants, fine clothes, the opportunity to travel and entertain in a manner befitting your rank, is what I ask really so much in return for all that?"

"I don't want *all that!* I never did and I never will." As she flung the words at him, Hadrian fancied her a defiant warrior queen. One of the Brigantes, perhaps, standing up to a Roman centurion. "That was why I came looking for you earlier. To tell you for the last time that I am not a fortune hunter. I want no part of this splendid house or the fine clothes you summoned a seamstress to make me. And I most definitely do not want Lee being tended by some strict old nurse who will keep me from him and train him to be a passive pawn in your grand schemes for the future. You cannot buy my cooperation or coerce it."

Artemis twisted his words in ways he'd never intended them. She refused to do the one thing for which he'd wed her. Yet Hadrian could scarcely keep his mind on those things because he yearned so urgently to kiss her. Why had his inconvenient desire chosen the worst possible moment to threaten his control? Was it because contesting the things they cared about most passionately provoked other kinds of passion as well?

He could not let that kind of passion overcome his zeal for the cause that had sustained him through the battlefield of tragedy and the wasteland of loneliness.

"I am not trying to buy you." He forced his hand to release Artemis, one stubborn finger at a time. "And I would never coerce you. I am only trying to make you see how important this is to me, and to a great many others. You said you wanted to help. Was that just idle talk? Does one child's future matter so much more than the lives and futures of thousands of other children, because he has Dearing blood and they haven't?"

He stalked past her, inwardly conceding that she had fought him to a bloody draw this time. But the campaign was far from over.

"You don't honestly believe that, do you?" Her words pursued Hadrian, reminding him of their agreement to make a fresh start.

He paused and glanced back at her, his shoulders raised in a helpless shrug. After all that had happened, was it possible the two of them could ever forge a steady cooperative understanding? Or would relations between them always be capricious and volatile? "What else am I to think?"

Artemis seemed to search for an answer that might alter his

opinion, but after a moment she gave up in defeat. With a stony nod to her, Hadrian retreated to consider his next move.

Without giving much thought to where he was going, he wandered up more stairs and down a long hallway that opened on to a high balcony with a breathtaking view of the dales. From that high perch, the rolling countryside looked like a patchwork in every possible shade of green, stitched together with seams of brown and gray stone fencing. In the wide blue sky above, plump clouds rolled before the wind like flocks of yearling lambs.

Off to the east was a different landscape altogether. Barren black slag heaps replaced verdant hillsides. Instead of snug cottages and cowsheds, shaft frames towered like the iron skeletons of hulking, hungry beasts. Tall chimneystacks spouted columns of black smoke that blighted the sky with a jaundiced haze.

But those visible signs of the Durham collieries did not weigh half so heavy on Hadrian as the scenes he could only see in his memory—young lads and lasses toiling in the stifling darkness, deep in the bowels of those hills. Hard as he'd worked the past seventeen years, they had been one long, sun-drenched holiday compared to the bone-grinding labor of his youth.

He could not bear to think how many more lads like his brothers would die in the dangerous depths of the earth before they had a chance to live, with no hope of escape.

Hadrian chided himself on not following through on his original plan for his young nephew. He should have gained custody of Lee by whatever means necessary then hired someone to raise him—someone who understood and approved of what Hadrian wanted the lad to do with his life. Someone more like *him*.

But where would he have found anyone more like him than Artemis? The woman was strong, stubborn and proud. Yet she was fiercely loyal and devoted to her family. She had known great loss and heavy responsibility from an early age. Though she'd tried her best to fulfill that duty and done a fine job by anyone else's standards, she remained acutely conscious of her failings.

Perhaps the combustible friction between them came not from their superficial differences, but from the many deep similarities in their character?

As he mulled over that intriguing, disturbing notion, Hadrian asked himself how someone might persuade *him* to change his mind about a matter of great importance. A direct confrontation would never work, so why should he expect it to work on Artemis? A better strategy would be to lay the facts before him in a way best calculated to appeal to his reason and sense of justice.

He had an idea how he might do the same for Artemis. But could he bear the jagged reminders of things he'd spent nearly twenty years trying to forget?

Chapter Ten

"Where are you taking me?" Artemis strove to disguise her uneasiness as they drove away from Hadrian's house in a two-wheeled gig pulled by a roan gelding. They were traveling in the opposite direction from the churchyard, where she had surprised him the previous day. "I'm sure Lee would have enjoyed the opportunity to see the Durham countryside."

"He'll have plenty of chances for that in the years ahead," replied Hadrian in a more amiable tone than Artemis felt she had any right to expect from him.

She had tossed and turned much of the night, fretting over the day's unsettling events. Ever since Hadrian Northmore had marched into her life, she'd felt as if a small part of her was being pulled in a different direction from the rest. Yesterday the division had become much more painful, as if powerful forces were tearing her in two.

With all her heart, she regretted the devastating losses Hadrian had suffered—both in his youth and more recently. Contrary to what he might believe, she was appalled by the notion of children working underground. Any minor deprivations she'd experienced paled in comparison to theirs. But she had known enough to make her feel for their suffering and want to be of assistance. And yet...

The notion that Hadrian only wanted Lee as a tool to achieve his aims sickened her. She knew all too well the pain of striving for love and approval, only to fall short, often for reasons over which she had no control. She could not subject her nephew to that. He must never doubt she thought the world of him and always would—not as a reward for fulfilling all her expectations, but as a gift bestowed without conditions.

Why must two such worthy desires run contrary to one another?

"As to where we are going…" Hadrian's words crashed in on her thoughts. "When we spoke yesterday, you seemed curious about my family and my past. I thought I could show you better than tell you."

Show her his past—how could he possibly do that? An ominous undercurrent lurked beneath Hadrian's offhand tone. Yet Artemis could not suppress her curiosity. The more she learned about this fascinating, complicated man she had married, the more she yearned to know.

A while later, they turned on to a bumpy, crooked road bordered by overgrown bushes that seemed determined to strangle it altogether. Artemis could imagine this path wandering back into the past. It certainly did not appear to lead anywhere else.

"Are you certain this is the right way?" she asked as the gig lurched over the ruts, jostling her hard against Hadrian. Every time her arm or leg pressed against his firm flesh, her heart gave an answering lurch.

"This is the way," he muttered, his gaze fixed on the road. "I'll not forget it as long as I live."

"The way to where?" Artemis gave a most undignified squeal as one wheel of the gig dipped into a deep furrow.

Hadrian answered with a single word that was clearly laden with meaning for him. "Fellbank."

A slab of stone seemed to settle on her chest—one inscribed with the words "Killed in the Fellbank Colliery Explosion."

She struggled to summon breath enough to ask, "So near Edenhall?"

Hadrian gave a grim nod. "Rich seams of coal hereabouts. Edenhall used to belong to the owners of Fellbank Colliery. Quite a difference, this place from Edenhall and Bramberley, isn't it?"

Forcing her gaze away from his hawkish profile, Artemis found herself peering down a narrow street that ran between rows of cramped, ramshackle dwellings, many of which had collapsed.

"The place didn't look much better than this, twenty years ago," said Hadrian. "The mine owners get pit cottages cobbled together as cheap as they can. I once asked my father why the cottages were put up in pairs like they are. He said it was so they could lean against each other to keep from falling down."

He reined the gelding to a halt beside one pair of pit cottages that looked reasonably intact. "Then Ma said no, it was so there'd be one wall out of four that didn't have a draft blowing through it."

"What became of your mother?" Artemis asked as he helped her out of the gig. "You've never mentioned her."

Hadrian looked toward the cottage with a distant gaze, as if picturing his brothers running through the broken door. "She died of lockjaw, a year before the explosion. It helped to think of her waiting in heaven to look after Pa and the lads."

He entered the abandoned dwelling and Artemis felt obliged to follow, though she feared the slightest breeze might bring the walls crashing down upon them.

"Eight people lived here?" Artemis shook her head in disbelief as she stared around a single room not much larger than the linen cupboards at Bramberley.

"We had more room than some." Hadrian pointed to a rough-cut hole in one corner of the ceiling. "At least there was a loft for us older lads to sleep in."

What sort of people had his parents been, Artemis wondered, to raise a son who could go from *this* to amass an enviable fortune? When she recalled the purpose that had driven him to make his fortune, a lump rose in her throat. Her reasons for opposing his plans for Lee suddenly seemed trifling.

"My arm hurt." Hadrian's unexpected words startled her. They came out in a low, half-stifled voice, quite unlike his usual vigorous, confident tone. It was not the voice of a powerful, arrogant man, but an uncertain boy whose whole world had been violently wrenched apart. "I broke it the week before when I took a fall on an underground bank. That put me on the *smart list* for eighteen days. So I was here minding Julian when the cottage shook and I heard a noise like cannons firing in the distance. I wondered what it could be, but deep down I knew."

There were many things she was curious to find out about Hadrian Northmore, but not the details of how his father and brothers had all been killed in a single moment. Artemis wanted to cover her ears and run away. But she knew he had come here for her benefit. She could not leave him if there was the slightest chance he might need her.

"I ran to the door and looked toward the works." He brushed past her and stumbled out through the empty door frame.

Artemis followed, grateful to escape the desolate pit cottage, painfully empty of everything but wrenching memories. She found Hadrian standing beside the gig, staring down the narrow road toward a cluster of buildings on the top of a nearby hill.

"I saw a cloud coming up from the pithead. It looked like a big black arrow pointing the way to heaven." Hadrian's voice trailed off.

He drew several shuddering breaths, then began to move forward with slow, shambling steps. "I shouted for Julian to stay inside. Said I'd wring his bloody neck if he came out. Then I ran to the works. The sides of the shaft frames were on fire and the heads had been blown clean off. The ground was covered with splintered hunks of wood, bits of coal and corves."

"Corves?" The question popped out before Artemis could prevent it.

Hadrian turned to stare at her as if he had never seen her before. Yet he answered her question like a child reciting lessons by rote. "Big baskets they load with hewn coal for the putters to drag up to the surface. Gus and Mark and me were putters. Titus and Quentin were trappers, the younger lads who opened and closed the doors when the putters came through hauling the corves."

The man had spent his youth dragging great baskets of coal up from the depths of the earth. No wonder he was so strong…and confident to the point of arrogance. After what he'd endured and overcome, it would take more than one intractable woman to daunt him.

He looked from her face to the buildings on the hill and back again. A spark of recognition kindled in the misty gray depths of his eyes. He seemed to be making a conscious effort to pull himself from the dark pit of his past.

"After the explosion, they had to seal up the mine for six weeks to starve the fire. When they opened it up again, I was part of the crew that went in to collect what was left of the bodies. They buried all the rest of the dead together in a mass grave, but I had Pa and the lads laid to rest with Ma at St. Oswin's."

He sounded exhausted, as if he'd just done all those things again.

Artemis held out her hand to him. "I believe we've seen enough for one day, don't you?"

Hadrian stared at her hand for a moment. Then he reached out to clasp it. "Reckon we have."

She led him back to the gig as if he were sleepwalking, the way Daphne had sometimes done as a child. He seemed dazed, held captive by the terrible events he'd relived.

"Up you go." Artemis coaxed him into the gig, then climbed up beside him and took the reins. "I'll get us home."

"Home?" Hadrian glanced toward the deserted pit cottage as they headed back toward Edenhall.

He had lost so much. Her arms ached to gather him close and

comfort him, though she doubted she had either the ability or the right.

"Not *that* home." She gave his leg a reassuring pat. "Your new one."

Her heart gave a broken-winged flutter when he placed one of his hands over hers. "The new one...of course."

His fine new mansion would never be *home* to him the way that drafty, tumbledown cottage had been. Or could it? Perhaps there was a way to atone for the most recent loss Hadrian had suffered.

She could make a home for him. She and Lee could become his new family...if he would let them.

What on earth had made him believe coming back here was a good idea?

As he and Artemis drove away from the abandoned pit village, Hadrian slowly emerged from the dark trance of his long-suppressed memories. What disturbed him almost as much as reliving the worst day of his life was that Artemis had seen him so confused and helpless, prey to emotions he could not control. He was tempted to resent her presence and the glimpse this had given her of his deepest fears and weakness. Such knowledge could be a dangerous weapon in the wrong hands. But were her hands the wrong ones in which to entrust his secret pain?

He stared at the one that held the reins. It was a strong hand, capable of pulling him from the grip of his nightmare, giving him something solid and steadfast to cling to. He felt her other hand beneath his, resting against his leg. With it, she had offered him sympathy and comfort without demeaning him.

This wife of his was proving an altogether surprising woman. He could not help feeling his parents would have approved of her. Though his return to Fellbank had stirred up many unwelcome memories, it also made him feel closer to his family than he had in a very long time.

He cleared his throat, making his voice come out deeper and gruffer. "That didn't go quite the way I planned."

"You and your plans." Artemis cast him a sidelong glance of exasperation mingled with something else. Could it be fondness?

The possibility made him a trifle tongue-tied. "I had...hoped...a visit to Fellbank might persuade you there are worse things our nephew could do with his life than take up the cause of the children who work in the mines."

"I can assure you, I need no persuasion of *that*," replied Artemis.

"You don't? But yesterday you said—"

"I said a great many things, but I fear I did not make myself very clear. For that, I apologize."

Once again it surprised him that a proud woman like her should be so willing to admit her mistakes. It did not make him think any less of her—quite the contrary. "You might have been able to explain yourself better if you had not been interrupted quite so much. Perhaps you could take the opportunity to enlighten me now?"

He hoped she would. The sound of her voice soothed him.

"Very well." Artemis drew a deep breath. "I want to raise our nephew to care about other people and be ready to offer his assistance to anyone in need of it."

Was it his imagination or did the pressure of her hand upon his leg increase, almost like a caress?

"When he is old enough, I want to take him to one of the mining villages to see and talk to children who work there. And, of course, I mean to show him the headstone you erected for your family at St. Oswin's."

"I could not ask for more than that." Perhaps their trip to Fellbank had succeeded better than he'd realized. Was it possible his betrayal of weakness had done more than a blustery show of force?

"Don't you see?" Artemis turned toward him with a plea in her eyes. So close, their color made Hadrian catch his breath. "I thought you were asking for much more."

In answer to his questioning look, she added, "I do not want to burden Lee with our expectations or make him feel this problem is his to solve all on his own."

"That was never my intention." Though the denial came readily to his lips, a seed of doubt found fertile soil. "Do you reckon that's how Julian felt and why he rebelled?"

Artemis shook her head. "If it was, that is all in the past. It is what we do from now on that matters. Is there anything we can do *now* to improve the situation? I cannot bear to let it go on for another twenty years without at least *trying* to help."

"What can we do? There are dozens of collieries in County Durham and hundreds, maybe thousands, all over the country. You must know the power of the forces that will oppose any reform." Even as he spoke, Hadrian's mind began to turn in new directions, seeking fresh channels.

"Then perhaps we should start small," suggested Artemis. "Lay a foundation so Lee will have something to work with when and if he is ready to take on the challenge."

"You know, lass, you may be on to something. Nothing ventured, nothing gained, as Pa used to say." Suddenly Hadrian could hear those words in his father's booming voice, clearer than he'd been able to recall it in many years.

"We could write letters to the newspapers." Artemis turned toward him with a smile that illuminated her whole face. "Or draft a pamphlet, like the abolitionists. My cousin Jasper is an abolitionist. He might be able to help us."

As she bubbled with ideas, Hadrian marveled at the change that had come over Artemis in the brief time he'd known her. Had she truly altered from that cool, disdainful lady he'd first met in the shadow of her family's ancient estate? Or had this fervor and compassion been there all along, imprisoned by pride or reticence?

It made him anxious to discover what other intriguing qualities might still be constrained within her, waiting to be liberated. Passion, perhaps?

That thought made him conscious of her touch upon his leg in a whole new way. The unwelcome attraction he had fought to suppress now burst from its cage, growling and roaring. He knew better than to hope the beast would be so easily tamed again. It would not rest until it had stalked, hunted and satisfied its ravenous hunger.

Now that his mistrust of his bride had abated, Hadrian feared he no longer had the strength to fight his desire. Nor the inclination.

But memories of his encounter with Artemis on their wedding night warned him he would need to proceed slowly and with great care.

The roan gelding turned off the main road toward Edenhall with hardly any urging from Artemis. That was fortunate, since she was still managing the reins with only one hand. The other one rested on Hadrian's thigh, with his hand covering it. This was by far the most prolonged physical contact she'd had with him. She had initiated it as an innocent gesture of comfort and reassurance, but somehow it felt different now—much less innocent. On her part, at least.

She could not ignore the heat of his skin rising through the fabric of his breeches to warm her palm. Or the muscular firmness of his thigh beneath her fingertips. Not to mention the size and controlled strength of his hand as it enveloped hers. Those sensations quickened her pulse and made her blood hum through her veins.

Her eager torrent of suggestions to help the young miners dwindled to a trickle, as she feared her breathless voice might betray her wayward thoughts. She felt vaguely ashamed of herself for entertaining such notions about Hadrian after what the poor man had just been through. A stolen glance at his rugged profile showed that he had lapsed back into his earlier daze. No doubt he was thinking more about the Fellbank Explosion and its wrenching aftermath.

Stopping the gig in front of Edenhall's main entrance, she tossed the reins to a boy who came running from the stable yard.

"We're home now," she murmured to Hadrian as they alighted.

"Would you like to lie down for a while before dinner? I believe it would do you good."

Hadrian nodded. "I feel tired to the bone."

Artemis recalled him telling her that strong emotion wearied him. After what he'd been through today, it was a wonder he remained conscious.

As they entered the house, Mrs. Matlock came bustling toward them. "Is something wrong with the master?"

It was clear from her sharp tone and stern frown that the housekeeper held Artemis to blame for whatever ailed him.

"Don't fret," said Hadrian. "It's nothing a bit of a lie down won't put right."

"No need to trouble yourself, then, ma'am. I'll see to the master." Mrs. Matlock approached with a brisk, determined air, clearly intending to take charge of the situation.

"It is no trouble for me to tend my husband." With a proud tilt of her chin, Artemis stared down Mrs. Matlock. "If I require any assistance, I shall be sure to inform you."

The housekeeper's eyes flashed with outrage.

"Mr. Northmore?" She appealed to Hadrian.

For an instant Artemis feared he might remember all the old hostility between them and turn away from her.

But he waved the housekeeper back. "I appreciate your concern, Mrs. Matlock. As you can see, I am in capable hands."

Artemis treasured his modest tribute. It meant far more to her than any dubious compliment on her appearance. Tightening her hold on Hadrian's arm, she steered him toward the stairs.

A few moments later, they reached his bedchamber, one door down from hers. The room was almost as large as the whole main room of the pit cottage in Fellbank.

"Let me help you off with your coat." She spoke in a gentle, matter-of-fact tone. "You will rest more comfortably that way."

Without a word, Hadrian let her remove his well-cut coat. While

she turned to lay it over the back of a nearby chair, he sank onto
the edge of the bed and began to pry off his boots.

Artemis hastened to assist him.

"And your neckcloth." She unwound the lightly starched fillets
of linen from around his neck, leaving his shirt collar hanging
open, snowy white against his sun-bronzed throat. Her fingers
trembled.

Hadrian stretched out on the bed with a drowsy sigh. Artemis
covered him with a light blanket. As she drew it up under his chin,
a bewildering impulse compelled her to raise her hand and smooth
a stray lock of dark hair back from his forehead.

"It feels quite pleasant, being tucked in like a wee lad. I'd almost
forgotten." One corner of his mouth curled into a crooked smile
that was dangerously endearing. "Do I get a kiss to sweeten my
dreams?"

The word *kiss* caused Artemis a spasm of alarm mixed with
a searing flare of desire. He did not mean that kind of kiss, she
chided herself. All he wanted was the sort of innocent peck on the
forehead she gave Lee when she put him to bed at night. Having
caught a heartbreaking glimpse of Hadrian's nightmares, she knew
he needed *something* to sweeten his dreams, if anyone did.

"If you like." The words came out in a tremulous whisper as she
bent over him.

Her lips grazed over his brow, relishing the warm smoothness
of his skin. She inhaled a deep draft of his spicy, smoky scent. Her
well-honed sense of discretion warned her that she should not linger
so close to Hadrian, but her body was slow to respond. After a brief
struggle with herself, she tried to pull away, only to feel the hot
mist of his breath and the velvet caress of his lips upon her throat.
The unexpected thrill of those sensations held her captive there,
hovering over him.

Though she could not break away, she was not entirely paralyzed,
either. His overture called forth an answer from her. Before caution
had a chance to intervene, her lips grazed the outer corner of one

devilish dark brow, then trailed down to the crest of his high cheekbone. As she moved, his kisses swept along the sensitive flesh just below her jaw, moving over her chin and finally upward to meet her approaching lips.

She'd received enough kisses from Hadrian by now so that this one had a deliciously familiar feel. But it held a subtle thrill of novelty, too. She sensed a tender restraint on his part, which appealed not only to her physical desires but also to her wary heart.

Her heart had good reason to be wary, painful memories reminded her—all the more because she had allowed herself to feel something for her husband. It was only a compound of compassion, curiosity and admiration, spiced with reluctant desire. But that could be more than enough to scorch her if she risked playing with fire.

Abruptly she drew back, ignoring the protest of her pleasure-starved senses.

"Rest well." She tried to pretend nothing of consequence had passed between them. But her ragged breath betrayed her.

Hadrian caught her hand. "Don't go."

It was not a command from the husband she'd vowed to obey, nor an order from the master of this fine house. It was an appeal to which she dared not respond, much as part of her longed to.

"I must." It required an enormous effort to extract her fingers from his tantalizing grasp. "I do not want to." She hadn't meant to speak those words, for they revealed divided desires, which he might exploit. Yet she owed him the truth. "I do not want to, but I must."

Chapter Eleven

Artemis hadn't wanted to leave him. Hadrian savored that thought as sleep overcame him. He savored her response to his kiss as well. It had mingled ripe promise with touching innocence in a way that made him want her more than ever. After that kiss and her parting words, he was convinced she wanted him, too.

So what was holding her back? Why had she told him she *must* leave, against her obvious inclination to stay? Was it pride, not wanting to back down from her earlier profession that she had no interest in consummating their marriage? Or had something made her fear a man's attentions?

He knew so little about her and understood even less. Part of him was inclined to resent that, after everything she'd discovered about him and none of it to his advantage. But his foremost reaction was tantalized curiosity. He longed to peel back her proud, proper facade every bit as much as he would like to unbutton one of her dark, dowdy gowns to explore the soft, fragrant woman beneath.

On that most appealing thought, he released his stubborn hold on consciousness and let himself slide into slumber.

He woke with a smile on his face, having dreamed of seducing Artemis, rather than of being trapped underground, as he'd feared he would after their trip to Fellbank.

The chorus of birdsong from outside and angle of light filtering around his window curtains told him it must be morning. The hollow ache in his belly confirmed that he had missed last night's dinner and urged him to go in search of breakfast.

Too hungry to shave or dress, he reminded himself that this was *his* house. If he chose to appear for breakfast with a shadow of whisker stubble and no coat or neckcloth, it was nobody's business but his own. So he pulled on his boots, raked his fingers through his disheveled hair then strode off to the dining room.

He found Artemis there, just finishing her breakfast.

"Good morning." He hurried to the sideboard and poured himself a cup of steaming coffee. "I beg your pardon for leaving you to dine alone last evening. It was not an intentional slight, I assure you."

"I was glad you were able to sleep." Artemis had to raise her voice to carry down the long table. "I wondered whether I ought to have you called for dinner. I hope you don't mind that I erred in favor of letting you rest."

"Of course not." Hadrian picked up his coffee cup and marched down to sit on the chair beside his wife. "There. Now we won't need to shout ourselves hoarse to carry on a conversation."

Artemis pursed her lips, as if fighting to suppress a grin. "I hope you slept well…with sweet dreams."

"Sweet enough." He made no effort to keep from smiling. "Thanks to you."

One of the maidservants appeared just then with a plate of bacon, buttered eggs and kippered herring for his breakfast. She seemed surprised to find the master not occupying his traditional place at the head of the table.

When the girl headed back to the kitchen, bearing Artemis's empty plate, Hadrian paused with a forkful of kippers halfway to his mouth. "I thought nothing could banish the memories that our visit to Fellbank revived. I am grateful to you for providing me with such a pleasant diversion."

His words appeared to throw Artemis into confusion. She

lowered her gaze and caught her lower lip between her teeth. And yet, he could not escape the conviction that some part of her was pleased.

That unaccountable certainty led him to add, "I did not mean to frighten or pressure you with the kiss we shared. But I must admit I am finding it more difficult than I expected to maintain a chaste marriage to such a beautiful lady."

He forked the salty kippers into his mouth, then washed them down with a mouthful of coffee. All the time he kept his attention fixed on Artemis, curious to judge her reaction. What he saw and heard puzzled him exceedingly.

Her brows drew together and her lips tightened into a fine line. "You did nothing to frighten me. Pray think no more of it."

She seemed offended rather than pleased by his mention of her beauty and the effect it had upon him. He would have to proceed carefully or he might put her off him altogether.

"As you wish." He hastened to change the subject to one of which he was certain she would approve. "How is the wee lad settling in? Does this place suit him better than old Bramberley? Has Mrs. Matlock had any luck engaging a nurse for him?"

"I meant to discuss that with you," replied Artemis in a brisk tone Hadrian was certain boded no good. "That was why I followed you to the churchyard the other day…and perhaps why I objected so strongly to your plans for Lee."

"Is there a problem?" Hadrian tucked into his breakfast, though the prospect of another *discussion* about their nephew threatened to spoil his appetite.

Why was it that whenever he and Artemis seemed to be getting on well together, something always came along to tarnish it? Every time that happened, it troubled him more than the time before.

Artemis picked up her spoon and began to stir her coffee. Hadrian could not keep his eyes off her delicate wrist and slender fingers. Yesterday he had noticed how capable and caring her hands could be. Now he appreciated how she accomplished even the most commonplace actions with such natural grace.

"I don't mean to complain, truly. This is a fine house. Everything is so new and well kept. I haven't felt a single draft or smelled anything musty or moldy."

"But…?" Hadrian prompted her, for he sensed it coming.

"*But*…Edenhall is so much bigger than I expected and Lee's nursery is so far from my bedchamber. Since the night he was born, he has never slept farther from me than the next room. I wondered if I might move over to the east wing to be closer to him, in case he needs me in the night?"

Was that all? Hadrian was about to assure her she was welcome to occupy any room she fancied, but he found he did not like the thought of her sleeping farther away from him than the next room. Indeed, he would prefer it if she slept closer still.

"There are empty rooms across the hallway from ours. Why not move the nursery there?"

When Artemis greeted his suggestion with a look of surprise, he added, "In case something serious arises and you need my help with the lad. Not that I doubt you can manage him on your own…"

"Do you mean it?" She rewarded him with a smile as dazzling as an unexpected ray of sunshine on new fallen raindrops. "I was going to ask if I might, but I did not want to risk Lee disturbing your sleep."

Hadrian shrugged, gratified that such a small thing pleased her so. "I doubt there's much chance of that. He and I are both sound sleepers."

"So you are." Her smile muted into something less brilliant, but warm and tender. "More and more I see how much alike the two of you are."

That was high praise indeed, to be likened to the child she doted on. Hadrian was hard-pressed to recall the last time he'd felt so flattered.

"As to the question of a nurse for Lee…" His wife's smile

vanished. "*Must* we hire someone? The reason I agreed to our… arrangement was so I could care for Lee myself. I know you lacked for many things when you were growing up, but being raised by loving parents rather than servants was no deprivation, I can assure you."

It staggered Hadrian to consider there might be anything about his childhood for a fine lady like Artemis to envy. But when he thought back over their trip to Fellbank, he recalled one or two happy memories it had revived in addition to the painful ones.

"You had a bad-tempered nurse when you were a child?" He tried not to betray *too* much interest for fear it might put her on her guard.

"Vile." Her delicate features clenched. "She'd raised my father and made a fine job of it. He thought she could do no wrong. But she never got on with Mother. Looking back, I think she may have been jealous. She was a horrid old martinet. I was never so happy as when Father finally dismissed her."

"What made him do that," asked Hadrian, "if he was so devoted to her?"

Artemis started at his question, as if she suddenly realized she had revealed something private about her family. To Hadrian's surprise, she gave him an answer. "Father overheard her saying something horrible about Mother, just after she died."

From the look on her face, Hadrian knew those were not the first horrible words the embittered old woman had spoken. Though he was desperately curious to know more, he did not ask for fear Artemis might withdraw behind her barriers again.

Though he refrained from saying the wrong thing, he had no idea what the proper thing might be. Unlike Artemis, he had never been any good at offering comfort. Poor Margaret had proven that.

He tried to think what Artemis had said yesterday to make him feel better. But all he could remember was the comforting reassurance of her touch.

Hesitantly, he reached out and patted the back of her hand.

"She said," Artemis continued in a choked murmur, "Mother had failed in her duty to the family by producing only one live heir in ten years of marriage."

"I'd have done worse than sack the old sow," growled Hadrian before he could stop himself.

Artemis gave a moist hiccough of laughter. "I'm sure you would."

When she glanced up at him, her magnificent eyes brimmed with gratitude—and it was the most breathtaking shade of violet Hadrian had ever seen.

"Master Lee seems to like it here, don't you think, Cassie?" Artemis popped a spoonful of porridge into her nephew's mouth while the girl folded his clothes, clean and fragrant from the laundry line.

"Oh, aye, ma'am." The girl beamed down at her small charge. "He's a busy wee one, but good-natured and full of spirits. I shall be sorry to quit looking after him and go back to housework. The sitting room floor doesn't reward ye with a smile like that after ye've scrubbed it."

"What if I were to make your duties as nursemaid permanent?" said Artemis. "Would you like that?"

"Do ye mean it, ma'am?" Cassie dropped the short frock she was folding into the clothesbasket. "I would like it right well and all. Only..."

"Only?"

"I'm sure it's not my place to say, ma'am." Cassie grabbed a small nightgown from the basket and began to fold it with exaggerated care.

"It most certainly is," said Artemis. "You are very good with Lee and I want you to continue helping me care for him. Does this have anything to do with Mrs. Matlock?"

For a moment Cassie did not answer. Artemis maintained an expectant silence, as Hadrian had done the day before. Somehow it had

coaxed her to reveal more than she'd ever intended about her childhood at Bramberley. Afterward she'd felt foolish for making such a
fuss about something that had happened so long ago. Considering
what he had endured as a child, she was afraid he would think the
whole matter a ridiculous trifle.

Cassie shook her head. "Mrs. Matlock works us hard and she
likes everything done up proper, but she's been good to me. It's the
woman Mrs. Matlock wants to put in charge of the nursery. She
has a right sharp tongue and never spared the rod with her own
brood."

"If that is all, you needn't worry." Artemis was so glad she'd discussed the matter with Hadrian. "I told Mr. Northmore I don't want
a nurse hired for Lee because I mean to look after him myself, with
your capable assistance. He told me I am free to do what I like. He
also agreed to let me move the nursery to the west wing so I can
be nearer to Lee at night. Wasn't that good of him?"

"Oh, aye, ma'am." Cassie's furrowed brow belied her words.

"Then what is the trouble?" asked Artemis. "And don't tell me
it is not your place, because I want to know."

"It's just…have you told all this to Mrs. Matlock, ma'am?"

"Indeed I have." Artemis scraped the last bit of porridge from
the bottom of the bowl and offered it to Lee.

"What did she say?"

"Not much of anything." It had been clear the housekeeper was
not pleased with the change of plans, but what did that signify?

"I hope she doesn't go to the Master." Cassie began to stow the
folded clothes in the wardrobe. "She was a friend of his mother's when he were young. That's how she got the position here.
There's been nobody but servants lived at Edenhall until you and
the Master came. I reckon Mrs. Matlock fancied herself mistress
of the place."

Why had Hadrian not mentioned Mrs. Matlock's connection to
his family? Artemis wiped her nephew's face, then handed him a

rusk to chew on. "Give him his milk pudding when he's done that, will you, Cassie? I just remembered something I must see to."

"Aye, ma'am." Cassie seemed to sense what her errand might be. "Good luck." She sounded as if Artemis would need it.

It cost Artemis every ounce of restraint she could muster to walk out of the nursery and down the stairs rather than dash as fast as her legs would carry her.

What might Mrs. Matlock be saying to Hadrian at this very minute? Might she be asserting her experience and seniority in the household to argue against the plans of her young mistress? Might she be imposing on her past connection with his family to get her own way?

Artemis recalled a similar situation from her childhood. How often had Father's old nurse made trouble between her parents? Because the woman was so strong-willed while they were both models of well-bred civility, the servant had often gained the upper hand over her master and mistress. Much as Artemis had revered her parents and lived in constant fear of disappointing them, she'd often wished Mother would raise her gentle voice or Father would put his foot down. When he'd finally exerted his authority, it had been too late.

But how could she expect Hadrian to take her part after she had insulted, misled and defied him? Especially against a woman of his own background and similar determined spirit, who represented his last tie with his dead mother?

Hearing voices from the study, Artemis moved toward it. Finding the door slightly ajar, she paused for a moment to decide what she should do.

Her feelings for Lee urged her to march in and do whatever she must to protect him. But deep-seated doubts held her back, warning her any effort to intervene would be futile. It would not change Hadrian's mind, but only damage the fragile bond they had begun to forge. And it would establish the housekeeper's ascendancy in the household beyond question.

"It is all most irregular, I'm sure." Mrs. Matlock's sharp voice carried out into the hallway. "Turning the entire household on its ear to suit one child who is far too young to know what's good for him. Where will that lead in time, I ask you?"

Put like that, her plans for Lee did sound like a foolish whim. Artemis shrank from hearing Hadrian's reply.

Before he had a chance to say anything, Mrs. Matlock continued. "I have been happy to work for you these three years, Mr. Northmore, preparing Edenhall for your family's return. It did my heart good to think of my old friend's children and grandchildren being masters of this fine place. But I cannot stand by and watch this house thrown in an uproar for the sake of a child like that, while a woman like her flounces about giving orders to decent—"

"Enough!" Hadrian's bellow made Artemis jump back with a muted gasp.

He must have made a conscious effort to lower his voice, for his next words came out much quieter, but no less firm. "I will not stand to hear my wife spoken of in that way, Mrs. Matlock. I am grateful for your loyal service and I will never forget what a good friend you were to my mother. But if you cannot show Lady Artemis the respect she deserves as mistress of this house, there is no place for you at Edenhall."

"You would turn me out for speaking my mind?" Mrs. Matlock sounded as stunned by Hadrian's decree as Artemis was. "I never thought I'd hear Eliza Northmore's son make such a threat."

"It is not a threat." Hadrian sounded regretful but resolved. "I have just told you what's what. Now I leave the decision to you. I shall be returning to Singapore in a few months' time, with no idea how long I'll be gone. I must be certain Lady Artemis can rely upon the people who will serve her in my absence."

"I see," the housekeeper answered in a reproachful tone. "So it is up to me, then, whether I stay or go."

"Entirely. I don't know how you got off on the wrong foot with Lady Artemis and I don't want to know. But if you can put that aside and make a fresh start, I'm certain she will meet you more than halfway. And I will forget we ever had this conversation. If not, I'll make certain you are well compensated for your past service and do everything in my power to find you a position elsewhere."

After a slight hesitation, Mrs. Matlock replied, "In that case, I reckon I must consider my situation."

The sound of footsteps coming toward the door made Artemis flee into the drawing room across the hall. She did not want either Hadrian or the housekeeper to know she'd overheard them.

But even from across the hall, she could hear Hadrian call out, "I only insist upon this because I know my wife is a fine lady and worthy of your respect."

As the housekeeper hurried away in a huff, she muttered something that Artemis did not catch.

Stumbling over to an armchair in the corner of the drawing room, Artemis sank onto it and tried to sort out her confused feelings.

She was so overcome with gratitude to Hadrian for the way he'd stood up for her, she longed to race into his study and hurl herself into his arms. What held her back, besides the strait-waistcoat of her reserved nature, was the fear he would take it as a sign that she wanted to be a real wife to him. Though the temptation grew stronger every day, she still had sense enough to know nothing good could come of that, for either of them.

As a distraction from enticing visions of herself in Hadrian's arms, Artemis turned her thoughts to the problem of their disgruntled housekeeper. Part of her hoped Mrs. Matlock would leave Edenhall so they could find someone more congenial. But congenial people were not always the most competent or dependable.

More than ever, she wanted to make a true home for Hadrian during his stay in England. If Mrs. Matlock left, some of the other servants might follow. Or they might stay and make life difficult for the new housekeeper. Neither would be conducive to domestic harmony.

For Lee's sake, she had managed to mend fences with his formidable uncle. Could she now try to win over the formidable Mrs. Matlock, for Hadrian's sake? She would have to swallow her pride and try to put aside the festering hurts of the past, neither of which had ever been easy for her. But she did want to be a good wife to him…in such ways as she was able.

For the next several days after his unpleasant interview with Mrs. Matlock, Hadrian felt as if he were perched on the rim of a seething volcano—knowing it would soon erupt, but not certain precisely when. Every moment he expected to hear shrieks rising from the housekeeper's parlor or the door of the service entrance slamming.

But Edenhall remained ominously quiet.

On Sunday, as he and Artemis drove to church in the gig they'd taken to Fellbank, he could not bear the suspense any longer.

"Are you getting settled in all right?" He tried to make his enquiry sound like casual chat. "Running the house, I mean—the servants and all?"

"Very well, thank you." Artemis sounded as if she meant it. "I went over the accounts with Mrs. Matlock and suggested a few economies we might make. I don't mind paying for good quality, but a higher price does not always guarantee it."

"I've seen the truth of that in my business," replied Hadrian. "How did Mrs. Matlock take it, you looking over her accounts and making…suggestions?"

"In a fine spirit of cooperation. You made an excellent choice by hiring her, especially considering you were thousands of miles away at the time. I wish we'd had someone of her caliber at Bramberley."

Was she having him on? Hadrian had come to appreciate his wife's subtle, ironic wit, but he could see no sign she was jesting now. "I didn't reckon the two of you had hit it off so well."

"We didn't." Artemis gave a soft, rustling chuckle that was rapidly becoming one of his favorite sounds. "No more than you and I did at first. But you have taught me not to trust first impressions. They are too often based on false expectations."

Certainly his first impression of her had been wide of the mark in many respects—though not all. He'd recognized at once that she was a woman of rare spirit, capable of standing up to him as few men had ever dared. And he had not been blind to her distinctive beauty, though it seemed to him she'd grown even lovelier since then.

"I wondered if Mrs. Matlock might have some misconceptions about me," Artemis continued. "So I sat down with her for a little chat, woman to woman."

Hadrian shook his head. "You're a brave lass."

She gave a cheerful shrug. "I had nothing to lose by trying. It turned out the poor woman did have the wrong idea about me entirely."

"In what way?"

"She hadn't heard the whole story about Julian and Daphne. She thought *I* was Lee's mother and that I had ensnared you somehow. Once I set her straight, she was so sorry for having misjudged me, she's gone out of her way ever since to be helpful."

"Well…bless me!" Hadrian found a spot to park the gig. "That *is* good news."

The volcano beneath him suddenly cooled. From its summit, months of domestic tranquility stretched ahead.

"Fancy me ensnaring a man with my nefarious charms?" Artemis shook her head in disbelief. "Our Mrs. Matlock has a more vivid imagination than one might suppose."

Hadrian came around to help her out of the gig. "I reckon you could ensnare a man if you had a mind to."

Fortunately she was not that kind of woman, and he was a man of strong will. Otherwise, he might be in danger.

When he offered Artemis his arm, she took it with a fond squeeze. "You are not obliged to flatter me. Our wedding vows made no mention of it."

They entered the small, ancient church where Hadrian had worshipped as a child. The last time he'd sat in one of these pews, it had been to bury his father and brothers. Today, he sensed many curious stares fixed upon him. Needing a distraction from those thoughts, he glanced at Artemis and lost himself for a moment in the admiration of her flawless profile.

Leaning toward her, he whispered, "Do you really not know how beautiful you are?"

She flinched. "You are not obliged to *flatter* me, but I would beg you not to mock me, either."

Before he could summon a strenuous denial of that charge, she nodded toward the altar window. It showed St. Oswin being visited by a heavenly messenger. "My sister was beautiful—like a stained-glass angel when the sunlight makes it glow."

The service began just then, so Hadrian only had time to mutter, "There's more than one kind of beauty in this world."

The kind that was in the eye of the beholder, perhaps? Hadrian put that uncomfortable thought from his mind. Anyone with two sound eyes and a groat's worth of sense could see Artemis was a damned attractive woman.

He'd thought his wife's lack of vanity one of her many appealing qualities. Now he began to see another side to it. Had she been an awkward child who never realized she'd blossomed into a lovely woman? Or had that malicious old nurse planted seeds of doubt in her impressionable young mind about her looks?

If she honestly doubted her attractions, then perhaps it was up to him to help her see the truth.

Chapter Twelve

Different kinds of beauty? Artemis mulled over that notion during the next busy week as she supervised work on Lee's new nursery, familiarized herself with the workings of the household and spent as much time as possible with her nephew. Though she still missed Bramberley, there was something wonderfully satisfying about being mistress of a house like Edenhall.

Here she was not constantly fighting a losing battle against decay, restricted by the unrealistic expectations of her uncles. They had required her to perform miracles of economy without sacrificing any of their accustomed comforts. Even when she *had* accomplished the impossible, they'd accepted it as a matter of course, never giving a thought to the effort and ingenuity it might have entailed.

By contrast, Hadrian seemed to regard her as some kind of marvel because she could run a household on a wildly generous allowance with an army of well-trained servants. It was so long since she'd received any kind of appreciation she could not help relishing it. She found it harder to accept his compliments on her looks and signs of his attraction. But even there, the constancy and sincerity of his attentions were beginning to have an effect.

Perhaps he was right about there being more than one kind of beauty. There was the indisputable kind on which everyone could agree. Like Daphne's golden, vivacious charm or the elegant symmetry of a house like Edenhall. But Artemis had also found beauty in the faded grandeur of Bramberley. Perhaps Hadrian recognized a kind of beauty in her, too. He was a remarkable man, so it followed that his tastes might differ from those of ordinary men.

"I smelled paint." Hadrian's voice broke in upon her secret thoughts, making Artemis start as if she'd been caught doing something shameful. "So I came to see how the work is progressing."

When she was absolutely certain her voice would not waver, she replied, "Very well indeed. Everything should be ready for Lee and Cassie to move in the day after next. The seamstress will be coming tomorrow with new window curtains. I ordered them in a nice thick brocade, to keep out drafts next winter, and a golden-brown color to darken the room for Lee's nap time."

Hadrian gave a favorable nod. "Thought of everything, haven't you? He's a fortunate wee lad to have you looking out for him."

"And you." She glanced around the newly enlarged room, freshly painted in a shade of creamy yellow. "I could not have provided him with any of this on my own. He'll soon be near us both and you will be able to look in on him whenever you like. I'm certain he would be happy to see more of you."

It puzzled her why Hadrian had spent so little time with Lee since they'd settled at Edenhall. He had been so good at keeping the child amused on their long carriage trip, Artemis wanted her nephew to continue having that fatherly presence in his life. She was certain it would be good for Hadrian, too—regaining a small part of the family he'd lost.

"When the seamstress brings those curtains—" Hadrian quickly changed the subject "—why don't you order some new clothes for yourself?"

Artemis had meant to speak to him about the new clothes, but there had been more pressing matters to settle first.

"Is there something wrong with the way I look?" Frustration sharpened her tone. "I thought you said I was beautiful."

Hadrian beckoned her into the hallway, out of earshot of the workmen. "I said *you* are beautiful, not your clothes. I hope you are not hanging on to your old gowns just to prove you are not a fortune hunter. I was...wrong to accuse you of such a thing."

Hadrian Northmore admitting to a mistake? Artemis knew what an effort it must have cost him and the gesture touched her. "I suppose I could order a few new gowns for going to church and such. I do not want you ashamed to be seen out with me."

"That would be impossible." The glow of admiration in his eyes was too sincere for her to doubt. "But I would like to see you dressed in a way that shows your looks to their best advantage."

"I must warn you," said Artemis, "I am not partial to the latest styles. They are too stiff and elaborate for my taste. It is that as much as a lack of money that has kept me wearing my old clothes for so long."

"If I am paying the seamstress's bills," replied Hadrian, "then you should have whatever you wish and fashion be damned. If you are too polite to insist on your own way, blame it on the whim of your old-fashioned, imperious husband."

Artemis rallied her composure enough to tease him a little. "You are not old-fashioned."

"But I am imperious?" He pulled a droll face like the ones he'd entertained Lee with on their journey north. "Fair enough. Then I insist you come for a walk in the garden with me. You put me to shame with your industry—supervising the household, overseeing this work on the nursery, spending every spare minute with Lee."

"I like to keep busy and make myself useful," said Artemis. "It is no reproach upon you. After working so hard for so many years, it is only right you should enjoy your leisure now. I would be happy to walk in the garden with you. Can we bring Lee with us? He loves the outdoors so and I believe the fresh air is good for him."

For a moment Hadrian looked reluctant, then he gave a resigned smile. "As you wish. Since all this is for his benefit, I shouldn't balk at anything that might do him good."

It was not only the fresh air and exercise that would be good for

Lee, Artemis reflected as they headed off to collect her nephew. His entire young life had been spent in the care and company of women. His obvious partiality to his uncle showed how much he craved a strong masculine presence in his life. And Artemis was convinced Hadrian needed Lee, too. The child was his last living connection to his lost brothers, one final chance to be part of a family again.

With Lee in tow, they headed out to the garden where everything was green and moist from a recent rain shower.

"I like to keep busy and make myself useful, too," said Hadrian. "Something else we have in common."

"So it is." Artemis ran after Lee, who'd managed to toddle ahead of them.

"All my life I took pride in being a hard worker," Hadrian continued. "Now suddenly I am at loose ends and I have no idea how to fill my time. How do gentlemen of leisure occupy themselves?"

Artemis thought for a moment. "My uncles spend all their time in the library, reading or playing chess. I cannot imagine you being content for long with such sedentary pursuits. Lee, come back here, you little rascal!"

"Don't coddle the lad." Hadrian's voice sounded a trifle sharp. Was it because he objected to her management of the child, or because Lee was diverting her attention from him? "He can't get far on those short legs of his."

"I'm not *coddling* him." She scooped up their nephew, who squirmed and fussed to be let down. "If he gets out of my sight, Lord knows where he might end up. Eating leaves off some poisonous plant. Wandering away to the stables to crawl under the hooves of those big horses, or down to drown in the beck. When he gets older I can teach him to keep out of danger, but for now he is too young…and too stubborn."

"Come here, then, you wee monkey." Hadrian seized Lee from her and lifted the child onto his shoulders. "I used to carry your father around like this when he was not much bigger than you."

Artemis feared Lee might be frightened to find himself up so high, but he seemed to enjoy the lofty view, squealing with delight and slapping his small palms on the crown of his uncle's head. She could not help but laugh at his antics even as Hadrian's mention of his late brother brought her a pang of regret.

To divert him from similar thoughts, she resumed their conversation about gentlemanly pursuits. "One of our neighbors from Sussex, Mr. Crawford, spends much of his time fishing. Of course, Lord Kingsfold keeps very busy managing his estate and your company's London office."

Hadrian's expression darkened at her mention of his partner.

"What's the matter?" Artemis asked. "Have I said something I oughtn't?"

Should he tell her? For a moment, Hadrian pretended he had not heard his wife's question. He'd spent years keeping his past and his troubles to himself. But something about Artemis invited his confidences.

"I was the one who said something I oughtn't…to Ford. I've been thinking if I cannot occupy myself like a gentleman, perhaps I ought to try opening a northern branch of the company. Most British goods for the East Indies trade are produced in the north, so why go to the expense of carting them down to London when they could be shipped cheaper out of Newcastle?"

Just then his nephew crowed, "Ya-ya!"

"I agree with Lee." Artemis chuckled. "It sounds like a fine idea. But what does any of that have to do with Lord Kingsfold? And what did you say to him that you shouldn't?"

"If I mean to embark on new plans for the company, I should consult my partner." Hadrian exhaled a sigh. "But I doubt he will want to talk to me and I cannot blame him. When I first returned to England, I went to see him at Hawkesbourne. It was Ford who broke the news of Julian's death to me. I was so stunned and enraged. I accused him of not doing enough to prevent what happened to my brother. I asked if that was because he considered himself too grand to be of service to people like us. I told him he'd let me down."

From the anxious set of her features, it was clear Artemis recognized the severity of his breach with Ford. Lee seemed inclined to punish Hadrian for his conduct, seizing a fistful of hair with one hand while smacking him hard on the head with the other.

"Lord Kingsfold did try to help," said Artemis. "Uncle Henry would not listen, nor would I. When matters finally came to a head, the Kingsfolds were abroad on their honeymoon. And it all happened so quickly, I doubt he could have prevented what happened, even if he *had* been at Hawkesbourne."

Hadrian gave a regretful nod. "Ford tried to tell me as much, but I refused to listen. I wish I could take back what I said and make things right with him."

"Then do it," said Artemis. "Write to Lord Kingsfold and tell him what you just told me. I'm certain he will understand it was the shock of the news that made you say the things you did. Perhaps he *does* blame himself, as I did, and needs to hear that you do not hold him responsible."

Hadrian hated to disappoint her. "You don't know Ford like I do. The best fellow in the world in many ways, but he is not one to forget a slight or forgive anyone he feels has wronged him. Besides, it is one thing for me to tell you all this, but quite another to tell him when I doubt it will make a difference. You may have noticed I'm not partial to begging. Not even if it is only begging another man's pardon."

"I have noticed." The teasing warmth of her smile assured Hadrian she did not think less of him for it. "It is yet another thing we have in common—our pride. But I wish you would make some overture to Lord Kingsfold. Not only for his sake and yours, but for mine. I owe him and his wife an apology, too. I should have listened to them when they came to Bramberley. But I resented them for meddling in my family's business…and perhaps for being so successful and happy."

Hadrian hesitated. He doubted a letter would suffice. If he apologized to Ford, it must be face-to-face. Even more than he disliked the thought of going cap in hand to his partner, he shrank from the prospect of leaving Artemis and their nephew.

From his perch on Hadrian's shoulders, Lee continued to babble away. Somehow the warm, solid weight of the wee boy eased the sting of Hadrian's self-recrimination and made him think there might be a crumb of hope for his fractured friendship. Even after the hateful things he'd said, Ford had been the one to give him the saving news that Julian had left behind a son.

"I have an idea!" Artemis cried. "What if we invite Lord and Lady Kingsfold to a house party here at Edenhall? We could ask her sisters, too, and her brother-in-law. If they refuse our invitation, we will know they are not disposed to forgive either of us. But if they accept…"

While Hadrian pondered the notion, she continued. "I could write to Lady Kingsfold. You men need not come into it until matters are settled one way or the other."

Hadrian's lips spread in a broad grin. Leave it to Artemis to come up with such a clever solution. "That way, if your invitation is refused, I do not lose face."

"Lose your face?" She stared at him as if he had lost his *wits*.

"Not in the way you think." Hadrian chuckled, his heart suddenly lighter. "It is something the Chinese and Malay people care a great deal about. To lose face means to be dishonored or humiliated. It is something they make every effort to avoid."

"No wonder you got on so well there," Artemis quipped. "Does that mean I may write to Lady Kingsfold?"

Hadrian pretended to consult his nephew. "What do you think of the idea, lad? Would you like pretty little Miss Eleanor to come visit us?"

Lee responded with a peal of blithe laughter.

"That settles it." Hadrian batted a roguish wink at Artemis. "Go ahead and write to Lady Kingsfold. I reckon saving a friendship may be worth losing face a little."

One evening the following week, Artemis made a face at herself in her dressing table mirror. Not because her reflection was ill looking. Indeed, she had never been better pleased with what her glass showed her.

It was more than her new gown of rich plum-colored taffeta trimmed with delicate ivory lace. It was more than the softer way of dressing her hair that her clever little lady's maid had suggested. Her face and figure had both filled out in becoming ways since she'd arrived at Edenhall. Her eyes and skin had taken on a fresh luster.

For all that, it made her feel strangely vulnerable to have put this much effort into looking well...for Hadrian. There could be no hiding from the truth—she had done this all for his benefit, though she was not certain why. Hard as she tried to pacify herself with all sorts of plausible excuses, deep in her heart she knew it was simply a blind compulsion she'd been powerless to explain or resist.

Her knees trembled as she opened her door and forced one foot in front of the other, heading toward the dining room. The trouble with putting this much effort into her appearance was that she could no longer pretend not to care what Hadrian thought of her. She had *tried* not to care. But of late he'd lavished her with such continuous approval that she had come to thrive on the steady, nourishing diet, just as her body flourished on the plentiful, toothsome meals from Edenhall's kitchen.

But what would become of her when Hadrian went away next winter? Would she starve for his appreciation? What if she angered or disappointed him? Would his criticism poison her budding confidence?

Her doubts grew by the second as she descended the staircase and approached the great double doors to the dining room. Sick with apprehension, she contemplated racing back to her bedchamber, pinning her hair in its usual severe knot and changing back into one of her unflattering old gowns.

Then she spied Mrs. Matlock coming out of the music room at the end of the main gallery. Though the two women had forged a respectful partnership, Artemis still had too much pride to let the housekeeper catch her in a cowardly retreat. Reminding herself that her ancestors had led armies and attended kings at their coronations, she marched into the dining room with her head high, though her insides quaked.

She found Hadrian standing by the sideboard consulting his watch. Was he annoyed that she had taken so long to dress for dinner?

Before she could stammer an apology, he spoke in a hoarse murmur. "Whatever I paid for that gown, pet, it was a proper bargain."

"You like it?" Lest he think she had squandered his money, she explained, "The seamstress got a very good price on the taffeta because of the color."

"What's wrong with the color?" Hadrian thrust his watch into his pocket.

"Most women prefer lighter shades for the summer, but they make me look sallow. Besides, the way time is flying, autumn will be upon us before we know it." That thought brought her a pang of regret.

"You made a fine choice." Hadrian studied her with a slow shake of his head, as if he could not quite believe the transformation. "It suits you very well indeed."

"I am glad you approve." Some baffling impulse made her sink into a deep, graceful curtsy. "I want to be a credit to you."

"You're all of that." Hadrian caught her hand and lifted it to his lips.

The gesture reminded Artemis of the first time he'd kissed her hand, at the White Lion Inn, before they'd struck their marriage bargain. Such a blaze of heat had surged through her when she felt the subtle pressure of his lips through her glove, she'd been afraid her hand would burst into flames!

Now he turned her hand to nestle her palm against his cheek, while his lips hovered over her wrist. Could he feel her fevered pulse racing through her veins?

As she stood there, frozen in the grip of powerful sensations, one of the serving maids entered the dining room, bearing a tray.

"Pardon my intrusion!" she cried the moment she spotted her master and mistress standing so close together. "Mrs. Matlock told us the mistress had come down and said you'd be wanting dinner sharpish. I'll go back to the kitchen and wait for you to ring."

"No need to rush away, Sarah," Hadrian called out in a hearty tone. "I was just admiring my wife's new gown. Don't you think it becomes her?"

Lowering her hand from his face, he led Artemis forward for the girl's inspection.

"Aye, sir." With a sigh of relief, Sarah carried her serving tray to the sideboard. "She looks a right picture."

Artemis wavered between embarrassment and pleasure at the girl's simple, honest praise.

"I suspect there is a conspiracy afoot in this house to turn my head," she replied as Hadrian escorted her to the table, her hand still clasped in his. "Or perhaps I looked so ill before that any improvement appears wondrous by comparison."

"Oh, no, ma'am!" cried Sarah. "I'm sure I meant no such thing."

"Of course you didn't," Hadrian reassured her as he held the chair for Artemis. "Nor did I. My wife is far too modest."

He sat down beside her, as had become his custom at mealtimes. "Now lay on our dinner, Sarah. Admiring such a pretty picture has whetted my appetite."

He cast a significant glance at Artemis as he spoke those words. For a fleeting instant, one corner of his mouth arched in a sly grin. Clearly the appetite to which he alluded could not be satisfied by braised pigeon breast or roast loin of veal. Only the sweets of her breasts and loins would suffice.

Had her efforts to look more presentable encouraged him to think of her in that way? And if they had, did she regret it...would she return to the safety of her former unflattering appearance? Artemis was not certain she *could,* any more than a hatchling chick could take refuge back inside its shattered shell.

As Sarah placed steaming bowls of lobster bisque before them, Artemis returned her husband's highly charged gaze. "I suspect that is a polite way of saying you are starved because I kept you waiting so long to dine. Now, tell me what you have found to occupy your time while we await Lady Kingsfold's reply to my invitation. I saw you ride out this morning."

Was it her imagination, or did his eyes shift furtively in the instant before he answered? "I had a commission to perform for my other partner, Simon Grimshaw. And I wanted to consult my solicitor about making Lee my heir and arranging financial provisions for you both."

Artemis was certain she detected a false note in his voice, as if he were trying to conceal something. But that was ridiculous. What could Hadrian possibly have to hide from her?

Chiding herself for her groundless suspicions, Artemis forced them from her mind. "I recall you mentioned your other partner. He must have his hands full back in Singapore managing the business alone."

"I reckon he does," replied Hadrian. "But it'll be the making of him. Simon's a capable fellow, but doesn't like to take a risk. He needs to understand there are times in business when being too cautious can prove the greatest risk of all."

Did that only apply to business? Artemis wondered. Was she clinging too cautiously to her virginity, needlessly afraid of rejection from a man who had shown her more respect and approval than she'd ever known? If she dared to risk her pride and her innocence, what might she gain by it? The possibilities took her breath away.

"A penny for your thoughts," Hadrian offered. "Judging by your secretive smile, I reckon they're worth more, but I've always prided myself on driving a hard bargain."

His gentle jest drove the smile from her lips. "My thoughts are no great secret and this gown is ample payment for them. I was thinking, once you finish your commission for Mr. Grimshaw, you might investigate what we can do to help some of the children who work in the local mines."

"By George, that is the best bargain I've driven in years!" Hadrian's gray eyes took on a soft, silvery luster.

Artemis suffered a qualm of guilt for palming off an invention in place of her true thoughts. In an effort to ease her conscience, she kept up an earnest dialogue on the subject with Hadrian throughout the rest of their meal.

After dinner they retired to the music room where she entertained him with several selections on the pianoforte. Every moment, she was acutely conscious of his gaze fixed upon her. By the time their accustomed hour for bed arrived, she was so keyed up she feared she would tremble at his slightest touch.

Since the afternoon she'd brought him home to Fellbank and tucked him in, she had managed to avoid retiring to her bedchamber at the same time Hadrian went to his. Sometimes she delayed for a word with Mrs. Matlock about some trivial household matter. Or she visited the nursery to check on Lee. Hadrian had conspired in her efforts, frequently retreating to his study for a glass of port while she went off to bed.

Tonight, neither of them mentioned his study, the nursery or the housekeeper.

As they climbed the stairs and walked down the west gallery to their bedchambers, Artemis strove to maintain her tenuous composure, though her heart raced as if she were walking toward the edge of a high, sheer cliff. If she succumbed to a mad impulse to jump, there could be no turning back.

"Thank you for a very pleasant evening," said Hadrian as they paused in front of her door. "I look forward to seeing your other gowns, though I cannot imagine any way you might look better unless…"

"Unless…what?" Artemis could not resist putting him on the spot. It made her feel a trifle less vulnerable.

For a moment, Hadrian looked as if he might decline to answer. Then he leaned toward her and whispered, "Unless you were not wearing a stitch of clothes at all. But since it wouldn't be proper for you to strut about naked, I like seeing you dressed in a way that makes you look your best."

Whatever gave him the idea that she might be the least bit attractive without these well-cut clothes? Even her old unfashionable gowns would be an improvement, hiding the worst of her deficiencies. The thought of Hadrian's disappointment was enough to make her want to bolt through the door and lock it behind her.

Then, as he drew back, Hadrian's cheek brushed against hers. Was it by accident, or did he intend to remind her how much pleasure his touch could bring her, if she let it? If that was his aim, he succeeded. For a moment, her preoccupation with her flaws faded and all Artemis could think about was *him*.

With a whole large house to rattle around in, she had not expected to feel the constant tug of awareness that had plagued her when she'd shared a cramped post chaise box with Hadrian for days on end. But she'd been wrong.

Every step she took toward knowing him better, every bit of consideration he showed her, every admiring word or glance he directed toward her, fueled the desire to which she had sworn she would not surrender. As she sought to restore something of the home and family he'd lost, Hadrian had become a constant stimulating presence in her thoughts. That included her dreams, where she had no control over his actions…or hers.

Raising her hand to his lips, he dusted kisses over her fingertips. "Are you not the least bit curious? Tempted? I promised it would be your choice whether or not you come to my bed. I only want to make certain you know you would be welcome. But perhaps you don't find *me* attractive? Or you think I am not good enough for you?" A shadow of uncertainty flickered across his features.

Those suggestions were so preposterous they almost made Artemis laugh. How could such an attractive, confident man of the world doubt the magnetic appeal he exerted upon her? Then she remembered the other Hadrian Northmore she had glimpsed— the boy who'd lived and worked under such harsh conditions, then suffered a greater loss than any young heart should bear.

Before he could release her hand, she reached out to cup his cheek. "*That* is not the difficulty, I assure you."

He searched her eyes. "What *is* the difficulty, then?"

Artemis sucked in a deep breath. The edge of the cliff seemed to crumble beneath her feet. "I fear I will only disappoint you."

Hadrian shook his head. "That is not possible."

She knew he believed it as much as she wanted to. "You cannot be certain."

"But you can?"

She gave a forlorn nod and lowered her hand from his face.

"How?" he demanded in an urgent whisper. "Why?"

Bent on escaping his questions, she reached for the knob of her bedroom door.

Then, as she pushed the door open, a flicker of wistful longing in the depths of his eyes compelled her to say, "Come in and I will tell you."

Chapter Thirteen

The sudden, unexpected invitation into his wife's bedchamber staggered Hadrian.

Did Artemis realize the step she was taking? If he could persuade her of his desire and prevail upon her to put aside her unaccountable self-doubts, there would be nothing to stop them consummating their marriage this very night. His body roused in anticipation.

Before Artemis had a chance to change her mind, he strode through her door.

The room was softly lit by a single flickering candle in one of the wall sconces. A faint aroma of lavender hung in the air.

"Pray take a seat." Artemis nodded toward the chair in front of her dressing table.

She closed the door and crossed to the bed, where she perched on the foot of the mattress.

"Go on, then," he prompted her, eager to refute whatever she might say. "Tell me what makes you so certain you would disappoint me. Everything I have learned about you leads me to believe quite the opposite. Time has proven my early prejudices against you wrong, while I have discovered new qualities to admire in you every day."

"That is kind of you to say." Artemis kept her gaze fixed on the rug at the foot of her bed, tracing the pattern with the toe of her slipper. "For such a dynamic, successful man, you have a great kindness about you. But you must not blame yourself for thinking ill of me at first. I gave you ample cause for it. Since then I have tried to atone for my past conduct."

"I hope you do not think you are obliged to atone for it in my bed!" The words burst out of Hadrian. "Or yours."

"Of course not!" she cried with a flash of the spirit that had first drawn him to her. "I want you far too much for my peace of mind. But I am certain if you come to know me too intimately, you will soon discover all my shortcomings as a wife."

"What shortcomings?"

"What shortcomings?" Artemis gave a bitter laugh. "My green-goose ignorance for a start. My advanced age, pasty face, maypole figure—take your pick."

"Is that what you think of yourself?" He wanted to wrap her in his arms and protect her from the harsh judgments of her self-doubt. "I thought it endearing that you were not vain and self-centered like so many beautiful women. But this? Why can you not see how desirable you are?"

"I treasure your opinion," she replied in a husky murmur. "When I am with you I begin to feel as if I truly am the way you see me. But I fear where my *attractions* are concerned, your view runs contrary to that of most men."

"Does it?" Hadrian bridled. "Then that is their loss, the damned fools! I am arrogant enough to reckon myself more discerning than *most* men. It is my judgment you may rely on. What do you say to that?"

She glanced up then, transfixing him with the radiance of her gaze. "You are the most uncommon man I have ever met, Hadrian Northmore. There is nothing arrogant about owning it. I envy your confidence and your certainty. I wish I could have your eyes for my looking glass."

Her words sent him flying out of the chair to kneel at her feet and lift his gaze to her. "You are welcome to use them for that purpose as often as you wish. Then I will have the pleasure of staring at you without having to look away in case you catch me at it."

Sweet, melodious laughter bubbled up from some secret spring deep inside her. "You have done that, too?"

"I couldn't help myself." A thought sparked by their earlier exchange suddenly came clearer to him. "Was there one particular man who had a harsh opinion of you?"

Her features froze into a tight, fragile mask. "What makes you ask?"

"You once told me you'd been deceived by someone you thought you knew. It was him, wasn't it? He made a fuss over you, then turned and showed his true colors?"

Artemis gave a shamefaced nod, as if she was somehow at fault for whatever had happened. "I was young and foolish enough to fancy myself in love. But my uncles disapproved of the match, so I refused his offer of marriage. I wanted to run away with him, but the family would have disowned me. I would never have been allowed to see Daphne again. She was so young. She needed me."

The poor lass, bound by duty, all the while knowing she might be forfeiting her only chance for love and a family of her own. Hadrian knew all about hard choices. He admired people who were willing to make them and do the right thing, no matter how difficult.

As for the man who'd won Artemis's heart only to lose her, he was torn between scathing contempt and irrational envy. "This suitor took your rejection badly, did he?"

"Very badly, though not because I broke his heart. Charles Nugent only wanted me for the distinction of having a titled wife. When I refused him as gently as I could, he took the opportunity to tell me his true opinion of my *charms*."

As she related, in halting words, the humiliating abuse heaped upon her by a man she'd trusted and cared for, Hadrian smoldered with indignant rage. Bad enough for the scoundrel to say such things if they'd been true. But to plant such malicious false doubts in a sensitive nature like hers, for no better reason than because she'd been loyal to her family, was downright wicked! If he could have got his hands on Nugent just then, he would have thrashed the bounder within an inch of his miserable life!

"Don't you see?" he ventured when her voice trailed off. "You cannot go by the judgment of such a conniving rascal. Not even if those were his true feelings, which I doubt. You thwarted his scheme. So he revenged himself in the only way he knew how. I hope you give my opinion more credence than his."

Artemis did not hesitate. "Of course! You are ten times the man Charles Nugent will ever be. But I fear you are partial in your judgment of me."

"Perhaps I am…now. But you must recall when we first met. Then, I detested you. I thought you were haughty and superior. I blamed you for what had happened to my brother. In spite of all that, I was drawn to you, against my will." He had long been ready to surrender to his physical attraction for Artemis. But there were other feelings he needed to guard against, for both their sakes.

The best way for him to resist might be to offer her some final words of reassurance, bid Artemis a chaste good-night and make his escape. When she had first invited him inside, he'd thought of her bedchamber as a glittering treasure box, ripe for plunder. Suddenly, he wondered if it might be a tempting trap.

Not that Artemis intended it to be. She was not to blame for his unruly desire or his insidious doubts. If he walked away from her now, when it was clear she wanted to let him stay, he would only confirm every miserable falsehood Charles Nugent had made her believe about herself. Not to mention that wretched old nurse and the well-meaning relatives who'd spent a lifetime telling her how little she resembled her beautiful sister.

Hadrian could not let that happen, no matter how it might complicate his life.

What had possessed her to invite Hadrian into her bedchamber so late at night? Artemis chided herself as she stared down at him, kneeling on her carpet with outrage and pity written plain on his bold, compelling features. Had she truly wanted to explain her reluctance to consummate their marriage? Or had she secretly hoped Hadrian would take that decision out of her hands?

Though she was fully clothed, every word she'd spoken about Charles Nugent seemed to strip away one more covering from her heart. If she kept on, she would soon leave it naked and vulnerable.

Her countenance must have betrayed her misgivings, for Hadrian rose from the floor and held his arms open to her. "Are you going to let a blackguard like Nugent continue to stand in the way of our pleasure? Or are you going to make us both pay the price for *his* sins? If you come to me now, I swear I will put all my skill and experience as a lover at your service. I will initiate you as gently and pleasurably as any maiden ever was."

His words set her desperate eagerness at war with her agonizing reluctance, wrenching her back and forth until she feared they would tear her apart. But when those two opposing forces were balanced in unbearable tension, Artemis suddenly felt herself no longer bound by either, but free to make a choice. In that moment she knew that although she could never banish all her doubts, she would regret it more if she did not act upon her feelings for Hadrian. Even if she was not entirely certain what all those feelings were.

Slowly she arose from the bed—not like the chaste huntress for whom she'd been named, but as the love goddess, Aphrodite, had emerged newborn from the sea foam. Slipping into Hadrian's waiting arms, she raised the chalice of her lips for him to fill with the rich, potent wine of his kisses.

For weeks, she had watched his lips whenever he spoke, remembering how they'd felt against her skin and the sensations they had kindled. How often she'd longed to feel them on hers again, not struggling to resist their attraction, but surrendering to it.

Hadrian obliged her with the delectable play of his lips and tongue until she was light-headed, giddy and almost satisfied. Surely a man could not kiss a woman that way unless she roused his desire to a fever pitch.

His fingers plunged into her hair, tugging out the pins that bound it up. Once he'd set it free to cascade over her shoulders, he lavished it with admiring caresses.

"I have wanted to do that almost from the moment I first set eyes on you," he whispered, releasing her lips to strew kisses down her cheek and neck. "A more glorious head of hair I've never seen on a woman. Puts silk clean to shame, it does. And the smell of it..." he inhaled deeply "...like a country garden after the rain."

She hid her face against his shoulder, intoxicating herself on breath after deep breath of *his* scent. "I rinse it with lavender water, the way my mother did. It reminds me of her."

"After this..." his deep velvety murmur made her knees grow even weaker than his kisses already had rendered them "...it will remind me of *you*."

He sounded so sincere that a lost, searching part of Artemis could not help but believe him. "Keep talking like that and you will make me insufferably vain."

"I doubt it." He nudged her chin with his shoulder, making Artemis lift her face to meet his admiring gaze. "You don't know how beautiful you are by half. But if you are still uncertain after I'm done with you tonight, I will have failed in my aim altogether."

With that, he scooped her into his arms and carried her to the bed. "You must know by now, I hate to fail. Especially at something so important."

He lowered her onto the bed with great care, as if she were a delicate treasure he wished to admire at his leisure. But the very next instant, he turned away from her and perched on the edge of the bed. Her bewildered body throbbed with an infernal compound of itch and ache.

One after the other, Hadrian's boots hit the floor with a soft, provocative thud. Then he slipped off his coat and tossed it onto the chair in front of her dressing table. His waistcoat swiftly followed. Did he mean to disrobe completely, in front of her?

What if he did? Curiosity sought to soothe her ruffled modesty. For all her innocence, she had seen a number of naked male figures in classical statues and paintings. There should be nothing about Hadrian's bare body to shock her. While he untied his neck linen, she wavered between averting her gaze and continuing to watch him undress. But when he pulled off his shirt, Artemis could not have looked away if she'd tried.

His torso was not as tanned as his face, but enough to give him the look of a Greek god, one carved out of rich, warm mahogany rather than cold, white marble. For a moment, she forgot all her earlier misgivings, lost in her admiration of the ideal proportion and contours of his physique: the spare masculine grace of his bare back, tapering from a magnificent pair of shoulders to a firm, trim waist; the hard, lean muscle rippling down his chest toward his taut belly, lightly shaded with fine dark hair; the powerful swell and sweep of his arms ending in large, strong hands, hands that nimbly unbuttoned his breeches and slid them down over lithe, smooth thighs.

With an abrupt, sickening jolt, all Artemis's doubts engulfed her once more. Much as Hadrian's glorious masculinity stirred her admiration and desire, it also intimidated her. What did she have to offer him in return?

The cruel words Charles Nugent had hurled at her ten years ago burst from the locked cupboard of her memory to taunt her. *The only way I could stand being wed to such a pallid, scrawny milk-and-water miss would be to engage a plump, pretty mistress at the earliest opportunity.*

All that had saved her pride was her relief at escaping the torment of marriage to such a scoundrel. She had never submitted to his mortifying caresses or let him deep enough into her heart to break it.

As Hadrian turned back toward her, Artemis caught sight of

something her stolen glances at antique statues had not prepared her for—the rampant shaft of arrogant manhood, rising from his loins. A gasp of awe and a shriek of alarm collided in her throat, threatening to strangle her! Forcing a deep draft of air into her lungs, she pulled herself upright and swung her legs over the opposite side of the bed.

An instant later Hadrian's arms twined around her. "You're not running away on me, are you? I didn't mean to frighten you, just now. But I cannot hide the effect you have upon me."

She was responsible for *that?* Preposterous as the notion seemed, it sent a heady surge of power through Artemis.

"I am not frightened." Dearing pride refused to let her admit otherwise. Besides, it was not her husband's size and power that intimidated her as much as the renewed consciousness of her own shortcomings. "I thought since you were undressing, I should, too."

"Taking your own clothes off?" Hadrian raised his hands to her hair and ran the back of one down her neck. "Where's the sport in that?"

The next instant he swept her hair to one side, draping it over her shoulder. "But since you're sitting up, I will take advantage of this opportunity to unfasten your gown."

His fingertips brushed against her back as he slid the mother-of-pearl buttons free from their ribbon loops. Then he eased the short sleeves off her shoulders and peeled down her bodice, exposing her chemise and short stays. A moment later he had her gown off and folded neatly over the back of the chair on which his garments lolled with such careless abandon.

Her slippers were next, and as he reached up under her chemise, the skimming caress of his deft, powerful hands sent shafts of pleasure racing up her legs to converge at the point where they met. At that instant, Artemis discovered a perfect balm for the itchy ache that had beset her earlier. It was her husband's touch.

Yet even as his touch soothed one yearning, it provoked another—a deep, desperate hunger for which even her self-conscious wariness was no match.

His upward journey halted at the top of her stockings. When his fingertips fluttered against her thighs as he untied the ribbons that secured her stockings, a soft whimper of need escaped her clenched lips.

"There, you see?" Hadrian murmured in a tone of warm satisfaction. "I knew you'd enjoy this."

Artemis tried to answer, but her mouth craved his kiss with such savage intensity, she could not coax out a single word. When Hadrian tugged the hem of her chemise upward to expose her naked loins, her head thrashed from side to side. She prayed he would not think she wanted him to stop.

"You needn't deny it." He nudged her legs apart and knelt between them, looming over her. "Your body will give the truth away."

He slid a finger into the crease between her legs, the center of her smoldering need. She gasped and writhed as it glided on the slick moisture.

Leaning closer, until his cheek rested against hers and the swift, hot breath from his nostrils tickled her ear, he whispered, "We both show the signs of wanting. Quite a wonder how a man and woman are made for each other, isn't it?"

A sound of inarticulate need escaped her lips. It was no use trying to deny the fierce passion he had wakened in her body. The proof was there, wet on his fingers, ready to ease the entry of his shaft deep inside her.

Until that moment, Hadrian had been so gentle and controlled even as he drove her mad with desire. But now a tremor rippled through his magnificent body. His voice grew harsh and husky as he whispered, "I wish I did not want you so badly. But I cannot help myself."

His lips moved down her cheek in search of her mouth. He found it open, her lips moving as if gasping for air. But it was not air she craved, only him. The insistent pressure of his lips upon hers and the ravenous thrust of his tongue filled some long-denied need in her.

Until that moment, she had kept her arms resting upon the bed lest they reveal her awkward inexperience. Hadrian's kiss shattered the bonds that restrained them. One hand rose to rake through his hair, ready to hold him if he tried to break from their kiss. The other found his smooth, taut torso, stroking it with greedy relish. Her mouth moved, too, her tongue caressing his. Her hips thrust against the sinful delight of his finger's velvet caress, even as she yearned for something more substantial.

"I wanted to…go slow." He panted the words into her mouth and she drank them like fiery brandy. "Make the first time…easy for you. But you are just too… I cannot hold back."

A voice that was not hers gasped, "Don't!"

Was she urging him on or protesting the abrupt, frustrating withdrawal of his finger at the peak of her need? Artemis was too deep in the grip of pure sensation to be certain. She only knew that her command or entreaty spurred Hadrian to renew their kiss with even more reckless passion.

In place of his finger, the searing, silken crown of his shaft rubbed against her, seeking entry. Spreading her legs wider and tilting her hips, she exposed the sensitive core of her yearning to the sleek friction of his thrust. A sharp burst of ecstasy merged with the hot stab of pain as he dived into her. With each reckless thrust of his hips, wave after shuddering wave of pleasure broke over her, drowning her, filling her.

Then his body wrenched and writhed in the grip of forces too powerful for him to control. Forces *she* had unleashed.

Afterward, as lazy ripples of delight pulsed through her body, Artemis looked forward to the next time Hadrian bedded her… and the next. Though she wondered how it could possibly be more satisfying, she nursed a sweet, secret confidence that it would only get better.

* * *

A sunrise concert of chaffinches, blackbirds and song thrushes woke Hadrian the next morning. For a disoriented instant he wondered why his heart responded with an answering trill of high spirits.

Then Artemis stirred in her sleep beside him, rousing lush memories of the previous night. Slumber enhanced her beauty, relaxing the guarded set of her features to something infinitely more approachable. It brought the pearly glow of dawn to her alabaster skin. While feasting his eyes on her delicate beauty, Hadrian recalled their midnight tryst with a mixture of delicious exultation and bitter shame.

He had not meant to take her with such wanton vigor. He'd promised to proceed with deliberate restraint, the way a gentleman should initiate such a rare lady. He hadn't wanted to alarm or repel her with his attentions, but to coax her to such a keen pitch of desire that pleasure would ease the sting of her first time. He'd also been thinking of himself, when he'd sought to maintain control. Like a rider on the back of a wild stallion, he'd been determined to master his passion. Otherwise it might run away with him...perhaps into dangerous territory.

A lock of his wife's rich dark hair lay upon the pillow beside him. Reaching up carefully so as not to disturb her, Hadrian twined the silken curl around his finger. Then he brushed it over his cheek and under his nose, where he caught a tantalizing whiff of lavender.

He had never expected Artemis to thaw so quickly to his touch... then take fire. For all he'd boasted of his experience, he'd never had an encounter so shattering in its intensity. Before last night, he'd always chosen the right instant to surrender control. But when his reluctant virgin bride had suddenly turned earthy temptress, she'd shattered his noble intentions and his iron self-control, making him passion's willing slave.

Much as Hadrian savored the triumph of rousing her to such pow-

erful heights and the tumultuous ecstasy they'd shared, he feared
he had made a grave mistake in consummating their marriage.

He considered stealing away before Artemis woke and he had
to face her reaction to his rough lust. But his father had taught him
to face the consequences of his actions. He could not turn his back
on that lesson now.

Her eyelids fluttered open, just then. For a breathtaking instant,
Hadrian gazed into an intricate, intriguing labyrinth hidden in their
amethyst depths. If he entered, might he penetrate all the way to
her secret heart? Or would he wander forever in a perilous twilight,
seeking in vain? Perhaps it would be best for both of them if she
despised him for the way he'd handled her last night.

"Good morning." His voice did not come out in its usual deep
pitch, but cracked like a stripling youth's. In his haste to release
the lock of her hair wound around his finger, he tugged too hard,
making her wince.

"Forgive me!" The words were out before he could contain
them.

But words alone were not enough. He pressed a kiss to Artemis's
head, where he'd pulled her hair. "Not only for that, but for last
night."

"Last night?" She brushed a stray curl off her forehead. "What
have you to be sorry for about last night?"

Hadrian hesitated. It galled him to admit he'd erred, even to
Artemis. "I did not keep my promise to initiate you as gently as
any maid ever was."

"Oh, *that*." She made it sound like a trifle. "I am quite content
that you kept the better half of your promise, to initiate me as pleasurably as any maid ever was."

Enough pleasure to outweigh the hurt? That reassurance brought
Hadrian a dizzying sense of relief. But it did not change his mind
about the danger of continuing what he'd so recklessly started last
night.

"Besides," Artemis added, "I have heard it gets easier after the first time."

She cast him a look that was far too inviting.

"So it does." He edged away from her, worried that the temptation of her nearness and willingness might overpower his honorable intentions. "But I reckon it would be better…if we…not…"

He struggled to find the proper words to free himself from the tangled maze into which he'd so eagerly stumbled.

"I understand. Once with me was enough for you." Artemis sat up abruptly and slid toward her side of the bed, leaving a rusty stain of dried blood on the sheets as proof that he'd taken her virginity. "I tried to tell you I would be a disappointment. Perhaps this time you should have heeded a naysayer."

After last night, could those old, poisonous doubts about herself still linger? Hadrian could not let her suffer for *his* mistake.

"Nay, lass!" He scrambled after Artemis, capturing her in his embrace before she could flee. "Disappointed is the last thing I was. I am not sure your parents named you after the proper goddess. Last night, I could have sworn I had Venus herself in my arms."

She looked every inch the love goddess this morning, with her wild, dusky curls unbound. Her loose white chemise and short stays even resembled a woman's garment of ancient times.

She did not melt into his arms as he'd hoped, but remained tense and wary, her face hidden against his shoulder. "Venus—isn't that what they call those women who hire themselves to men? I knew I behaved too wantonly! I made you doubt my innocence. But I swear, it was *because* of my inexperience. If you will only have patience and teach me how I should behave, I will do my best to please you."

Raising her face, she fixed him with a gaze that pleaded for another chance. How could he find the will to resist when his body ached to surrender?

Perhaps he could let Artemis have her way long enough to quell any lingering doubts she might have about her ample attractions. "I promise you, there was nothing wrong with your behavior. It was what any proper man would want from a beautiful woman in his bed. And better than most would dare hope."

"Then why did you not want to...try again?" Artemis sounded torn between hope and uncertainty.

She was too clever a woman to be persuaded by anything but the truth...at least part of it. "You made me lose control of myself last night. No woman has ever done that to me before."

"And you did not like it?"

"Quite the contrary! Have you ever done something that scared you half to death, yet gave you such a thrill you'd never felt more alive?"

After a moment's thought, she replied with a furtive nod. "One winter when I was young, Papa unearthed an old sleigh from the stables and took me for a drive over the high weald. I'd never gone so fast. I squealed and screamed the whole time, certain we would crash and I'd be dashed to pieces. But when we were safely back in the courtyard, I begged Papa to take me again."

She glowed with the delight of that long-slumbering memory. "And I made you feel that way?"

Even as he nodded, Hadrian sensed only one thing would truly convince her.

Running the tip of his forefinger up her arm toward her shoulder, he flashed a crooked grin. "Would you like to try again? Not quite all the way this time, though. I reckon I can bring you pleasure while still giving your sore parts a rest."

"Indeed?" She gave his bare chest an admiring caress. "And how do you propose to accomplish that?"

"Like this, for a start." He inclined his head to graze his cheek over the linen chemise that covered her bosom. His grin widened when she let out a soft gasp and her nipples strained against the fine cloth, demanding his attention.

"That is a fine start." Artemis gave a voluptuous sigh as she sank back onto the pillows. "I am curious to see what else you will do."

She might not believe he owed her any recompense for his earlier loss of control, but Hadrian believed otherwise. He owed her another debt for enticing her into bed, despite her reluctance. He could not cast her aside simply because he was afraid of getting in too deep.

To prevent himself from dwelling on all the mistakes he'd made with Artemis, he cupped her chin and gently tilted her face until it was at the perfect angle for kissing. Then he kissed her, again and again, longer and deeper, until he could no longer think of anything else.

Chapter Fourteen

"Hadrian!" Artemis ran into her husband's study, as she never would have dared into her uncles' library, her voice louder than had ever been permissible at Bramberley. "Mrs. Matlock just brought me the post."

Evidently the housekeeper had delivered his correspondence, too. The moment Artemis appeared, he thrust three letters into the top drawer of his writing table and pushed it shut.

"They're coming!" She fluttered her letter under his nose. "Lord and Lady Kingsfold and all her family. Her ladyship wrote the most gracious reply, accepting our invitation. I never expected to hear from her so soon."

For a moment he looked preoccupied, as if his mind were elsewhere. Then a silvery twinkle lit his gray eyes. "Splendid!"

He rose from the writing table, scooped her into his arms and twirled her around. "Well done, pet!"

It lasted only a few seconds, but to Artemis it seemed longer, though not half as long as she would have liked. She felt as if she were flying—weightless and carefree. But all too soon her feet hit the floor again, and her soaring spirits with them.

It had been over a week since Hadrian had truly made her his wife. But since then, though he'd been kind and attentive, he had not visited her bedchamber again. Warmly as she would have welcomed him, Artemis could not bring herself to beg for his company. Instead, she savored this fleeting moment in his arms, hoping it might lead to something more.

They were both breathing fast when they came to a stop. Hadrian still clasped Artemis around the waist, while she clung to his shoulders. He leaned closer, until she was lost in the impenetrable gray mist of his eyes. Her lips parted. She trembled in anticipation of his kiss.

Instead he let her go and stepped back so abruptly that she almost pitched to the floor.

"We have preparations to make." Hadrian spoke in a tone of false heartiness. "When did you invite our guests to come?"

Artemis struggled to master her voice and her sickening disappointment. "I suggested several possible dates and let Lady Kingsfold choose. She writes that they can come three weeks from now and stay for at least a fortnight."

"Perfect." Hadrian backed toward his writing table. "That will give us time to order provisions, and get the old nursery converted into proper guest quarters. I was thinking, perhaps we could invite Ford's old friend, Blade Maxwell, too. Blade was in Singapore during the very early days and used to stop by our *godown* most evenings for a drink. I'd like to see him again. He was always good company."

That gave Artemis an idea. "Is Mr. Maxwell a single gentleman? We could use one. Otherwise poor Susannah Penrose may feel like a complete gooseberry with three married couples."

"I hadn't thought of that." Hadrian shook his head. "I'm afraid Blade will not suit your purpose. I heard he got married upon returning to England. He is now the Earl of Launceton."

"Oh." A brief pang of disappointment gave birth to a new possibility. "Then would you mind if *I* invite someone? If I can persuade him to come, I believe he would be an ideal addition to our house party."

"By all means," said Hadrian. "Who are you thinking of?"

"Jasper, Viscount Ashbury. I mentioned him to you once. He is a cousin of mine on my mother's side."

Hadrian chuckled. "Everyone of consequence in this country is a cousin of yours. Tell me, what makes Viscount Ashbury such an ideal guest?"

"Cousin Jasper is a Member of Parliament and a devoted abolitionist. He is something of a black sheep in our family on account of his radical Whig politics. I believe he would be as outraged as I was to hear how the mining industry employs young children. If we were to gain his support, Jasper might begin the work you intended Julian to undertake in Parliament."

That would remove the full weight of responsibility from Lee's small shoulders. Then perhaps Hadrian could begin to see their nephew for what he was—a little boy who needed a father's love.

"You truly care about this cause." Hadrian regarded her with a look of genuine admiration. "Perhaps if Julian had been raised by someone like you, he might have come to understand and care about the mission I wanted him to fulfill."

Was that all she meant to him, Artemis wondered, a useful tool to further his plans?

"I have another reason for wanting to invite my cousin," she explained. "For all his fiery oratory in the Commons, Jasper has always been painfully awkward with women. A vivacious girl like Susannah Penrose might be just the sort to draw him out."

"Matchmaking, are you?" Hadrian shot her a teasing grin that lofted her spirits to dizzying heights. "That can be a dangerous occupation."

Could anything be more dangerous, Artemis wondered, than losing her heart to a husband who might not want it?

With preparations to make for their house party, the summer days flew by faster than ever. While Artemis ordered supplies and planned menus, Hadrian drew up plans for a northern office of Vindicara. He wanted to be ready with facts and figures to discuss the venture with Ford. He also prepared for the discussion he hoped to have with Viscount Ashbury, gathering information on the numbers and ages of children employed in local mines.

A week before their guests were due to arrive, he met one afternoon with a pair of earnest young Methodists who were endeavoring to establish Sabbath schools in several mining villages. It was difficult to judge who left the meeting happier—the young men who received a generous endowment to assist with their work, or Hadrian who gave them the money. Bringing an end to the practice of employing children underground would be as long and difficult a task in its way as dragging those heavy-laden corves up from the coalface. Yet it heartened him to take this first small step.

He could hardly wait to tell Artemis about it over dinner. He knew she would share his enthusiasm. With a spring in his step, he bounded up the stairs and strode toward his bedchamber where he would wash up before dinner.

The nursery door stood ajar and as he passed it, the sweet gurgle of his nephew's laughter wafted out. Lured by the sound, Hadrian approached quietly and peeped inside.

A porcelain bath basin sat on the floor, while Artemis knelt beside it cuddling their nephew. His small, plump body was swathed in towels, his skin bright pink and his wet hair a mass of soft curls. He laughed with giddy glee as his aunt kissed him again and again and blew raspberries against his cheeks.

Artemis was laughing, too. Not her usual self-conscious chuckle, but a warm, hearty gush of laughter.

"You are a silly goose, Lee Northmore." She jiggled him in her arms, rubbing her nose against his. "A silly goose without a bill or a single feather. But you love to splash in the water, don't you, my sweet little goosie?"

Lee squealed and giggled uncontrollably.

An almost forgotten brooding sensation swelled in Hadrian's heart as he watched them. It reminded him of the first time he'd seen Margaret holding their infant daughter. That memory revived a host of buried regrets and fears.

He tried to steal away unnoticed. But when he stepped back, one of the floorboards betrayed him with a loud creak. Artemis glanced up and spied him. With a grimace of embarrassment, she hid her face in Lee's towels.

Before Hadrian could retreat farther, she scrambled up from the floor and approached him, carrying the child. "Look, Lee. Uncle Hadrian has come to see you. Poor child, how old will you be before you can say our names properly? Bob and Ann would have been so much easier than Hadrian and Artemis."

By the time the boy could pronounce his name, Hadrian knew he would be back in Singapore.

"Ba!" Lee flailed his arms toward Hadrian. "Ba-ba-ba!"

"There, you see," said Artemis. "That could be Bob or perhaps… Papa."

That word drove an icy blade into his heart. "I did not mean to disturb you." He backed away. "I was just passing."

"And a lucky thing, too." Artemis bundled his nephew into his arms. "Lee has hardly seen you lately. I believe he's missed you."

"Rubbish." Hadrian tried to resist the fresh-scrubbed smell of Lee and the warm weight that filled his empty arms. "He is too young to have any idea who I am."

"He may not be able to say your name properly or understand what relation you are to him, but he's taken to you in a way he has to few other people." Artemis sounded as if she were telling him something he might want to hear. "It began that first afternoon we met you on our way back to Bramberley. Remember how he latched on to your leg and clung for dear life? I was afraid I might tear your breeches prying him off."

"I remember." Trying to curb the grin that tugged at the corner of his mouth, Hadrian pretended to scold his nephew. "You were a naughty wee scamp, putting your poor aunt in such an awkward position."

Some children might have thought he was in earnest and taken fright, but not Lee. He flung his arms around Hadrian's neck, squeezing hard. "Papapa!"

"You see?" Artemis's voice rang with a note of triumph. "He does know you. Could you not find a bit more time to spend with him?"

"What would be the use?" Hadrian's mock scowl clenched into the real thing. "I will be gone before he is old enough to remember me."

Artemis flinched. "So it doesn't matter how you neglect him because he is only young? You sound like Uncle Henry."

The warm, demonstrative woman Hadrian had come to know in the past several weeks seemed to retreat behind a stout barrier.

"That is not fair, and you know it. What good will come of encouraging an attachment, then disappearing out of his life?" Hadrian wished he'd thought of that before he made his way into her bed.

"You went to such great lengths to get Lee." Artemis sounded puzzled and hurt. "I thought you cared about him. But all you really cared about was continuing the Northmore bloodline, wasn't it? That and taking over the mission you set for his father." She seized the child back from him. "Apart from those things you don't give a damn about him, do you?"

He turned away. "You don't understand."

Lee did not like being taken from his uncle. He began to fuss. Hadrian fought the urge to cheer him up by making comical faces. He longed to wrap the child in his arms and protect him from anything that might harm or grieve him. But how could Hadrian do that when *he* was one of those hazards?

"You're right," said Artemis. "I do not understand and he cannot. All the same, I believe young children sense things at a deeper level than words or reason. Things that may influence how they grow to view themselves."

Was she talking about their nephew, now, or herself? For all the deprivations of his early years, Hadrian had known deep in his bones that his parents loved him and believed in him.

"He has you to give him all those things, Artemis. I undertook to provide for his material needs. Remember our bargain?" Sensing this was a battle he could not win, Hadrian forced himself to walk away. If he did not retreat, his gallant opponent might exact a disastrous surrender.

"Of course I remember." Her passionate reply dogged his footsteps, harrying his resolve. "At the time, I thought it was the perfect solution. I wanted Lee all to myself to love and care for. But you have shown me he needs more than that. He needs a father's love and guidance...and firmness when it is warranted. He needs those things more than whatever luxuries your fortune can provide."

She'd said far worse things to him when they'd first met, but Hadrian had been able to dismiss them without a qualm. Since Artemis had come to know him so well and he'd come to value her judgment so highly, that was no longer possible.

Did Hadrian view her darling nephew as nothing but a means to further his aims? That night Artemis tossed and turned in her bed, tormented by uncertainty. There'd been a time, not so long ago, when she would have believed it without question and despised him. Now that she knew the tragedies of Hadrian's past and his dreams for the future, her feelings were vastly more complicated and she could not be certain of anything.

After several restless hours, she rose and donned her dressing gown. Then she crept down the stairs, hoping a breath of cool night air might soothe her troubled heart.

Her hand was on the latch of the great front door, when a quiet query reached out of the darkness behind her. "Not running away, are you?"

Her heart gave a fearful jolt against her ribs. Struggling to catch her breath, she spun about to face Hadrian. "I could not sleep, so I decided to step out for a bit of air. You are a fine one to talk of running away after the way you ran from Lee and me this afternoon."

"You're right." He stepped into a pool of moonlight. "I should have stayed and explained myself. But you caught me off guard. I needed some time to think about what you said. That is why I am up so late—doing a bit of thinking while the house is quiet."

There was something about being alone with him in the darkness while the rest of the household slept. It took Artemis back to the other time they'd been alone in the dark—sharing a bed. It stirred up wanton yearnings she could not afford to indulge.

"Shall I leave you to continue thinking in peace?" She turned toward the door.

"I reckon I've done enough thinking for one night—too much, perhaps. It's time I did some explaining instead. May I come out with you?"

The hushed intimacy of his tone made her heart speed up again. "If you wish."

Quietly they let themselves out. Artemis sank onto one of the wide stone steps beneath the semi-circular portico. Hadrian stood for a moment, leaning against one of the tall pillars. Then he sat down beside her. They kept silent for a while, breathing the cool night air while the shrill chirping of frogs rose from the beck at the bottom of the garden.

"It's not that I don't care about the lad," said Hadrian at last. "I do worry about him getting attached to me, and me to him."

Could he not see that would be the best possible thing for both of them? "But he is all the family you have left."

"And all you have left," Hadrian replied. "Apart from your uncles, though I reckon they have never been much of a comfort."

Artemis heaved a rueful sigh. "No indeed. Lee *has* been a comfort to me, though, and a great diversion. I cannot imagine how I would have borne the loss of my brother and sister without him."

She longed for Hadrian to know that kind of consolation. "Even with him, there was still a void. I wanted so desperately to fill it, I was not very particular about what I used—anger, bitterness, blame. Those made bad patching materials."

"At least they last."

If anyone could understand about the emptiness of loss, it was Hadrian. His mother's death must have gouged a deep hole in his heart. Before it had begun to heal, the sudden violent loss of his father and brothers must have blasted a bottomless crater.

"But at what cost?" asked Artemis. "They are so…corrosive. They eat away at the edges of the hole, making it bigger and bigger until it becomes impossible to fill. I believe reaching out to others provides a better remedy. After my mother died, Papa relied on me for so many things. It helped, somehow, being needed. After he died, Leander and Daphne needed me. Now Lee does."

"All very commendable. But it can be a dangerous business, using other people to fill the void. What happens when you lose *them?*"

A shiver ran through Artemis at the thought of losing Lee. What would she do? To whom would she turn in the forlorn hope of filling that emptiness?

She could think of only one person. "Surely there will always be someone who needs our help, if we are willing to look. But there are other things that can fill the void. Lasting things that heal rather than harm."

"And what might those be?" Hadrian sounded doubtful.

"You should know." Artemis drank in a deep breath of night air fragrant with the wholesome sweetness of clover. "It was thinking of you that brought them to my mind. Hard work, for one. A worthwhile cause. Fond memories."

"You may be right. Those first two served me well for many years. Perhaps if they had not been tainted with resentment and guilt, they might have done a better job."

They fell silent again. Not the tense, expectant silence that had once bristled between them, but a tranquil hush in which they could ponder their thoughts.

"I have tried your way of filling the void," said Hadrian at last. "Almost ten years ago. Her name was Margaret. Her father worked for the East India Company. I was young enough that the memories of what happened to my family had begun to fade. I'd gone into business and was making a success of it. So I thought, why not get married, have a family of my own, continue the Northmore line in case anything…ever happened…to Julian."

His words knocked the air out of Artemis. She remembered him calling Margaret's name on their wedding night when she was in his arms.

"What happened to your wife?" she whispered.

Hadrian stared up at the pale, melancholy face of the moon. "One of those infernal fevers that are the scourge of tropical countries. They come on without any warning and before you know it—" he snapped his fingers "—the person you love is gone. A young life snuffed out like a candle."

Artemis wanted to tell him how sorry she was to hear of yet another tragic loss he had suffered. But her lips refused to form the words. Could that be for the heartless, shameful reason that she was *not* entirely sorry Hadrian had been free to wed her?

He gave no sign of noticing her lapse, but continued to recount his litany of heartbreak. "The baby caught it first. The doctor told us nothing could be done. He said we should let the *ayah* tend Elizabeth so we wouldn't catch the fever. Margaret refused to heed his advice, said she could not bear to have her child die in any arms but hers."

Suddenly Hadrian's first wife was no longer a threatening shadow from his past, but a real woman with whom Artemis could not help but sympathize. The summer moon became a soft, silver blur as tears filled her eyes. "I do not blame her. I would feel the same about Lee."

So her husband had been a father once, however briefly. He knew how it felt to place his heart and his hopes in a pair of tiny hands… then stand by helpless while a fever consumed them. She could not blame him for being reluctant to risk what little of himself he had left. Not even for the sake of her adored nephew.

As for anything she might have been foolish enough to hope for herself…

"Tell me about Margaret." Artemis could not coax her voice above a whisper. "What was she like?"

Hadrian heaved a slow sigh. "Many of the things you told me about your sister, I could say of Margaret. She had high spirits, a strong will and a good heart. I cannot fault Julian for being smitten by a woman like that. We Northmore men must fancy the same kind."

Artemis swallowed a pathetic whimper that rose in her throat. Why should it matter if Hadrian's heart belonged to his late wife—a woman as different from her as her sister had been?

It *should* not matter at all. But it did—far too much.

Margaret. Elizabeth.

He had finally spoken their names aloud for the first time in far too many years. For Hadrian, those names were like enchanted keys, unlocking long-imprisoned memories of his young wife and daughter. With them came echoes of the profound sorrow and bitter regret their loss had caused him. But there was a strange sense of relief, too, an elusive whisper of peace.

"So you see how it is, then?" He slanted a glance at Artemis, all silvery-white in the moonlight, her arms clasped around her knees. "Caring for someone…loving them…doesn't mean giving them everything they long for. Sometimes you have to do what you know in your heart is best for them."

"I do see how it is," she answered in a voice like the sigh of a midnight breeze.

"Then I reckon we ought to get back in." Slowly he rose to his feet and offered her his hand. "We've been out here long enough."

Without another word, Artemis let him help her up. Quietly they entered the house and crept through the darkened entrance hall, up the staircase and down the west gallery. Would he dream of Margaret and Elizabeth tonight? Hadrian wondered. Would he relive those anguished days in Madras? Or would his slumbering mind reach back to happier times, savoring their hopeful joy, until he woke to the crippling realization that they were gone?

When he and Artemis reached the door to her bedchamber, he asked, "Can I come in? I know I've no right to ask, but…"

"It is not a question of having the right," she replied in a weary-sounding whisper. "But I do not think it is a good idea under the circumstances. Do you?"

"I don't want to bed you." He could not deny it was a tempting diversion, but Artemis deserved so much more than that. "I just want to be close to you. This is the first time I've spoken about Margaret and Elizabeth in years and I don't want to be alone with my memories."

She exhaled a soft sigh. "I'm not sure you know what you're asking."

"Forgive me." He backed away. "I am being selfish. You need your rest. It's just that you are the only one I've ever been able to tell—first about the Fellbank Explosion and now about this. After all you have been through in your own life, I believe you understand better than anyone else can. Good night, Artemis."

He turned to go.

"Hadrian?" she called softly after him. "Are you saying you need me?"

It was an unsettling admission, but how could he deny it? "I am."

Her door swung open. "Come in, then."

How had an acquaintance that had begun with so much mutual hostility blossomed into this? Hadrian did not even try to puzzle out the mystery as he followed her inside. Instead he cherished a sense of gratitude for all the gifts Artemis had brought into his life.

At the same time, she made him achingly aware of his emptiness and tempted him to risk filling it with the very things he had sworn to avoid.

Chapter Fifteen

Hadrian needed her, but not in the way she wished he might. Their talk about his wife and daughter had helped her understand where she and Lee stood with him.

Artemis mulled over that thought as she sat hemming a nightshirt for Lee, who staggered around his nursery making noises that occasionally sounded like words.

Hadrian did care about them, in his way. But his heart belonged to the family he had lost. They were his true family. The high-spirited, golden angel he had wed for love, and the precious little daughter their love had begot. Not the illegitimate offspring of a brother he could barely remember and a remote stranger whom circumstances had forced him to wed. It was a tribute to his generous nature that they had managed to form a makeshift bond—one based on necessity and physical attraction and their common history of bereavement.

That was as much as he could give. Though she wanted more for Lee, Artemis was enough of a realist to accept what she could get for herself and be content with it. A few months of half marriage to a man like Hadrian Northmore would be better than a conventional union of many years with any other man.

The nursery door opened then and Hadrian strode in, looking so cheerful and handsome, he lit up something inside of her. "Hi-ho, my lovely lady and my fine young master! Why are you shut up inside on such a splendid summer day?"

"We were planning to take a walk down to the beck as soon as I finish my sewing." Artemis greeted him with a fond smile, determined not to spoil the time they had by pushing for more. "What are you doing home? I thought you had a meeting today."

The moment Hadrian entered the room Lee toddled toward him with his arms raised. "Papapa up-up!"

As Artemis looked on in amazement, Hadrian picked up their nephew and swung him high in the air. "Not very eloquent, but you get your point across, lad! I'm not your papa, but I will admit 'Uncle Hadrian' is a mouthful at your age."

He turned toward Artemis. "My meeting will keep for another day. There's somewhere I've a fancy to show the pair of you, if you'd care for an outing."

If they'd care? For weeks she'd been pressing him to spend more time with Lee to no avail. Now, just when she'd resigned herself that it would never happen, here he was.

Artemis was not about to refuse a gift, simply because it was unexpected. "I'm sure Lee will be delighted to go anywhere with you. But I thought…that is…you said…"

Hadrian gave a rueful nod. "I know what I said. You said a few things, too. They made a good deal of sense, once I took the time to think them over. I reckon I do owe this wee lad more than what my fortune can buy him. He may not remember, but you will be able to tell him when I'm gone."

When he was gone. That thought made her throat tighten. This unexpected outing did not signify any change in Hadrian's plans. But it was more than she'd dared to hope for half an hour ago.

"Let's be off, then." Hadrian headed for the door, bouncing Lee in his arms. "The gig should be harnessed by the time we get down to the stable yard and Mrs. Matlock had Cook pack us a lunch."

* * *

A short while later, they drove past St. Oswin's. Lee perched on his aunt's knee, taking in everything around him.

"What sort of place are you taking us to?" asked Artemis.

His childhood home, perhaps—the farm his father had lost, forcing the family to find work at Fellbank? Surely Hadrian would not be in such high spirits if they were going there.

"It's a place you'll appreciate with your love of history," was Hadrian's cryptic reply. "I want you to bring Lee back here again, when he's old enough to understand."

"Ee! Ee!" cried the child, clapping his hands.

"That's right, you wee monkey." Hadrian ruffled his hair. "I want your auntie to bring you here when you're about eight. That's the age I was when my pa first brought me. What I saw that day sparked my fancy and stayed with me the rest of my life."

He glanced up at Artemis. "I want you to take him to Fellbank, too, when he's older. I'll leave it to you to decide when he's ready."

His gray gaze fairly glowed with trust.

A few moments later, he steered the gig onto a narrow path that wound around the base of a hill overlooking the church. After driving a little farther, he stopped and climbed out. He held his arms open to take Lee. "We shall have to walk the rest of the way. It's not far. If you can carry the basket of food, I'll tote this young fellow."

Lee was only too happy to go to his uncle, who swung him onto his shoulders and set off up the hill. Following with their lunch and the picnic rug, Artemis basked in the warm caress of the summer sun and the cooling rustle of the breeze. Only when she reached the flattened summit of the hill and glimpsed the tumbled, overgrown outline of ancient stonewalls did she realize where Hadrian had brought them.

"This must have been a Roman fort." Setting down their picnic gear, she stared around in wonder.

"That's right." Hadrian's voice rang with pride, as if he had built the place with his own hands. "Vindicara they called it. I named my company after this place."

"I wondered how you'd come by that name." Artemis pictured the fort as it might have looked many centuries ago, with Roman soldiers standing guard, practicing with their weapons, marching in drills. "It means 'to avenge,' doesn't it?"

"That is one meaning," said Hadrian. "Another is 'lay claim to.' I believe that's how this fort got its name."

"Does it have anything to do with how you and your brothers came by *your* names?" Artemis asked. "It is not every day one meets a man called Hadrian."

The name had associations of strength and authority that suited him, though.

He nodded. "As a lad, I got a good many bruises sticking up for my name when my friends made fun of it."

"And *gave* a few as well, I imagine."

"So I did," he admitted. "Pa said it was a name to be proud of, a name to live up to."

"He was right," said Artemis. "And you have."

Hadrian looked torn between pride and embarrassment.

"See there, Lee?" He pointed to a large, squared-off stone in what was left of the eastern wall. "The inscription has worn away more in the past thirty years, but I can still make it out."

Lee was too young to understand. Yet the intensity of his uncle's tone seemed to engage his attention. "*LEG VI*—that means the Sixth Legion. Some of them likely built this place sixteen hundred years ago. That's even older than me."

Lee chortled, as if he understood his uncle's wry quip.

Hadrian turned his attention back to Artemis. "St. Oswin's was built out of stones taken from here. Some of them have words carved on them, too. Remind me next Sunday and I'll show you."

He swung Lee off his shoulders and eased the child to the ground, keeping hold of one small hand. Lee wasted no time toddling toward a slender block of carved stone set out from the fallen wall.

"This is some kind of altar," said Hadrian. "The inscription is to the god Vitirius, by a tribune called Titus."

They spent a delightful afternoon exploring the ruins. Lee roamed about to his heart's content, happy to be out of doors in the company of his aunt and uncle. As Hadrian had predicted, Artemis appreciated the vivid history he brought to life for her. But more than that, she savored the indescribable sweetness of being a family—even if it was only a fleeting mirage.

When Lee's boundless energy began to flag, they settled in the shade of a section of wall and ate a hearty luncheon of cold meat pies, bread and cheese, washed down with cider.

"I have something else to show you." Hadrian fished in his pocket and pulled out a coin about the size of a sixpence. Balancing it upright between his thumb and forefinger, he held it out for Lee and Artemis to get a good look. "This here is a silver denarius. The Romans used them to pay the soldiers. That man on the front wearing the helmet is Emperor Constantine the Second. Looks a bit like your old uncle, don't you think?"

Artemis peered closer. "The profile does look rather like you. Did you find that coin here?"

Hadrian shook his head. "My father found it when he was a lad. He thought old Constantine looked like *his* father. It made him wonder if our family might have Roman blood. That inspired him to study Latin and history from the local vicar. The more he learned about the Romans, the more he admired them. It made him resolve to raise our family up."

"He sounds like a very determined man," said Artemis. Both Hadrian and Lee had inherited that sometimes-exasperating virtue.

Hadrian nodded. "He was all of that. Some of the miners spent more of their pay at the public house than their families could afford. Pa never darkened its door. He said he had better things to do with his time and brass. The money he might have spent on a pint, he put away for Julian's schooling. The time he might have idled away there, he spent teaching us to read and write."

Hadrian flipped the coin into his palm and clenched his fingers over it in a protective fist. "Pa gave this to me on the day he first brought me to Vindicara. I've carried it with me ever since to remind me where I come from and what I have to do."

Another woman might not have understood that urgent sense of duty to secure his family's legacy. Not only did Artemis understand, she admired it. "I am certain your father would be proud to know how well you've fulfilled his dream to make something of your family."

"I've a ways to go yet. But with your help I'm making progress." Hadrian reached out and dropped the denarius into her palm. "Keep that safe for Lee, will you? Give it to him when you bring him here again and tell him the things I've told you."

"I will." Artemis nodded toward their nephew, who had drifted off to sleep in his uncle's arms. "I will also tell him all about this day and what a wonderful time he had with you. Though he may not remember, I'm certain that somewhere inside he will carry a special sense of you."

Hadrian glanced down at the child, then raised his eyes to her. As always, a potent physical awareness stirred between them.

His firm, wide mouth arched in a devilish grin. "What would you say to coming here late some warm night and performing the sacred rites of Aphrodite?"

"I should be scandalized, of course!" Artemis tried to look as shocked as she once would have at such a suggestion from him. Unable to support the pretense, she sputtered with wanton laughter. "Deliciously scandalized. Name the night and I shall be yours!"

More and more, she yearned to be his—fully and forever. But since Hadrian's tragic past had made that impossible, she must try to be content with as many days like this one as he could give her.

* * *

When he heard the first of their guests had arrived, Hadrian sent Mrs. Matlock to fetch Artemis, while he took up his place on the steps of the front portico. He preferred that this first meeting with his estranged partner take place amid the bustle of their arrival. Hopefully it would ease any awkwardness between them.

The first one to alight from the carriages was Susannah Penrose, holding a small boy by the hand. "Thank you for inviting us, Mr. Northmore. It is a pleasure to see you again. This is my nephew, Master Phillip Crawford. Phip, make a nice bow to our host, like I taught you."

The child abruptly doubled over at the waist, then straightened up and retreated behind his aunt's skirts.

Hadrian dropped to his haunches. "A pleasure to meet you, Master Phillip. My nephew Lee is near your age. He'll be keen to play with you."

Lady Kingsfold appeared next, carrying her young daughter. "This has been a great adventure for Phillip and Eleanor—their first journey from home. Mr. Northmore, may I present my sister Belinda and her husband, Sidney Crawford?"

"Welcome to Edenhall, Mr. and Mrs. Crawford. Thank you for accepting our invitation."

"Our pleasure." Sidney Crawford returned Hadrian's bow. "A fine-looking place you have here. Is the fishing good?"

Hadrian nodded. "I am told the trout are running very well down in the beck."

Ford stepped past Mr. Crawford to offer Hadrian his hand. "My brother-in-law is a keen angler. The skill of your cook and the quality of your wine cellar matter far less to him than a plentiful supply of fish nearby. I'll wager his enjoyment of your hospitality is assured."

"I'm glad to hear it." Hadrian gave his partner's hand a hearty shake. "Would the two of you care to walk down to the beck? If you're anything like me, you'll be anxious to stretch your legs after a long carriage ride."

Mr. Crawford greeted the suggestion with an eager nod.

"In that case," said Lady Kingsfold, "my sisters and I will take the children inside and get them settled."

"My wife is waiting to welcome you." Hadrian gestured toward the large front door. "She will be pleased to see familiar faces from Sussex."

As the women and children headed inside, Sidney Crawford strode toward the beck, leaving Hadrian and Ford to follow at a more leisurely pace.

For a few moments they walked side by side without speaking. Then Ford broke the silence. "I must say, *this* is not where I pictured you'd be after you stormed out of Hawkesbourne."

"Where did you picture me, then?"

"The truth?" Ford gave a hoarse chuckle. "Swinging from a gallows for murdering Lady Artemis Dearing."

There was a time Ford's prediction might not have sounded so far-fetched. Now the thought of harming one hair on her head made Hadrian's blood run cold.

"She was not to blame for what happened to my brother." Hadrian glanced toward his partner. "Neither were you. I was a blinkered fool to say otherwise. I know you are not a man to easily pardon such a grave insult, but I regret what I said to you that day. Whether or not you are willing to accept my apology, I'm offering it."

Ford halted abruptly and turned to fix him with an incredulous look. "Who the hell are you? And what have you done with the *real* Hadrian Northmore?"

"I beg your pardon?"

"So you have." Ford broke into a bewildered grin. "And I cannot believe my ears. Laura insisted you must have invited us here to make amends, but I had my doubts. I should know by now that she is usually right. Tell me, what made you willing to apologize? During three years in India and two in Singapore I never once heard you beg anybody's pardon for anything. The most you ever did was dispatch Simon or me to smooth things over."

Hadrian knew what—or rather *who*—had brought about the change in him. But he could scarcely admit it to himself, let alone Ford. "Perhaps my brother's death has made me realize there are worse things than losing face."

Ford's dark brows rose. "Such as...?"

"Losing a friend."

For an instant Ford looked overcome with a mixture of emotions. Then he gave Hadrian a hearty clout on the arm. "That sounds like the sort of good sense I would be prepared to drink a toast to."

"Then drink we shall." Hadrian nodded toward the beck and the two men resumed their walk. "We never did get to hoist a glass of arrack in honor of Singapore being officially recognized."

He inhaled a deep draft of late-summer air, redolent with the scent of things ripening. "Something tells me you and I have a great deal of good fortune we should drink to."

"Your guests have arrived, ma'am." Mrs. Matlock appeared at the drawing room door to inform Artemis. "The master sent me to tell you."

Artemis jumped from her chair, where she'd been trying to concentrate on a bit of needlework. The house party had been her idea and she hoped it would promote reconciliation between Hadrian and his partner. But she dreaded having to face the Kingsfolds again after the way she'd treated them.

Though she had changed in many ways since leaving Bramberley, she was not a naturally sociable person and probably never would be. The prospect of formal entertaining, even a small group of people with whom she was fairly well acquainted, still alarmed her.

Hadrian was relying on her, Artemis reminded herself, inhaling a deep breath and smoothing her skirts. "Thank you, Mrs. Matlock. I trust everything is ready to make our guests comfortable."

"Indeed it is, ma'am." For all her brisk, capable manner, the housekeeper had not been able to hide her excitement over Edenhall playing host to a baron, a viscount and an earl. "Your guests will find nothing lacking in our hospitality."

With that reassurance to shore up her courage, Artemis contrived a smile of welcome and hurried to the entrance hall to greet her guests.

She found Lady Kingsfold holding her small daughter in her arms, while Mrs. Crawford carried a baby. Susannah Penrose brought up the rear, clutching the Crawfords' elder son by the hand.

In spite of her earlier misgivings, pleasure welled up inside Artemis at the sight of their familiar faces. "Welcome to Edenhall. It is a pleasure to see you all again. I hope you had a good journey."

"It was quite tolerable." Lady Kingsfold exchanged looks with her sisters and they all began to laugh. "I believe that is the best one can hope when traveling with small children."

"I'm certain the trip will be well worth it." Mrs. Crawford endeavored to soothe her baby, who had begun to fuss. "I have scarcely been a step from home since Phip was born and Laura is just as bad. It will do us good to have a change of scene."

"We can get the children settled in the nursery before I show you to your rooms." Artemis led her guests toward the main staircase. "My nephew will be delighted to have some playmates of his own age."

She felt rather apprehensive about mentioning Lee. Would the ladies object to their respectable little darlings sharing a nursery room with an illegitimate child?

If they did, Lady Kingsfold gave no sign of it. "Your nephew and my Eleanor are of an age, aren't they? It will be good for her and Phillip to make a new friend."

When they reached the nursery, two capable-looking nursemaids were waiting to take their young charges in hand after the excitement of their journey.

Artemis showed Mrs. Crawford and Miss Susannah to their rooms first, then seized the opportunity of a moment alone with

Lady Kingsfold. "I cannot thank you enough for accepting our invitation. I would not have blamed you for refusing after the way I spoke to you and your husband when we last met. I understand now that you had everyone's best interests at heart. I only wish I'd had the sense to heed your advice."

Lady Kingsfold reached for her hand and gave it a warm squeeze. "It was a difficult situation and I cannot blame you for taking exception to our interference. I might have done the same if you had tried to give me unwanted advice about my family. I was delighted to receive your invitation. It gave me hope that our husbands might mend their friendship."

A weight lifted from Artemis's heart when she heard that. She and Lady Kingsfold were near in age and had been neighbors for almost ten years. Though their younger sisters had been great friends, there had always been a polite coolness between them.

That was her fault, Artemis acknowledged. When Laura Penrose had come to Hawkesbourne as the young bride of a much older husband, Artemis had privately condemned her as a fortune hunter. Later, when the widowed lady had wed her late husband's heir, it had seemed to confirm all Artemis's worst suspicions. As with Hadrian, her uncharitable assumptions had been quite wrong.

"Ford has been so out of spirits since he quarreled with Mr. Northmore," Lady Kingsfold continued. "I urged him to make some overture, but he can be very stubborn when he believes he has been wronged."

Artemis nodded. "Hadrian has difficulty admitting he has done wrong. I knew he wanted to make amends, but he could not bring himself to make the first move."

"They are too much alike, that is their trouble." With a chuckle of exasperated fondness, Lady Kingsfold linked arms with Artemis and they continued down the wide gallery of the east wing. "That is the price we pay for having married such dynamic, ambitious men."

"Perhaps so." It gave Artemis a sense of bittersweet satisfaction to talk with Lady Kingsfold about their husbands, as if she and Hadrian had a true marriage, rather than a convenient arrangement for their nephew's sake.

"Clearly you have much more influence over your husband than I have with mine," said Lady Kingsfold. "You were able to persuade him to invite us here. If it had been left to me, I fear their estrangement would have continued, growing more difficult to resolve as bitterness hardened between them."

Artemis detected a note of regret in the lady's voice and wondered at its cause. "Here is your room. I hope you and Lord Kingsfold will find it comfortable and that you will enjoy your stay at Edenhall."

"I'm certain we shall."

As Artemis turned to leave, Lady Kingsfold called after her, "I hope you will not mind my saying so, but marriage seems to agree with you."

A few months ago, Artemis might have resented such a well-meant observation. Now she welcomed it. "Thank you. I believe it does."

Marriage to Hadrian Northmore, even a sham one, did agree with her. If only she had as much influence over him as Lady Kingsfold seemed to think she did, then perhaps she could persuade him to reconsider his plans for the future.

Chapter Sixteen

The Earl and Countess of Launceton and their small son arrived at Edenhall not long after the Kingsfold party. Hadrian was pleased to find the young earl had changed very little from the affable Blade Maxwell he'd known in Singapore. He had rather mixed feelings to discover Blade's wife was the former Miss Genia Vernon, a lady he'd known in India.

That evening as they assembled for dinner, the countess confessed, "I wasn't certain what to say when Blade told me he'd received an invitation from someone he'd known in Singapore. I was afraid I shouldn't know anyone else in the party. But when he mentioned your name, I told him we must accept at once. It is so good to see you again, after all these years, Hadrian. I have often thought of you and wondered how you were getting on."

"As I have of you." Hadrian hoped he delivered the polite falsehood with a convincing smile.

It was not that he'd ever disliked Genia or wished her ill. She'd been Margaret's dearest friend, a witness at their wedding in Madras. His memories of her had been locked away as deep and tight as those of his late wife and infant daughter. With help from Artemis, he'd begun to unearth those memories and to learn to live with them. But Genia was a vivid reminder of the carefree days before his life had shattered for the second time.

Hadrian welcomed the distraction of Lord Ashbury's arrival. The young viscount entered the drawing room with a rangy, loping stride. His sandy-brown hair was disheveled and his eyes held a look that might have been bristling irritation or abject terror. Artemis introduced her cousin to Hadrian and their other guests.

The young man responded to their greetings with terse civility, his reply to Miss Penrose scarcely more than a grunt. Clearly Artemis had not exaggerated her cousin's unease around young ladies. Susannah Penrose did not seem any more taken with the viscount than he was with her. Her tight little smile looked brittle enough to shatter.

Hadrian feared his wife's matchmaking plans were doomed to failure. Then again, Lord Ashbury and Miss Penrose were not off to any worse start than he and Artemis had been. And think how far they had come. A good deal further than he had ever intended or wanted. Yet where would he be without her? He would not trade the past months for anything.

The Crawfords appeared just then, and they were all able to go in to dinner. Over the first course, Lady Kingsfold and her family kept up a flow of easy conversation. Their attempts to include Lord Ashbury met with scant success. Hadrian might have dismissed the young nobleman's aloofness as haughty superiority, but his deepening understanding of Artemis had given him a more sympathetic perspective.

When the viscount's sullen silence threatened to dampen the evening, she cast Hadrian a look that he recognized as an appeal for his help. Though he doubted his ability to prevail where the others had failed, he could not disappoint her. What would draw *him* out, Hadrian asked himself, if he were ill at ease and not inclined to talk?

"Lord Ashbury, my wife tells me you are a great admirer of Mr. Wilberforce. Do you reckon Parliament will pass a law to abolish slavery in his lifetime?"

"I do indeed, sir." The young man sat up with a jolt, as if Hadrian had jabbed him with a fork. "Though Mr. Wilberforce has been ill of late, his supporters are spurred to action by the hope that he may live to see that long-overdue legislation passed."

The earnest fervor with which Lord Ashbury spoke quite transformed him. And Hadrian was not the only one to notice.

"I am a great admirer of Mr. Wilberforce." Miss Penrose looked at the viscount with sudden interest. "He appeared at a meeting in Horsham last year and spoke so movingly."

Lord Ashbury turned to stare at her as if he could not believe his ears. "*You* attended an abolition meeting?"

"Is there something wrong with that?" The young lady's eyes flashed with proud defiance. "Many women have made vital contributions to that great cause."

"Hannah More has had great influence, as have several others," Lord Ashbury conceded, "though Mr. Wilberforce fears the ladies are inclined to go too far."

"You agree, I suppose." Susannah Penrose stabbed her fork into a veal cutlet. "Men are eager enough to accept women's help when you need it, but heaven forbid we should express an opinion."

"On the contrary, Miss Penrose. I have nothing but admiration for those ladies, Hannah More in particular. Have you read any of her writings?"

Artemis turned to Ford. "Lord Kingsfold, I hear your daughter is quite the belle of our nursery. All the little boys are vying for her attention."

"I feared as much," Ford replied. "Eleanor is a strong-willed little creature and a beauty to boot. I suspect these will not be her last conquests."

"Nor are they her first." Lady Kingsfold chuckled. "Thanks to her adoring papa, our daughter is accustomed to having a powerful man wrapped around her pretty little finger. I shudder to think of the havoc she will wreak in the assembly rooms of London one day."

As the other married guests joined in this conversation about their children, Miss Penrose and Lord Ashbury continued talking together in hushed but emphatic tones.

From the opposite end of the table, Artemis flashed Hadrian a smile of gratitude for rescuing their party from the doldrums. As he tossed off a quip in answer to one of Blade's, he could not help feeling at ease in the company of happily married couples. Yet Genia's presence was a faintly disturbing reminder of how swiftly his newfound happiness could vanish.

If anyone had told Artemis she would one day be happy to entertain a houseful of strangers, she'd have thought they were mocking her. But that day *had* come. And the acquaintances she'd long kept at arm's length were bidding fair to become something she'd never had before—friends.

After several days spent taking the children for outings and evenings making music and playing cards, she was now on familiar terms with the countess and the Penrose sisters. She found all four ladies very congenial in different ways. Laura was the most like her, responsible and loyal. Genia was clever and forthright, Belinda gentle and amiable, while Susannah had a vivacious charm like Daphne's. Artemis wished she'd made an effort to cultivate a closer acquaintance with Laura and her sisters years ago.

Now, while the men were down at the beck fishing, the ladies brought the children outside to play in the garden.

"You have such a pretty place here, Lady Artemis." Susannah gazed around as she walked with her young nephew clinging to her hand. "Hawkesbourne is lovely, too, of course. But I have been there so long I scarcely notice it anymore."

Was it possible part of the charm of Edenhall lay in the presence of a certain awkward but ardent young politician? Artemis found herself eager to promote a match that might lead to the sort of true, lasting marriage she now longed for.

"If you like it here, you must return for a longer visit after Christmas." She stooped to dust off Lee, who had fallen on his bottom. "I shall want company once Mr. Northmore goes back to Singapore."

"Did you hear that, Laura?" Susannah called to her sister. "Lady Artemis has invited me to visit her this winter. I'd be delighted to. Winter passes so slowly at home since Daphne…I mean…now that I have no particular friends to call on."

When Artemis let a faint sigh escape her lips, Susannah reached for her hand. "Forgive me! I did not mean to bring back unhappy memories at such a pleasant time."

"Do not fret, my dear." Artemis strove to raise a smile. "I have far more happy memories of my sister than unhappy ones. Lately it is the former I recall most clearly. You remind me of Daphne when she was in her brightest spirits. Having you here makes me feel close to her again."

Susannah looked torn between her own grief for her friend and pleasure at having cheered Artemis. But before she could reply, little Phillip spotted a squirrel perched on a nearby garden seat and darted after it. His aunt was obliged to lift up her skirts and give chase.

No sooner had she gone than Laura and Genia joined Artemis.

"Did I hear you correctly?" asked Laura. "Mr. Northmore is going back to Singapore while you and Lee stay behind? How soon do you expect him to return?"

Those questions troubled Artemis far more than Susannah's mention of Daphne. Hadrian's departure would be a bereavement of sorts. Would she come to accept it in time, as she had the deaths of her brother and sister? Or would she wait and pine, living for that annual letter from Singapore, hoping he might return or send for her?

"Not for many years." Her voice caught in her throat. "If ever."

"And you cannot go with him?" Laura stooped to show her daughter a butterfly perched on a nearby shrub. "Is that your inclination or his?"

"I cannot leave Lee," replied Artemis. "And Hadrian would never risk taking him to the tropics. He says the climate is very hard on English children."

Hearing his name, Lee began to tug on her skirts, wanting to be picked up. Artemis welcomed the distraction.

"That is true." Genia kept a keen eye on her young son, who was pulling a toy boat on wheels. "Especially if they are accustomed to northern climates. Hadrian knows better than most, poor man. One can hardly blame him for not wanting to go through that again."

"Did you know his first wife well?" Artemis could not resist asking, though she knew she was only torturing herself to hear Genia sing Margaret's praises.

Genia nodded. "We were as close as sisters. Did Hadrian not tell you? I was Margaret's bridesmaid. Her death came as such a shock I went rather wild afterwards. Hadrian couldn't bear to stay in Madras. He moved his business to Penang and I did not see him again until the other day. I never thought he would wed again. It has done my heart good to see him so happy with you and your little nephew."

Before Artemis could digest all that and form a proper response, Laura chimed in. "Ford says Hadrian is quite a changed man and all for better. That is why I was so surprised to hear you are to be parted. Perhaps it is not my place to ask…" she lowered her voice "…but do you *want* him to go?"

Artemis stiffened as she used to do when anyone approached too close for her comfort. "It is necessary."

"That does not answer the question," said Genia in a gentle but firm tone.

Artemis hesitated, torn between contrary inclinations. It was against her reserved nature to confide in others, yet she craved an outlet for her feelings.

"No," she whispered, holding their nephew as tightly as she wished she could hold Hadrian, "I do *not* want him to go, but there is nothing I can do to prevent it."

"Are you quite certain of that?" Laura challenged her. "Often we have more choices than we realize, if only we dare to make the difficult ones. Have you told Mr. Northmore how you feel?"

"Men are admirable creatures," added Genia, "but they sometimes have difficulty divining a woman's feelings if she leaves the slightest room for doubt."

"It would do no good," Artemis insisted. Did these women not understand how impossible a thing they were suggesting? "Hadrian and I have an arrangement to which we both agreed. I cannot change the conditions now."

"Are your feelings the same as they were when you made this arrangement of yours?" Laura's candid blue gaze would accept nothing less than the truth.

Artemis shook her head.

Laura exchanged a subtle nod with Genia as if to say she had guessed as much. "Are his?"

"No, but that signifies nothing. We detested one another at first. Just because we have overcome our differences and made an effort to be civil—"

"Civil?" Genia laughed. "My dear Artemis, if all married couples were as *civil* as you and Hadrian, the courtesans of London would starve for want of patrons!"

How could Genia taunt her with what she so desperately wanted to hear? "You should know better than anyone, his heart belongs to Margaret. Even if I wanted to I cannot fight a ghost...or an angel! Pray excuse me."

She set her nephew on his feet. "Could you please watch Lee for me?"

Hoisting up her skirts, Artemis dashed away before her composure deserted her entirely. She finally staggered to a halt a few minutes later under a stout old oak tree beyond the stables.

But before she had a chance to catch her breath, Genia appeared, breathless and anxious looking. "Forgive me... my dear! I did not mean...to distress you...truly. I have...a habit...of letting my tongue...run away with me."

Too winded and agitated to reply, Artemis could do no more than stand there, shaking her head like a perfect ninny while her galloping heart slowed.

Genia recovered her voice first. "Perhaps I should not behave like such an infernal busybody when we have known each other such a short time. But I felt so sorry for what Hadrian suffered and it has gladdened my heart to see him so happy with you. Margaret was a dear girl and I believe Hadrian loved her very much.

"But you must believe me." She fixed Artemis with her expressive hazel eyes. "I never saw him happier with her than I have seen him since I came here. Margaret used to wonder if he had some secret sorrow and fretted that he would not share it with her."

Could it be that Hadrian had never told his beloved first wife, the mother of his child, about the tragedy that had befallen his family? Artemis was almost afraid to believe it. Then she recalled something he'd said on the night he told her about Margaret and Elizabeth. *You are the only one I've ever been able to tell—first about the Fellbank Explosion and now about this. After all you have been through in your own life, I reckon you understand better than anyone else can.*

Perhaps Genia saw some change in her expression that offered hope. Reaching for Artemis's hand, she gave it a reassuring squeeze. "Laura was right, you know, about daring to make difficult choices. Love like yours is worth fighting for."

"Did you have to fight for yours?" Artemis could scarcely believe she was inviting such an intimate confidence from someone who was little better than a stranger. Yet she felt an inexplicable connection to Genia and Laura, as if they were all part of some secret sisterhood.

"I did indeed." A shadow of past distress dimmed Genia's eyes for a moment. Then a blaze of remembered strength and triumph lit them brighter than ever. "I believe Laura did, too. And after what you have accomplished already, I am certain you can."

She had accomplished a great deal, Artemis realized as she looked back over the past weeks, both with Hadrian and with herself. It had not been easy, but the rewards had been worth the struggle. And the struggle had made the rewards even sweeter.

Did she have the courage to fight all the ghosts from Hadrian's past and her own, for the sweetest reward of all?

"I say, Jasper." Hadrian took advantage of finding the young viscount sitting by himself reading the newspapers, rather than enjoying a flirtatious argument with Susannah Penrose. "There's some place I'd like you to see, if you wouldn't mind taking a drive with me. Artemis thought you might find it of interest."

Jasper looked up from his paper with an eager glint in his eyes. "Will the ladies be joining us?"

"Just you and me, I'm afraid." Hadrian strove to suppress a knowing smile. Did the fellow not realize how obviously he was smitten with Ford's pretty sister-in-law? "Where I plan to take you...it's not a very agreeable sight for ladies."

Before Jasper could reply, Ford and Blade strolled into the drawing room, back from an afternoon ride.

"That sounds intriguing." Blade broke into a sly grin. "Where are you planning to take our young friend, Hadrian?"

"Can we come along?" asked Ford.

"It's only a local colliery." Hadrian wished the pair of them had stayed out riding a little longer. "I doubt you'd find it of much interest."

Ford shrugged. "It will be a novelty to me. With all the new industries running on coal-fired engines, it is something I should learn more about."

"Very true," said Blade.

Hadrian cudgeled his brains for an excuse to put his friends off without offending them. He had resigned himself to telling Jasper how he'd once lived and what had happened to his family. But Ford and Blade had long known him as a successful man of business.

He wasn't sure he wanted them acquainted with the details of his early life.

Then he fancied he could hear Artemis whispering in his thoughts, reminding him that his old friends were now peers with seats in the House of Lords. If they took an interest in the plight of young mine workers, their influence could be a great asset.

"Stay or come as you like," he muttered. "I warn you it'll be no pleasure excursion."

The pair of them were obstinate enough that his reluctance made them all the more determined to go.

An hour later, the four men were on the road to the Stanehead Colliery, near the Northumberland border.

"Do you mean to keep us in suspense?" asked Blade. "Or are you going to tell us why you want Ashbury to see this coal mine?"

Hadrian inhaled a deep breath and forced himself to speak. "Jasper is an abolitionist. I thought he might care to know there are children as young as six spending most of their lives below ground, cut off from fresh air and sunshine, exposed to dangerous conditions that maim and kill many every year. They are not slave children in some distant colony, but native British, born and bred, enslaved by their poverty and ignorance."

"*Six* years old?" Blade repeated as if he'd misheard. "Surely not!"

"If you don't believe me," said Hadrian, "you can see for yourselves when we get to Stanehead. The shift should just be coming up."

"If it's true it is an outrage!" The words burst out of Jasper. "Why have I heard nothing of it until now?"

"Because people like you never go to places like Stanehead or Fellbank or Kellsend. And because so few people ever get out of those places to tell their stories. Even when they do, they may think you won't care."

That kept all three of the others quiet for a minute or two. Then

Ford ventured to ask, "Hadrian, how do *you* come to know so much about all this?"

"Because I started work as a trapper when I was eight years old—sitting in the dark from six in the morning until six at night, opening and closing the ventilation doors. After a couple of years I got big enough to become a putter—crawling through the tunnels on my hands and knees, hauling corves full of coal with a girdle harnessed around my waist."

The unspoken revulsion of his companions hung over the carriage like a thick cloud of noxious gas. And they hadn't heard the worst. If he stopped now, Hadrian feared he might never be able to speak of it to them again.

He forced himself to continue as he knew Artemis would urge him if she were there. "When I was seventeen, my father and four of my brothers were killed by a gas explosion, along with thirty-three others. At the time of their deaths, the eldest of my brothers was fourteen and the youngest was eight. In another year Julian would have been down there with them. If an injury had not kept me from work that day, so would I."

"Good God, man!" Ford broke the stunned hush that greeted Hadrian's confession. "You've never mentioned a word of this to me in all the time I've known you. I thought we were friends."

"We are," said Hadrian, relieved by his response. "It is not something I care to talk about, or remember. But I reckon it is necessary to speak of now, if it might prevent the same thing from happening to others.

"And you need not take my word alone," he added, nodding toward a cluster of pit cottages ranged on either side of the road ahead. "You can see and hear for yourselves from the young ones who are about to come off their shift."

He had timed it well. As they drew near the pithead, the mine began disgorging its captives. They were blacker than tinkers and all seemed to walk with a stoop, a limp or an exhausted shuffle.

Fortunately, there was still enough light for Hadrian's companions to see how small some of the children were.

"Girls, too?" Blade muttered a curse. "Some of them look no bigger than our Theo."

Jasper vaulted out of the carriage and waded among the workers, firing off questions about their ages, hours, wages and tasks they performed. Most of the adults gave him a wide berth and dark looks, but many of the children answered with brutal honesty.

By the time he returned to the carriage, he was bristling with indignation. "This cannot be allowed to continue! Not in our day and age."

"Is there anything you can do, Ashbury?" asked Ford.

"I shall raise some pointed questions during the next session of Parliament," replied Jasper. "But there is so much badly needed legislation that has no hope of passing until Parliament itself is reformed. You must know the power of the forces arrayed against that."

Both Ford and Blade gave dispirited nods.

"So that's it, then?" His lip curled in a disgusted sneer, Hadrian turned the carriage back toward Edenhall. "You're not even going to try because it might take a bit of effort? I should have known. This place is owned by the Earl of Jarrow—a crony of yours, no doubt. Lord Gateshead and Lord Bournemore made their fortunes from Durham coal, as well. You wouldn't want to risk offending those fine gentlemen. I tried to tell Artemis that with Julian gone, his son is our only hope of changing things."

Jasper began to protest, but Ford broke in. "Was *this* why you spent every spare penny on your brother—sent him to the best schools, pushed him into politics?"

"That's right." Hadrian softened his tone a little. Discouraged as he was by the others' response, he didn't want to destroy a friendship so recently mended. "You could say it was the reason I set out to make my fortune."

He glanced back at Ford, only to glimpse a look of deep chagrin on his partner's face. Had Ford's ambition sprung from some less noble motive?

"We must do *something,*" insisted Jasper. "Otherwise the prosperity of this century will be built on the backs of those children, as that of the last was built on the backs of slaves."

"Well said, Ashbury!" cried Blade. "You must use that line during your speech in the Commons. I fear this will be a long fight. Just think how many years it took the abolitionists to see any results."

Ford heaved a sigh. "And remember how they've been attacked by their opponents—branded as traitors and half-mad revolutionaries."

"I've been called worse than that." Blade gave a derisive chuckle. "And not in such a good cause, either. Count me in for whatever I can do."

"And me," said Ford. "I am all for progress, but not at this price."

For a moment, Hadrian did not dare speak, lest his voice break. But he soon regained his composure enough to say, "It seems Artemis was right about you lot after all."

Blade laughed and slapped him on the back. "When you've been married a bit longer, you'll discover wives are always right."

Chapter Seventeen

Had she done right to tell Hadrian's friends that he and Cousin Jasper were planning an excursion? Artemis watched anxiously for the men to return that evening.

She knew Ford had a good heart and cared about the welfare of his tenants. Surely he could not help but be moved by the plight of the young miners? And Blade was so devoted to his young son. How could he fail to picture Theo laboring under such conditions? With two such influential peers supporting him, Cousin Jasper would stand a much better chance of making headway in his efforts to bring about reform.

But how would Hadrian feel about having to reveal the tragic details of his past to more people? And what if she'd been mistaken in her belief that his friends would be willing to help? Would it create a new, deeper breach between them? And would he blame her for forcing the issue, destroying any hope of winning his wary, battered heart? Those worries plagued Artemis as she dressed for dinner.

The muted clatter of horses' hooves and the distant sound of men's voices sent her flying to the window, her heart thudding against her short stays. She glimpsed the four-wheeled trap coming up the lane, its passengers talking eagerly together. If they were still on speaking terms, surely that was a good sign.

Struggling not to let her hopes get too high, she sent her lady's maid off and stood with her bedroom door slightly ajar to watch for Hadrian. The moment she caught sight of him striding up the gallery, looking ruggedly handsome and pleased with the world, Artemis could not restrain herself.

"How did it go?" She sprang out into his path. "Is Jasper willing to help? And the others?"

He started at her sudden appearance and checked his brisk stride. Even so, he might have knocked her down had he not possessed the presence of mind to grasp her by the arms. Though Artemis managed to catch her balance, his sudden nearness made her knees weak.

"It was a bit of a shock to them," Hadrian answered. "But they all came around better than I ever hoped. Here, now—how did you know about Ford and Blade coming along? It was only supposed to be Jasper and me. You were behind it all, were you? I should have known."

"I did send them your way, hoping you might take them along," she admitted. "Are you vexed with me for interfering? I was only trying to help."

"Vexed with you?" Hadrian pulled her into an enveloping embrace. "Don't be daft. If we had more time before dinner, I'd whisk you back into that bedchamber and show you how pleased I am."

Raising one hand, he tilted her chin and kissed her. Artemis thought she'd grown accustomed to his kisses by now. But in some blissful, bewildering way, this one felt different and better than any other they had shared. Did it signify a change in his feelings toward her, even if he was not aware of it? Or had the change taken place in *her?*

Before she could unravel the mystery, Hadrian released her lips and held her out at arm's length, his gaze sweeping over her from head to toe. "This gown is new, isn't it? It becomes you even better than the wine-colored one I like so well. It's fortunate our lady guests are not the envious sort or they'd be green over how you'll outshine them tonight!"

"Nonsense!" Artemis protested as a fiery blush flared in her cheeks. "Laura and her sisters are three of the prettiest women I ever met and you told me Genia was hailed as the most beautiful Englishwoman in India. They have nothing to fear from me."

It was quite true, yet bubbles of delight fizzed inside of her at the notion that Hadrian considered her their equal in loveliness. She had only to peer into the silver mirror of his gaze to know his praise was sincere. Her misty-green gown with a gauzy overskirt was not vivid or dramatic, but it had an airy elegance that suited her to perfection. Between her enchanting new gown and Hadrian's enthusiastic approval, she could not help feeling truly beautiful.

"Now," she continued, "you must go dress for dinner. Shall I order champagne to drink a toast to our friends and the great things we hope they will achieve?"

"An excellent idea." Hadrian drew her hand to his lips for a final kiss.

Then he walked backwards down the gallery, as if he could not bear to take his eyes off her.

It seemed to Artemis their dinner that night was the most convivial so far, perhaps because they had become so well acquainted and happily reacquainted during the past fortnight. Or perhaps the trip to Stanehead had reminded the gentlemen to relish their good fortune. Whatever the reason, their table talk flowed with high-spirited wit.

After dinner they bandied about ideas on how to pass the rest of the evening. Sidney Crawford was in favor of cards while Ford called for music. Genia suggested charades while Susannah mentioned drawing shades. To everyone's surprise Jasper proposed dancing, which Hadrian was quick to endorse.

"A clever lad, this cousin of yours," Hadrian murmured to Artemis as the party retired to the music room. "I did say we must find more opportunities for you to dance."

She did not lack for opportunities that night. The ladies each took a turn playing the pianoforte for the other four couples to dance.

"You are an excellent dancer," said Hadrian a while later, as he sat on the bench beside Artemis. "Graceful and sure of your steps."

She cast him a playful smile as her fingers galloped over the keys, producing a jaunty melody. "This is the first time I have danced at such an informal gathering. Before, it was always at stuffy balls and assemblies with partners who were either reluctant or vastly uncongenial."

"I am not reluctant to dance with such a charming partner." Hadrian batted a roguish wink at her. "And I hope you do not find me vastly uncongenial these days."

It was a heady delight, flirting with such a handsome man who was already her husband. "Quite the contrary. The better I know you, the more congenial you become."

Leaning closer, he spoke just loud enough for her to hear over the music from the pianoforte. "Keep talking like that and I shall be in danger of vexing my friends. Almost as much danger as you were in earlier, when I first caught sight of you in this gown."

His words sent a dark, delicious thrill through her. The warm tickle of his breath against her ear stirred a sensual flutter in her bosom and her loins. It was fortunate she was playing a very familiar piece or she might have got into a hopeless muddle.

"What danger was that exactly?" Her breath raced faster than the music.

He gave a low husky chuckle that was like a suggestive caress. "Why, the danger that I would whisk you into your bedchamber and ravish you repeatedly while our poor guests went hungry."

That notion brought a feverish flush to her cheeks, even as it sparked an impish grin. "I'm sure Cook would have fed them sooner or later."

"Scandalous disregard for propriety and the welfare of our guests!" Hadrian whispered in mock outrage. "When did my well-bred lady become such a shameless wanton?"

At one time his jest might have offended her, making her scurry back behind the pristine barrier of her reserve. But tonight Artemis could only relish his nearness, the bantering caress of his voice and the fact that he had called her *his lady.*

Perhaps there was hope for her to make theirs a true marriage after all, if she dared to ask for what she wanted from Hadrian.

To hell with being a good host! Hadrian darted up the main staircase following a final brandy with the other gentlemen.

Blade had suggested they share a drink after the dancing concluded and the others had all agreed. That left Hadrian with little choice but to join them when he would have much preferred to retire to bed with his beautiful wife. While the others discussed plans for political and social reform, he had sipped his brandy and pretended to listen. But his thoughts had been otherwise occupied... with Artemis.

During the second week of their house party, she had blossomed before his eyes into the woman he'd sensed she was meant to be— capable, caring and confident. She had managed the whole event with such assurance, never seeking attention but not shrinking from it, either. Though he knew better than to claim all the credit for her transformation, Hadrian congratulated himself on accomplishing what he'd set out to do.

And yet there was one consequence of this change in Artemis that he had not foreseen. It made him want her more than ever. That desire now smoldered within him as he strode down the west gallery, hoping to find her still awake and ready to welcome him into her bed.

When he reached her door, he tapped softly upon it, then waited. Receiving no answer, he knocked again, a little louder. Still the door remained shut and his straining ears detected no sound from within. Perhaps she'd fallen asleep waiting for him.

He considered entering quietly and stealing into bed with her so they might enjoy an early-morning frolic. But fearing his uninvited arrival might disturb her, Hadrian continued on to his own chamber.

When he spied Artemis rising from his bed, Hadrian let out a gasp of the most delighted surprise. With only a sheet draped about her and her dark curls falling over her shoulders, she looked for all the world like a goddess come to life.

The sight of her so captivated him that he could scarcely speak. "I—I stopped by your room. I thought you'd gone to sleep. I never expected to find you here."

"How could I go to sleep after you whipped up my desire with your outrageous flirting?" Holding the sheet around her, she advanced slowly toward him with a bewitching sway in her step. "Are you sorry to find me here?"

Not long ago, if she'd asked him such a question it would have betrayed her doubts about herself and him. Tonight, clearly certain of her welcome, she meant only to stir the fire beneath the simmering cauldron of their mutual attraction.

He stepped toward her, opening his arms so she might slip into them, where she fit so well. "I'll show you how sorry I am, my Lady Temptress!"

She must have known what he had in mind, for she raised her chin and tilted her head, presenting her lips in the most unmistakable invitation to a kiss he'd ever received. Hadrian wasted no time accepting. Unable to keep his mouth from hers, he captured her lips in a hot, hungry kiss. She welcomed the thrust of his tongue, caressing it with hers.

For several blissful moments, Hadrian was aware of nothing but the silken warmth of her mouth and her intoxicating scent. Then he felt a series of deft little tugs over his chest and realized she was unfastening the buttons on his coat. He was not accustomed to having a woman undress *him*. It made for a novel and stimulating change.

He concentrated on his amorous quest of her mouth while she finished with his coat buttons and went to work on his waistcoat. When both his outer garments had come undone, she tugged the bottom of his shirt free of his breeches and slid her hands beneath it to caress his bare chest.

He greeted her rousing touch with a sharp intake of breath that muted into a rumbling purr deep in his throat. Shrugging off his coat and waistcoat, he let them fall to the floor behind him. "I must... untie this damned cravat," he panted, reaching up to tear apart the fastidiously tied fillets of linen, "before it throttles me!"

The instant it gave way, he pulled it off and hurled it to the floor. His shirt followed a moment later.

Whisking Artemis into his arms, he feathered her neck and shoulder with kisses as he carried her to the bed. Passion throbbed through his veins as he pried off his boots and dispatched his breeches. Then he turned his full attention back to his goddess, offering her the practiced homage of his lips and fingertips.

She did not merely accept his attentions with her usual bashful delight, but stoked his desire with admiring caresses.

"You are splendid," she whispered, rubbing her body against his, "beyond anything I ever imagined a man could be. You make me feel like a true love goddess...or perhaps a nymph, cavorting with her lusty satyr."

"You are trying to make me lose control of myself, with talk like that." Hadrian rolled onto his back, flipping her up to straddle his belly. "But you will not succeed. I am determined to take my time and leave us both well and truly sated."

Sated enough to last them all the years they would be apart? a plaintive little voice cried out from its prison in the deepest reaches of his heart. Ruthlessly he silenced it. He would not permit looming clouds on the horizon to mar his enjoyment of present pleasures.

Artemis seemed content with their arrangement—why should he not be?

Desperate to distract himself from any more such thoughts, Hadrian embarked upon his quest to make this a night they would both remember for a very long time.

After they had dallied together for what seemed like hours, more than once rousing each other to the brink of ecstasy before easing off to prolong their pleasure, neither could bear to hold back any longer. Arching her hips to meet him, urging him on with a soft mew of need, Artemis took the hard, potent part of him into the secret, vulnerable part of her. This time he was certain she did not suffer even the faintest twinge of pain, but shared his primal delight, culminating in wave after wave of searing, shuddering rapture.

It was he who felt the sting later when he withdrew from inside her and they were no longer one.

Hadrian had certainly kept his promise. As Artemis lay in his arms afterward, a secretive little smile hovered on her lips. She was well and truly sated. Echoes of pleasure still rippled through her body as she recalled the exquisite caresses of his lips and tongue, the gentle eagerness with which he'd fondled her breasts.

Yet, as pleasurable the sport was she had enjoyed with Hadrian, to her it represented something more. When she'd stroked his skin, run her fingers through his hair and nuzzled his neck, she'd been trying to communicate so many feelings she could not bring herself to express in words.

Her compassion for all the hardships he had suffered. Her respect for the courage, ambition and tenacity that lifted him so far above his humble beginnings. Her admiration for his efforts to right a great wrong. Her envy of his wit and zest for life. Did all those things together add up to love? If, as Artemis suspected, they did, then this passionate encounter truly had been *lovemaking*.

And if he felt as relaxed and carefree as she did just now, there could be no better time to broach the subject she'd been mulling over since her conversation with Genia.

"Hadrian," she whispered.

"Mmm?" He sounded half-asleep. Would he understand what she was about to say?

"I know when we first met, I said I didn't want you dragging Lee halfway around the world. But I've been thinking—there is probably nothing he would like better than to board a ship and sail to faraway lands, to see all sorts of strange new sights."

"What's got into you, Artemis?" Hadrian gave a drowsy chuckle. "You're talking daft. That little imp would shimmy up a mast or throw himself overboard before the ship even weighed anchor."

The thought sent chills through her. But so did the thought of Hadrian sailing out of her life. "We could rig up some sort of tether for him. Our guests all brought their children from the south to Newcastle by sea and none of them came to any harm."

"What about you, though?" It was clear from his bantering tone that Hadrian did not take her seriously. "You never sleep well in a strange bed. Imagine weeks on end in a ship's bunk. It would drive you mad."

He was right, but that was no consolation to Artemis at the moment. She did not trust her voice to argue further.

"It's not that I wouldn't enjoy having the two of you with me in Singapore." He pressed a kiss on the crown of her head. "But I have to think of Lee's welfare and yours. I'd never forgive myself if any harm came to either of you."

His words spawned a question in her thoughts and Artemis could not stop herself from asking it. "Have you never forgiven yourself for what happened to Margaret and your daughter?"

His stony silence was as good as a confession.

"That was not your fault!" She was torn between her instinct to comfort him, and the urge to shake some sense into the man. "There was nothing you could have done."

"I could have protected her." Abruptly he pulled away from

Artemis and rolled out of bed. She could hear him groping for his clothes in the darkness. "I could have kept my distance. It's not a mistake I mean to make again!"

What was he talking about? Her deeply ingrained reserve pleaded with Artemis to keep silent. After all the tragic secrets Hadrian had confided in her, this was clearly something he did not want to discuss.

"Kept your distance?" She sat up, wrapping the bedclothes around her. "Did you have the fever first? Were you contagious?"

"I wasn't ill!" Hadrian growled. "Not a day. But I was contagious for all that. People I get too close to end up dead."

His words left Artemis stunned. "Surely you cannot believe you are to blame for the Fellbank Explosion or your mother's death or Julian's."

"Why not?" Hadrian strode away. "There was a time you held me responsible for Julian's death and your brother's and sister's. Remember?"

"Of course I remember," Artemis called after him. "But I was wrong and willing to admit it. You should consider whether you might be wrong about this. Or do you mean to spend the rest of your life punishing yourself for a crime you did not commit?"

She braced herself for the door to slam and the receding thunder of Hadrian's footsteps as he stormed away. Instead, a precarious silence settled over the darkened room, like freezing rain that left a cold, brittle coat of ice over everything it touched.

Why had she not kept silent? Artemis scarcely dared breathe for fear a cowardly whimper would escape her lips. Hadrian had shown her more respect, affection and kindness than anyone ever had. Far more than she deserved, no doubt, after the damage her family had inflicted upon his and the way she had treated him in the beginning. She should have been content with that and not greedy for more than he could give.

If she had, then she might have reveled in several more months of the kind of happiness that she'd so recently enjoyed. Now, she would not have that to relish while it lasted and to savor the memory of it after he'd gone. What was worse, her selfish outburst might have cost Lee the continued company of his adored *Papapa*.

Moments of silence stretched until they ached with tension. Then Artemis heard the soft tread of approaching footsteps and felt the mattress settle under Hadrian's weight.

He heaved a sigh so deep it seemed to fill the whole room. "I know I didn't cause the explosion…or the epidemic…or the duel. But the dangers of taking you and Lee to Singapore are real enough."

Artemis could not gainsay that. And after this undeserved reprieve, she was not about to risk saying anything that might turn Hadrian against her.

He fumbled in the darkness for her hand. "I am touched that you'd be willing to put yourself and Lee at risk for me. But it is not a chance I can take. Do you understand?"

Did she? Artemis struggled with that question even as she slipped her arms around Hadrian's neck and pressed her cheek to his, so he could feel her nod.

To her, caring for people meant holding them close and doing everything in her power to give them what they needed. But Hadrian seemed to be saying he must leave her and deny her the one thing she wanted most from him *because* he cared for her.

Chapter Eighteen

What had put the mad whim of going to Singapore into Artemis's head?

Hadrian spent the final few days of the house party doing everything possible to keep from thinking about her offer. But late on the last evening, when he and the other men gathered in his study to drink their brandy, his powers of diversion failed him. While the others talked about business, politics and fishing, he fell to brooding.

His wife's gentle whisper in the darkness had caught him off guard. At first he'd thought he must be dreaming—or caught in a nightmare. It was a powerfully tempting fancy, to take his little family away with him. Show them all the wonders of the wide world. Have them to come home to after a long day's work. Watch Lee learn and grow.

But that's all it was—a fancy.

The truth was what he'd forced himself to remember and to remind Artemis. The likelihood of Lee falling overboard and drowning. Their ship attacked by pirates or wrecked by a violent storm. Artemis catching some fatal fever. How could she expect him to consider a course of action so fraught with danger?

And why did she want to go? Did she think he needed her so desperately that he could not manage without her? The way her family had needed her? Well, he didn't! Her family's need for Artemis had been entirely selfish—taking everything she'd so capably provided without sparing a thought for *her* needs. He was not about to place her in jeopardy, no matter how much he cherished her company.

Hearing his wife's name suddenly spoken jarred Hadrian back to his friends' conversation.

"I have known Artemis since we were children," said Ford, "but I never heard her laugh until the other day when we were larking about over the pall-mall wickets. You know, my grandmother once hoped I'd marry her."

"You and Artemis?" Hadrian scowled at his partner. "Absurd!" The thought of any other man married to Artemis made his jaw clench and his fists itch.

"That's what I thought." Ford shrugged. "Though she was younger than me and quite pretty, she seemed almost like a mother to Leander and Daphne. Not to my taste at all."

Blade and Sidney sputtered with laughter.

"Then you were a damned young fool," Hadrian growled. Much as he disliked the idea of Artemis with another man, he resented Ford's casual dismissal of her charms.

"My cousin certainly was different from other young ladies." Jasper drained the last of his brandy. "She was the only one who didn't make me feel as if I had two left feet, ten thumbs and a tied tongue."

"The *only* one?" asked Blade with a sly grin.

"Yes…well…" Jasper ducked his head. "Until very recently, I mean."

Ford and Sidney exchanged a knowing look, as if placing a silent wager on how soon Lord Ashbury would join their close-knit family circle.

"Be that as it may," Jasper persisted, "I always thought it a shame that none of the family ever paid Artemis much heed, other than expecting her to look after them. I am delighted to see her so happy with you, Hadrian. I often thought she deserved a husband and family who adore her."

Jasper's kindly meant words drove a stab of guilt deep into Hadrian. That *was* what Artemis deserved…but could never have from him. And since he had chained her in the bonds of matrimony, she would never have the opportunity to find a man capable of cherishing her without putting her in danger.

"Adore?" He gave a dismissive grunt that did not sound all that convincing, even to him. "I agree she is a fine woman and we get on well together. But we married for the sake of our nephew. It was never meant to be a love match."

"It may not have meant to be—" Blade wore an insufferably smug grin "—but somewhere along the road your feelings changed, didn't they?"

Hadrian would rather have had a blacksmith pull his teeth than submit to this good-natured ragging on such a private subject. "I cannot deny we've put our differences behind us and grown rather close."

"Rather close?" Blade let out a whoop of laughter that Hadrian longed to cram back down his throat. He raised his glass toward Jasper. "Our young friend may not have much experience in such matters, but I reckon he's struck pretty near the mark. You adore the woman. Admit it. You're besotted with her."

"They are right, old fellow," Ford weighed in. "You love your wife. It's as plain as the scowl on your face! No need to be ashamed of it. Blade, Sidney and I love our wives and it hasn't done us a bit of harm."

"Not yet, perhaps." Hadrian slammed down his glass and stalked toward the door. "But let some harm come to them, then see what you have to say about it!"

A few days after their guests departed, Artemis sat at her dressing table one evening, wishing Genia and Laura were still there so she could seek their advice. Though they'd promised to write and had invited her to come south for a visit, those were no substitute for their presence—the camaraderie, advice and support they'd offered. Never had she needed those things more.

That morning, after wakening with a queasy stomach for the third day in a row, she'd consulted her calendar and realized something she'd been too busy to notice during the house party. For the first time in over ten years, her monthly courses were more than a month late. She was going to have a baby!

The prospect of bearing Hadrian's child brought a rush of intense contradictory emotions. Indeed, all her emotions seemed more intense of late. Was that an effect of her condition or was it Hadrian's fault for breaking through her reserve and making her care so deeply for him?

One minute she was elated at the thought of bearing a child who would need her and love her in the innocent, uncomplicated way Lee did. A child who would be like a brother or sister for her beloved nephew, giving him a taste of the closeness she'd shared with Leander and Daphne. A child she might not have to share with anyone else—not even its father.

Part of her was attracted by that thought. It was everything she'd once dreamed of and more—two dear children, a comfortable home in which to raise them and the means to give them every possible advantage. And no one to interfere or tell her how best to bring them up. But now that she had come to know and love Hadrian, her old dream no longer seemed so idyllic.

Would the pure and uncomplicated love of her little ones be enough, or would she yearn for the complex passion and powerful intimacy she had known with a man? She would miss watching him play with them, guide them and love them in a different way than she did—but a way she sensed they needed. She would miss watching them grow with him, talking over all their small doings, sharing the pride in their accomplishments.

And when she thought of how much Hadrian would miss by being so far away, knowing the children only through a yearly letter, it made her heart ache for him. He had lost two families already. Would those tragedies compel him to turn his back on a third? She feared it might.

She had sensed a growing closeness to him in the past weeks, as they'd fit so well into the company of other happily married couples—until she had made the mistake of asking him to take her and Lee to Singapore. From that moment, a subtle but distressing coolness had crept into their relationship, like the first hint of autumn frost after a sun-drenched summer. Though Hadrian was as kind and attentive as ever in some ways, she felt a distance widening between them and did not know how to bridge that gulf. She was afraid even to try, fearing she might do or say the wrong thing and make matters worse.

She sought comfort in the reassurances of her new friends.

"Of course he cares for you," Laura insisted when Artemis had reluctantly confided in her. "That's why he would do anything to protect you. Ford was just the same when he believed he'd been tainted by scandal. He tried to drive me away…for my own good, of course."

"Men." Genia shook her head. "They are such dear, exasperating creatures, always certain they're the only ones who know what is best for us."

She, Laura and Belinda all went on to tell of risks taken and obstacles overcome in their quests for lasting happiness with the men they loved. Though their stories inspired her admiration, Artemis feared she did not have their courage.

"Of course you do." Laura gave her hand a heartening squeeze. "You have been through such a lot, yet still carried on taking care of everyone else, trying to make them happy. Is it not time you put as much courage and effort into securing your own happiness?"

Was it not, indeed? Artemis asked her reflection in the glass. Thanks to Hadrian, she'd gained new confidence in herself—confidence in her looks, her abilities and her judgment. She must not let him undermine her newfound sense that she was worthy of love, even when she did not cater to every whim of those she cared for. She felt certain that was the last thing he would want.

"Will you be wanting to dress for dinner this evening, ma'am?" asked her lady's maid. "With all the guests gone and only you and the master dining?"

Artemis thought for a moment. She had more than just herself to fight for. There was Lee and her unborn child and Hadrian, too. "I believe I will, Emily. The wine-colored taffeta, I think. Can you dress my hair the way you did the first evening I wore it? Mr. Northmore admired it very much."

But her effort to attract Hadrian's attention did not work. At dinner that evening he gave no sign of noticing her gown or her hair, but sat eating in preoccupied silence. During the house party, he'd taken up the host's customary place at the head of the table. Since then, he had not returned to his prior custom of sitting beside Artemis. It was as if his heart and mind had already sailed off to Singapore, leaving behind a handsome but lifeless statue in his place.

If this was all their marriage would be for the next three months, what did she have to lose by confronting him? Emboldened by that thought, Artemis picked up her plate and silverware. Marching to his end of the table, she sat on the chair to his right.

"There." She echoed the explanation he'd given the first time he'd come to sit beside her. "Now we won't need to shout ourselves hoarse to carry on a conversation. Not that we've done much talking of late."

Hadrian shot her a wary look. "I've had a lot on my mind."

"If I offer a penny for your thoughts," she asked under cover of a falsely bright smile, "will you drive me a harder bargain?"

"I'm an honest merchant." A welcome glimmer of warmth crept back into his eyes. "I wouldn't want to overcharge you. I was only thinking I must go to Newcastle for a few days on business. I spoke to Ford about opening a branch of Vindicara here in the north and he reckons it's a fine idea."

Why did she get the uneasy feeling there was something more he was keeping from her?

That vague suspicion fled her mind when she realized Hadrian had given her a perfect opening to broach the subject that had occupied her thoughts for some time. "If you have a branch of the company here, won't you need someone to manage it?"

Hadrian nodded. "I'll hire someone. I plan to make enquiries while I'm in town."

"What sort of person would you be looking for?" Artemis picked up her fork and took a bite of her dinner, to make it appear as if her question was only casual mealtime conversation.

Hadrian did not seem to guess it might be anything else. "Somebody who knows both the East Indies trade and northern industries for a start. He must be able to get a good day's work out of the men under him and show some initiative. If he does a good enough job, we might consider taking him on as a partner."

"You could be describing yourself." Artemis raced on before Hadrian could protest. "Wouldn't *you* be the perfect man to run a northern branch of Vindicara?"

"I might..." Hadrian bolted a mouthful of wine "...but I can't very well be in two places at once, can I?"

"Then why not stay in the one place where you're needed most— here, with Lee and me?" It was on the tip of her tongue to mention the baby. But she could not be certain whether it would persuade him to stay or drive him away.

"You're not on about that again?" he muttered. "I thought we agreed."

"I agreed not to badger you about taking us to Singapore." Artemis reached for his hand and clung to it when he tried to pull away. "I understand why you object to that. But why could you not stay here? It would not put Lee and me in any danger. And it would keep you *out* of danger. If you go, I shall worry all the time about some harm coming to you."

"No harm ever comes to me." He squeezed her fingers. "Only to the people around me, the ones I care for."

The next instant he ripped his hand from her grasp and pushed his chair away from the table. Its feet scraped harshly against the floor as he rose and backed away from her. "I *must* return to Singapore, Artemis. You've known all along that was my intention. What makes you want me to change my plans now?"

Though she longed to go to him, to hold him so tightly he would never break free, Artemis stayed in her chair. If she pursued him, he would flee. But if she kept her distance, perhaps she could hold him with her words and make him understand.

"I want you to change your plans because I have changed and so have you. We are not the same people we were when we first met and our feelings for one another are not what they were then."

Should she tell him what else would change by next spring? Surely a man so desperate to continue the Northmore line would want to be on hand for the birth of his child. What more compelling reason could she give him to alter his plans? But if she did and if he stayed, she would always be haunted by the fear that his feelings for her had not been enough to hold him.

"If it is a matter of your fortune," she continued, "what does that signify compared to your happiness and mine and Lee's? Edenhall is a lovely house and it has become even more of a home to me than Bramberley. But it is not the portico or the rooms or the grounds that make it so. It is the three of us being here together! Playing in the nursery, going for walks in the garden, taking an outing to Vindicara. I would be happier in a tumbledown pit cottage with you and Lee to cook and care for than I could ever be in this fine house with you thousands of miles away. If that is not what you want, too, you should never have made me love you!"

There it was, that wonderful, perilous word, spoken aloud at last after being locked in her heart for weeks like a precious child growing inside her, waiting to be born. Like a newborn infant, it was so fragile and vulnerable, exposed to the cold, harsh world outside. But from the look of anguish in Hadrian's eyes, it might have been a full-grown warrior, armed to slay him.

"No," he choked out. "I should not. I should have left you alone as you should have left me. And I would have, I swear, if you'd been any other woman. I would have kept you at arm's length and never taken the chance of something like this happening. But, with all the differences between us, and all the strife between our families, I was certain you would be the last woman in the world I'd ever have to fear that from."

"You *fear* someone loving you?" Artemis struggled to hold together the tattered shreds of her composure. "Why in heaven should you fear that? I have spent my whole life craving it. I hoped perhaps I had found it at last. It seems I was mistaken."

"The mistake was mine," Hadrian confessed in a hoarse voice as he headed for the door. "Forgive me."

It had been bad enough to let himself fall in love with Artemis. As he rode to Newcastle, Hadrian faced the harsh tribunal of his conscience. To hear from her own lips that he'd encouraged her to fall in love with him, when he had no business doing anything of the kind, was more than he could bear.

He trotted out a dozen excuses in his defense, each more lame than the last.

He'd meant to help Artemis, to make her realize what a beautiful, desirable woman she was. He'd counted on her being too sensible to lose her heart to a man she knew would eventually sail out of her life. But that responsibility should never have rested with her. He was the one who'd known what was at stake. He should never have taken the chance.

He'd thought that what she felt for him and he for her was only passionate attraction…and mutual understanding…and the enjoyment of one another's company... and... How could he have been so blind not to recognize love when he saw it?

Upon reaching the city, he strove to put the matter out of his mind and concentrate on what he'd come to do. He would lay the groundwork for a branch of his company and interview the women who'd answered his newspaper notice in order to find a suitable mistress for Simon Grimshaw.

But putting Artemis out of his mind was not so easily done. Every warehouse he inspected, and every merchant he spoke with, made him more and more eager to stay here and build a business, perhaps invest in other industries, like the new locomotive engines that were all the talk.

Every time he made enquiries about a potential manager for the branch, he ended up comparing the fellow unfavorably with himself. Artemis had been right, as she was so often—he would be the perfect man for the job.

When it came time to interview the women who wanted to become Simon's mistress, Hadrian found himself comparing each of them with his wife.

One or two were attractive enough, though in a conventional, obvious way that could not hold a candle to the luminous grace of Artemis. For all that, they were so vain about their looks that Hadrian feared they might stoop to entertaining other men behind his partner's back. Having suffered an unfaithful wife, the last thing Simon needed was an unfaithful mistress.

Most of them jabbered on without saying a single clever or interesting word. It made him recall all the conversations he and Artemis had shared about history and books and their lives. Even when they'd argued, she had challenged him to see things in new ways.

But his plan to return to Singapore was one he could not permit her to make him question. Could he?

"Come in," he called in a dispirited voice when the final applicant knocked on his door. If she was no better than the rest, he was not certain what he'd do.

The door swung open, admitting a fresh-faced lass with red-gold hair and a wholesome country look about her.

"Miss Bethan Conway?" He rose, waving her toward an empty chair opposite his. "It is a pleasure to meet you. My name is Hadrian Northmore. I'm acting on behalf of my partner, Simon Grimshaw, to find him a suitable…companion."

Miss Conway bobbed a curtsy and settled onto the chair. Perhaps because she was his last hope and her looks reminded him vaguely of Margaret, he felt more nervous about interviewing her than he had the others.

"As I mentioned in my newspaper notice, Mr. Grimshaw resides in Singapore."

Her lips spread into a wide smile. "Yes, Singapore."

"You've heard of it, then?" Two of the other applicants had not. When he'd informed them it was between India and China, they'd decided the situation would not suit them after all. "You know where it is?"

"Of course, sir." She sounded surprised by the question, as if anyone should know.

Her short and direct answers were a refreshing change from the flighty chatterboxes before her.

"And you would be prepared to go to Singapore, even though it would require a voyage of many weeks?"

"Yes, sir!"

She certainly sounded eager. Perhaps she'd read about Singapore in the newspapers and taken a fancy to the place. Miss Conway seemed to have a cheerful, obliging disposition. That would be good for Simon, who had turned rather severe since the troubles with his late wife.

"I reckon you'll suit Mr. Grimshaw very well, Miss Conway." Hadrian extended his hand. "The position is yours if you want it."

"Oh, yes!" She wrung his hand with surprising strength. "Thank you, sir!"

"Thank *you,* Miss Conway. You have no idea the trouble you've saved me." He took out a handful of gold guineas. "This should cover whatever kit you'll need for the voyage. I'd suggest you have a number of serviceable, lightweight gowns made up."

Her gray-green eyes widened as he dropped the coins into her hands. "Thank you, sir!"

Hadrian handed her a card with the name of a respectable inn near the docks. "Meet me at this place on the third of January."

"Yes, sir." Miss Conway stuffed the card and the money into her reticule. "The third of January."

"That's right. I shall look forward to seeing you then." Hadrian rose and bowed. "Good day, Miss Conway."

She jumped from her chair with a delighted but vaguely bewildered look, as if she could not believe her good fortune. "Good day, sir!"

Without another word she rushed off, leaving Hadrian to sink back onto his chair and heave a sigh. He wished *he* were as eager to get back to Singapore as Bethan Conway.

She seemed a pleasant, respectable young woman, better suited to be a wife than a hired mistress. Perhaps Simon would recognize that, too, and make an honest woman of her. Hadrian hoped so, for Simon's sake and his little daughter's. The child's *amah* was devoted to her, but that could not make up for the lack of a mother's love… and a father's.

Though Simon was too decent a fellow to intentionally turn his back on his own child, the little girl's uncanny resemblance to her beautiful, wayward mother made it impossible for him to look at her without stirring painful memories. Unable to glimpse the least likeness to himself, Simon could be forgiven for doubting he had sired the child in the first place.

Hadrian hoped Miss Conway might persuade his partner to give marriage another try. Just because one woman had betrayed him did not give Simon grounds to mistrust the entire sex and declare he would never wed again. It would not be an easy job convincing him, though. As Hadrian had told Artemis, his partner had a deep aversion to risk.

Was he any better? a rebellious part of Hadrian demanded. Was it any more reasonable to believe that because he had lost so many loved ones in the past, he was doomed to lose anyone he let himself care for? Reason told him it was absurd. But there was a place inside him, deeper than reason or discretion, black as a mine pit, ruled by sensation, raw instinct and gnawing fear. A dark vein of despair ran through that place, fueling his fatalism.

With all that was left of his heart, he yearned to stay in the land of his birth, after so many years of exile. He wished he could love Artemis and his nephew as they deserved and be everything they needed. But it was for their sake, *because* he loved them so much, that he dared not tempt the hand of Fate to strike them.

Was he truly acting out of concern for Artemis, trying to protect her? Or out of cowardice, fearing the devastation of losing her?

Chapter Nineteen

"Your uncle said the most foolish things before he went away." Artemis pressed her cheek to her nephew's silky hair as she sat in the nursery rocking chair with him on her lap. "He said he'd made a mistake in making me love him. Can you imagine? And he thought I could never love him because there are so many differences between us."

Lee fussed a little, popping his thumb out of his mouth to whine, "Papapa?"

"Whisht, now!" Artemis tried to soothe him with the word Hadrian often used. "I know you miss Papapa. So do I. We may seem as different as two people can be in background and situation. But beneath all those outward trappings, we are very much alike. We are both interested in history and books. Our families matter a great deal to us and we take our responsibilities to them very seriously. We are both rather proud and neither of us gives our affections easily. But when we do—"

"Papapa," said Lee again in a more demanding tone.

"He's only gone to Newcastle." Artemis patted her nephew's back. "Whatever he may say to the contrary, I know you will miss him terribly if he sails off to Singapore. I wish I knew how to persuade him to stay, for all our sakes."

Lee's eyelids were starting to droop, but he struggled to resist sleep. Did he think Hadrian might come home while he was napping? "Papapa. La-eeoo."

"I know you love Papapa," Artemis whispered. "Whether he says so or not, he loves you, too. There is nothing in the world he would not do for you. He is so afraid of losing you and me through some calamity, he would rather lose us by sailing away to the other side of the world."

Was she being selfish, asking Hadrian to stay and live with the constant fear that she and Lee would be taken from him? And what if something did happen to one or both of them? There were so many illnesses that afflicted small children. Many women died in childbirth or afterward of milk fever. The thought of dying troubled Artemis less for her own sake, than for Hadrian's and Lee's and her baby's.

If only Laura and Genia were still there to offer wise advice and staunch support. Artemis felt desperately in need of both. Perhaps one of her friends had written to her.

She glanced down to see that Lee had fallen fast sleep, like a proper little Northmore. He did not stir when she carried him to his cot.

Once he was resting there, Artemis hurried downstairs in search of Mrs. Matlock. She found the housekeeper just outside Hadrian's study.

"Has the post come yet, Mrs. Matlock?"

The housekeeper cast a skittish glance over her shoulder. "Not long ago, ma'am. I just put the master's correspondence on his writing table."

Artemis wondered why such a simple question appeared to ruffle the woman's usual brisk composure. "Were there any letters for me from Lady Kingsfold or the Countess?"

"I don't believe so, ma'am." Again Mrs. Matlock gave a furtive look, as if something were bothering her conscience.

"You don't sound very certain." Artemis peered around her into

Hadrian's study. Was the housekeeper trying to hide something? "Are there or not?"

"One letter was in a woman's hand." Mrs. Matlock sounded as if the information were being extracted from her by torture. "But it came addressed to the master."

"Perhaps Lord and Lady Kingsfold both wrote to us and her ladyship addressed the letter." That made sense. Artemis could not wait to read it. Laura's kindly good sense might help her decide what to do. "I'll have a look."

She slipped past the housekeeper and headed for Hadrian's writing table.

"I'm certain the writing is not her ladyship's." There could be no mistaking the alarm in Mrs. Matlock's voice. "Let it be, ma'am... please. I fear the master wouldn't like you reading his post."

"Why should he mind?" Artemis extracted a pair of folded, sealed letters from under Hadrian's heavy pewter inkwell. "Unless he has something to hide. We both know Mr. Northmore is far too honorable for..."

Her voice trailed off as she stared at the second letter. Not only was it addressed in a woman's hand, the faint but unmistakable scent of eau de cologne rose from the paper. The smell revived her morning nausea. It also revived the memory of Hadrian thrusting several letters into the top drawer of his writing desk.

When Artemis could open her mouth without fear of vomiting, she looked up at the housekeeper with a reproachful stare. "This is not the first such letter my husband has received, is it?"

Mrs. Matlock shook her head. "There were several others, perhaps a dozen, all within a fortnight. But that was over a month ago and nothing more until today. I hoped he might have thought better of it. He didn't go to any great effort to hide what he was doing. I thought you must know, but you don't, do you?"

Know what? Artemis feared her brain would burst from struggling to make sense of all this in a way that would not break her heart. There'd been one or two incidents that had given her passing qualms of suspicion. They had come and gone so quickly she could not recall the particulars, just the vague sense that something was not right.

With a violent tug, she jerked open the top drawer of Hadrian's writing table and pulled out every piece of paper she could lay her hands on. There were some notes about Sunday schools for children in mining communities, the draft of a letter to the local Members of Parliament, a note from his solicitor about changes to his will, but no other letters from women. Then her eyes fell upon a scrap of newsprint.

It was a notice of employment for a personal companion—a healthy woman between the ages of twenty and thirty to go to Singapore, all expenses paid, generous terms offered. Interested parties were instructed to write Mr. Hadrian Northmore for particulars.

Personal companion, indeed. A *mistress*—that's what Hadrian was looking for. Was that the true reason he'd gone to Newcastle—to hire a young woman to accompany him back to Singapore? No wonder he'd refused her offer to go with him and her plea for him to stay.

Artemis sank onto Hadrian's writing chair, assailed by memories of their disastrous wedding night when she had coldly advised him to find some strumpet to gratify his desires. Had he taken her at her word, even after she'd surrendered her body and heart to him? At the moment, her heart felt as if he'd ripped it from her chest and flayed it raw.

"Such goings-on," the housekeeper muttered in a tone that mingled exasperated censure with grim sympathy. "Eliza Northmore would turn in her grave. She raised those boys proper, even after they went away to Fellbank. I know rich folk have their own ways and all, but..."

Though Mrs. Matlock's words fell on her ears, it was Charles Nugent's scathing abuse that echoed in Artemis's heart—*The only way I could stand being wed to such a pallid, scrawny milk-and-*

water miss would be to engage a plump, pretty mistress at the earliest opportunity. It appeared her husband shared that sentiment.

Then why had he gone to such lengths to persuade her of his passionate admiration and entice her to consummate their marriage? Another qualm of nausea reminded Artemis of the tiny life growing inside her. Was that all Hadrian had wanted her for—a brood sow on which to beget another Northmore heir? She'd longed for him to need her, but not for that alone. Even when Charles Nugent had denounced her so cruelly, she had not felt so worthless. An anguished sob rose in her throat and a tear as hot and caustic as acid trickled down her cheek.

"Come away from here and let me fetch you a cup of tea." The housekeeper's unusually gentle voice called Artemis back from the brink of despair. "I know you and I got off on the wrong foot at first, but you deserve better than this from him."

Perhaps Hadrian had not given her what she longed for from him, Artemis reflected, but he'd helped her discover something precious within herself. The assurance that she deserved to be loved, not contingent upon what she did, but because of who she was. If she truly believed that, she could not allow his betrayal to take it away from her.

"You're right, Mrs. Matlock." Slowly she rose, like a newborn filly testing her legs. But when she got them under her, they held firm. "I *do* deserve better."

It rained all the while Hadrian was in Newcastle. Thick clouds had shrouded the northern sky, mirroring the doubts and fears in his mind. The wind had sighed around the eaves of his inn at night like a broken-hearted lover. Raindrops had trickled down windowpanes, the way his tears might have fallen if he'd ever been able to weep for his lost loved ones.

Now as he rode home over muddy, rutted lanes, his heart ached with longing for Artemis and Lee, as if he'd already lost them, too. But he hadn't lost them yet—at least he hoped he hadn't. The tragedies that had twice robbed him of his family were not his fault. Indeed, one of the worst things about both was that there'd been nothing he could do to prevent them. This time would be different.

The rain ceased and the clouds began to disperse. Shafts of golden sunshine burst through, striking raindrops that clung to leaves and branches, giving the world a fresh, clean shimmer.

The moment he reached the stable yard at Edenhall, Hadrian sprang from his saddle and rifled his pack for an item that had caught his eye in a shop window. By the time he found it, the stable boy had come running to attend his horse.

"If ye're looking for missus and the wee lad—" the young fellow pointed toward the garden "—I spied them out walking not long ago."

Hadrian nodded and smiled. "I'm obliged to you for saving me the trouble of hunting them down."

Catching the sound of his nephew's infectious laughter in the distance, he followed it and soon found them.

Lee spotted him before Artemis did. Wriggling out of his aunt's grasp, he pelted toward Hadrian. "Papapa! Papapa!"

"That's right, Papapa's home." Hadrian swung the child up into his arms. "I hope you were a good boy for your auntie while I was gone. I brought you a present from Newcastle—a boat with wheels and a string so you can pull it around, just like your friend Theo had when he was here."

Lee gave a shriek of glee when he saw the toy, but he seemed even more delighted to have his uncle home. Hadrian returned the sentiment. He bounced and swung the child around, making comical faces and strange noises until Lee could scarcely catch his breath for giggling.

"There, now." Hadrian held his nephew to his shoulder and rubbed his back to calm him down. "I mustn't get you too wound up to eat your supper or your auntie will have my head."

He risked a glance at Artemis, wondering if she would have his head. Would he blame her if she did?

She started when their eyes met, but quickly composed herself. "Welcome home. I trust you accomplished everything you wanted in the city."

Though her lips curved in a faint smile, she was clearly not as happy to see him as he was to see her. It was as if, in his absence, Artemis had reverted to the cool, formidable lady she'd been when they first met.

"It was a very productive few days." He moved toward her, hoping a kiss might thaw the frost in her manner.

But Artemis averted her face and took a quick step backward. "Were you able to find someone suitable for the position?"

"To manage the northern branch, you mean?" He shook his head. "I didn't meet anyone who quite fit the bill. I believe you were right about who would be best suited for the job. But I don't want to talk about business now. How have *you* been? I thought about you a great deal while I was away and the things you said."

"Did you?" she replied in a brisk, biting tone. "I am surprised you had the time or the inclination with so many more agreeable things to occupy you."

Hadrian tried to defuse the growing tension by addressing Lee. "You know, lad, I get the feeling there's something troubling your auntie. Has she told *you* what it is?"

"Ee-oo!" echoed Lee.

"Me?" Hadrian gave an uneasy chuckle. "I was afraid of that. Tell her I'm sorry for what I've done to vex her. I'd like to make it up to her if she'll let me."

He hoped an appeal through their nephew might soften her resistance. Instead it seemed to have the opposite effect.

"I will thank you not to drag the poor child into the middle of this sordid business." Snatching Lee out of Hadrian's arms, she set the lad on his sturdy little feet and gave him his toy boat to play with.

Then she turned her attention back to Hadrian. A fierce amethyst spark flashed in the depths of her eyes. "You need not pretend to care how I feel. I know the true reason you went to Newcastle. A letter arrived while you were away, from another applicant for the position you posted in the newspapers."

The position he'd posted? She must have found out he was trying to hire a mistress and assumed the woman was for his own amusement. "Artemis, you mustn't fret on that account. I can explain, pet."

"I am not your pet!" she bristled, wrapping her arms around her slender torso. "And I don't want your...explanations. Perhaps I have no right to complain, since I told you on our wedding night to get yourself a mistress. But I will not stand to be treated like a fool!"

"A fool? But I never—"

Artemis was clearly in no mood to listen. "If you never wanted a real marriage with me, you should have said so. Instead you made me feel sorry for you by pretending to believe you were under some sort of curse. Claiming you must stay away from Lee and me for *our* protection, when all the time you were methodically going about hiring a mistress under my very nose. You did not even try to hide it from the servants!"

He wanted to explain, if she'd let him get a word in. But stubborn pride froze his tongue. How could Artemis think so ill of him after the closeness they'd shared and everything he had confided in her? Why should he grovel to a woman who thought of him as an unfeeling upstart, unworthy of her trust?

His fears made one last desperate appeal. If he still wanted to return to Singapore, it would be a great deal easier to face living without Artemis if he could convince himself she despised him.

But how could he believe it after he'd come to know her so well? Beneath her proud antagonism, he glimpsed the true source of her anguish and uncertainty. It was not his integrity she doubted, but her capacity to inspire and keep his love. Could he blame her after the way she'd been treated in the past and his recent intention to desert her?

He managed to untie his tongue and was about to speak when Artemis suddenly looked around, her splendid eyes widening in alarm. "Lee! Good God, where is he?"

Hadrian swept a glance around the grassy nook, bounded by hedges and shrubs. Only an instant ago, Lee had been happily pulling his toy boat in circles around his aunt and uncle, paying no heed to their sharp exchanges. Now there was no sign of him.

A stunning blow seemed to catch Hadrian from out of nowhere. Like the sudden rumble and shaking of his family's cottage, and Margaret's first mention that the baby seemed unwell—was it going to happen again? Was the life Artemis had coaxed him to rebuild about to crash down around him?

Artemis struggled to breathe.

"He was just here." She dashed to the nearest hedge and looked behind it while Hadrian ran to check behind a pair of rhododendrons. "I only took my eyes off him for a second. I should never have made you set him down. If any harm comes to him…"

She knew this was what Hadrian had feared—what he'd been trying to spare her and himself. Whatever his plans to take a mistress, he had not deceived her about his true reason for wanting to keep his distance from her and Lee.

"No harm will come to him." Hadrian strode to her side and clutched her hand in a grip as fierce as his resolve. "We will find him and all will be well. I'll head down toward the beck—that's the greatest danger and he may have taken a notion to sail that boat of his."

His urgent but positive tone restored her shaken composure. "I'll call the servants out to look for him and tell the groom to bring his dog."

Raising her hand to his lips, Hadrian pressed a swift, ardent kiss upon it that Artemis took as a promise. Whatever happened, he would not let it destroy the bond between them.

The next instant he strode away, calling, "Lee, where are you? Lee, come to Papapa!"

As she lifted the hem of her gown and raced toward the stables, she heard Hadrian in the distance, trumpeting like an elephant and gibbering like a monkey. Had he gone mad?

Then she heard another sound that ripped a sob from her throat and brought tears to her eyes—Lee's sweet, bubbling laughter.

Spinning about in midstep, she raced in the direction of the sound, wading through herbaceous borders, dodging around shrubs, catching her gown on rose brambles. Then suddenly, she rounded a hedge and there he was, without a scratch on him, still clutching the string of his boat and laughing at his uncle's comical animal noises.

"Thank God!" She swooped down on Lee, gathering him into her arms, laughing and sobbing with relief.

Hadrian appeared an instant later and wrapped his arms around both of them. "Still laughing are you, naughty little monkey? You think this is a fine game, making your poor auntie and uncle frantic."

As he gave the child a cheerful scolding, his voice sounded husky. And when Artemis grazed his cheek with her lips, she tasted tears that were not hers.

"Dearest!" she crooned. "Angel!" She meant those endearments for both of them.

For it was not only Lee who'd been delivered from harm, but all of them, including the tiny flicker of new life within her. During those brief, terrifying moments, when their future had seemed under threat, she'd realized nothing meant more to her. And there was nothing she would let stand in the way of their happiness. Not her doubts, nor Hadrian's fears, nor their pride.

Drained by their alarm and outburst of intense emotion, she and Hadrian sank onto the grass, their arms still entwined around each other.

"Dry your eyes, pet." Hadrian pulled out a handkerchief and

offered it to Artemis. "You'll have no more reason to weep today, I promise you. About this mistress nonsense—"

"You needn't explain." Artemis wiped her eyes. "I know love and faithfulness were never part of our original bargain, but you gave me so much more than you ever promised."

"You exceeded our bargain, too, pet." A silvery mist rose in his eyes, which glowed with love. "Somehow you eased the burden of my past and leeched the poison from my wounds. You brought back to life the parts of me I thought had died with each member of my family. It is a debt I can never begin to repay."

Artemis shook her head. "Not a debt. It was a gift that brought me happiness and fulfillment in the giving. We *can* make each other happy, Hadrian. I know we can, if only you would let us try."

"I never doubted that." He raised a hand to stroke her cheek. "It was the price I might pay in heartbreak if I lost you that made a coward of me. But I've come to realize whatever time we have together will be worth even that."

He'd promised she would have no further cause to weep, but he was wrong. His words brought fresh tears to her eyes, but they were happy tears. Cleansing tears. Like welcome rain on drought-parched fields.

Lee seemed to sense something momentous was passing between the two people who loved him most. He did not make a sound, or squirm to escape their embrace, but snuggled into it with a contented sigh.

"Do you remember," murmured Hadrian, "when I told you I had a commission to perform for my partner, Simon Grimshaw?"

Though she did not understand why he'd changed the subject, Artemis nodded. She recalled everything from the night he'd first come to her bed—every look, every touch, every word.

"Simon asked me to fetch him back a mistress from England. He was badly used by his late wife and wants nothing more to do with marriage. I reckon it was a daft way to go about finding one, putting a notice in the papers, as if I was hiring a cook or a laborer.

I didn't tell you about it because I thought you wouldn't approve. But I didn't try to hide it, either, because it never occurred to me how my actions might look."

A hiccough of laughter bubbled out of Artemis. The world suddenly looked brighter, its colors more vivid, as if her tears had washed away a film of dust from her eyes…and from her heart.

"As for me…" Hadrian caressed her tear-streaked face with his eyes "…there is only one mistress I will ever want. Only one woman I will ever love. That is the one I'm married to."

Even as her heart swelled so full of joy Artemis feared it would burst, one final foreboding chilled her. Hadrian loved her and she loved him. That changed many things, but not everything.

"Then you will take us with you to Singapore?" she whispered, half-afraid to ask.

Hadrian shook his head. "I shall have to find someone to escort Simon's mistress to Singapore, because I have no intention of leaving you and Lee. I mean to stay here, do everything I can to help the young mine workers and start up a new branch of Vindicara. Mind you, I do not expect to work the long hours I once did. I have found a great many pleasanter ways to spend my time."

Taking Hadrian's hand, Artemis slipped it behind Lee to rest against her belly. Now she had no qualms about sharing her happy news with him. "By next spring, we should have one more thing to keep us both happily occupied."

A look of dumbfounded delight warmed Hadrian's features as he caressed her taut, subtly rounded belly. When he recovered his voice at last, it was husky with emotion. "I hope it will be the first of many."

As he inclined his head for a kiss that would seal their new commitment to one another and to the family their love would create and nurture, Artemis whispered, "Bless all Northmores!"

Epilogue

Newcastle, England—January 1825

"That's it, then. They're off." From the quayside, Hadrian waved toward the brig *Godspeed* easing out of the Tyne channel.

From the ship's taffrail, four half-grown boys and a young woman waved back.

Hadrian turned toward Artemis, who stood by his side, swathed in a fur-trimmed wrap that modestly concealed her growing belly. "That was a fine idea you had about hiring those lads from the mines. I reckon Simon will find plenty of work for them in Singapore. In the meantime, they can keep an eye on Miss Conway during the voyage out and she can look after them."

"I hope so," murmured Artemis, her delicate brow furrowed as she gazed toward the departing ship.

"What's the matter, pet?" Hadrian slipped a protective arm around her waist. "Have you caught a chill? I knew I shouldn't have let you persuade me to bring you to town in this cold weather."

With the passing weeks of autumn, his happiness and contentment had ripened. He'd worked hard to banish the fears that might mar his enjoyment of each new day with his family. Though he was getting better, it did not take much to make him fret over their well-being.

"This trip has not done me the least harm." Artemis cast him a fond smile. "I was just thinking about Bethan Conway."

"What about her?" Though his wife's words reassured him, he still kept his arm clasped around her. "Is that why you insisted on coming to town? Were you afraid I'd be tempted to sail off to Singapore with Miss Conway?"

"Don't be silly." She pressed against him, making Hadrian impatient for bedtime, which was still far too many hours away. "You are the most devoted husband I could wish for. I would trust you on a ship full of women. I insisted on coming to town because this may be our last opportunity to enjoy a little honeymoon off by ourselves for a while. And because I wanted to talk to Miss Conway before she sailed. I don't much care for the idea of sending a young woman halfway around the world to become the mistress of a man she's never met. I wanted to make certain she knows what sort of situation she is getting herself into."

"And what did you conclude?" Hadrian led her back toward their waiting carriage. Much as he loved their nephew, he looked forward to this few days alone with his beautiful wife.

"I cannot make her out at all." Artemis shook her head. "She seems so respectable...even innocent. The only answers I got to my questions were 'Yes, ma'am' and 'Thank you, ma'am.'"

"It was the same when I met with her." Hadrian helped Artemis into the carriage, then covered her legs with a blanket. "But I confess, I was thinking more about you than about her, poor lass. I didn't pay much heed."

"Her name and accent are Welsh," mused Artemis. "Perhaps she doesn't know much English."

As he climbed into the carriage, Hadrian thought back over his brief meeting with the young woman. "She wrote a good letter in reply to my newspaper notice. Though I suppose someone else might have written it for her."

Artemis turned toward him and clutched his hand. "We must do something—send someone after her or get a message to the ship!

Miss Conway may not understand where she is going or what will be expected of her."

"Calm yourself, pet." That was so like his wife, to care deeply about the welfare of anyone who might need her help. A rush of tender feelings made Hadrian's heart swell until he feared it would burst his ribs. "The lass may not speak much English, but I reckon she knows her geography. She seemed very keen to get to Singapore for whatever reason. As for Simon, he's a decent fellow. He won't force her into anything she doesn't want. Perhaps it will all work out for the best."

The concern in her eyes melted away, replaced by a sparkle of fond merriment. "Hadrian Northmore, have *you* taken up matchmaking? Did you not once tell me it was a dangerous occupation?"

He flashed a devilish grin, then pressed a gentle kiss upon her brow. "If she might make Simon as happy as you have made me, I will happily run that risk!"

* * * * *

HISTORICAL

Novels coming in January 2011

LADY FOLBROKE'S DELICIOUS DECEPTION
Christine Merrill

Confronting her errant husband after being snubbed, Lady Emily
Longesley finds that he has been robbed of his sight and doesn't
know her! Emily longs for a lover's touch. If she plays his
mistress, can he finally begin to love his wife?

BREAKING THE GOVERNESS'S RULES
Michelle Styles

Governess Louisa Sibson was dismissed for allowing Jonathon,
Lord Chesterholm to seduce her. Now she lives by a strict set of
morals. But Jonathon *will* get to the bottom of her disappearance
—and will enjoy breaking a few of her rules along the way…!

HER DARK AND DANGEROUS LORD
Anne Herries

Exiled Lord Stefan de Montfort rescued Englishwoman Anne
Melford from the sea, taking her to his French château. The
spirited beauty fires within him a forbidden desire. Now he's
determined to break one last rule and claim her as his bride!

HOW TO MARRY A RAKE
Deb Marlowe

Mae Halford mended her heart after rejection by Lord Stephen
Manning. Now she's ready to find a husband—only the first man
she bumps into is Lord Stephen himself! Romance may blossom
once more—but will their adventure lead to the altar?

MILLS & BOON

HISTORICAL

**Another exciting novel available
this month:**

LADY ARABELLA'S
SCANDALOUS MARRIAGE

Carole Mortimer

You are cordially invited

to the marriage of

DARIUS WYNTER, DUKE OF CARLYNE

to

LADY ARABELLA ST CLAIRE

What is Lady Arabella letting herself in for? Sinister whispers surround the death of Darius' first wife—could Arabella be in jeopardy? Or will the infamous Duke prove all Society wrong?

One thing's for sure—after the compromising situation that led to this marriage, Arabella will soon discover the exquisite pleasures of the marriage bed…

The Notorious St Claires

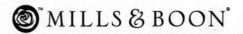

HISTORICAL

**Another exciting novel available
this month:**

DANGEROUS LORD,
SEDUCTIVE MISS

Mary Brendan

Lord…libertine…lawbreaker?

Heiress Deborah Cleveland jilted an earl for Randolph
Chadwicke. He promised he would come back for her.
But then he disappeared…

Seven years later Randolph, now Lord Buckland, bursts
back into Deborah's life! She's unmarried and penniless,
he's as sinfully attractive as ever—but this time he isn't
offering marriage… Worst of all, he seems to be involved
with the murderous local smugglers. Can Deborah resist
the dark magnetism of the lawless lord?

**Regency Rogues
Ripe for a scandal. Ready for a bride**

HISTORICAL

**Another exciting novel available
this month:**

BOUND TO
THE BARBARIAN

Carol Townend

Out of her depth and into his arms…

Sold into slavery, maidservant Katerina promised one day to repay the princess who rescued her. Now that time has come,
and Katerina must convince commanding warrior
Ashfirth Saxon that *she* is her royal mistress.

Spending balmy days and long sultry nights with this man
make Katerina's task increasingly impossible. How long will
she be able to keep up her deception? And how long before
she finds herself willingly bedded by this proud barbarian?

**Palace Brides
Beauties of Byzantium—claimed by warriors!**

MILLS & BOON